The Empress Irini Series

Betrothal & Betrayal
Poison Is A Woman's Weapon
Seizing Power
The Price of Eyes

By Janet McGiffin
Illustrated by Harry Pizzey

Book IV

The Price of Eyes

Scotland Street Press

Published in 2025 by
Scotland Street Press
Edinburgh

All rights reserved
Copyright © Janet McGiffin
Illustrations © Harry Pizzey

The author's right to be identified as the author of this book under the Copyright, Designs and Patents Act 1988 has been asserted.

A CIP record for this book is available from the British Library.

ISBN: 978-1-910895-825

Typeset by Tommy Pearson
Printed on responsibly sourced paper

Cover image and design by Harry Pizzey

Many thanks to Jean, Paddy, Harry, Alex, Susan, Katerina, and Nellie.

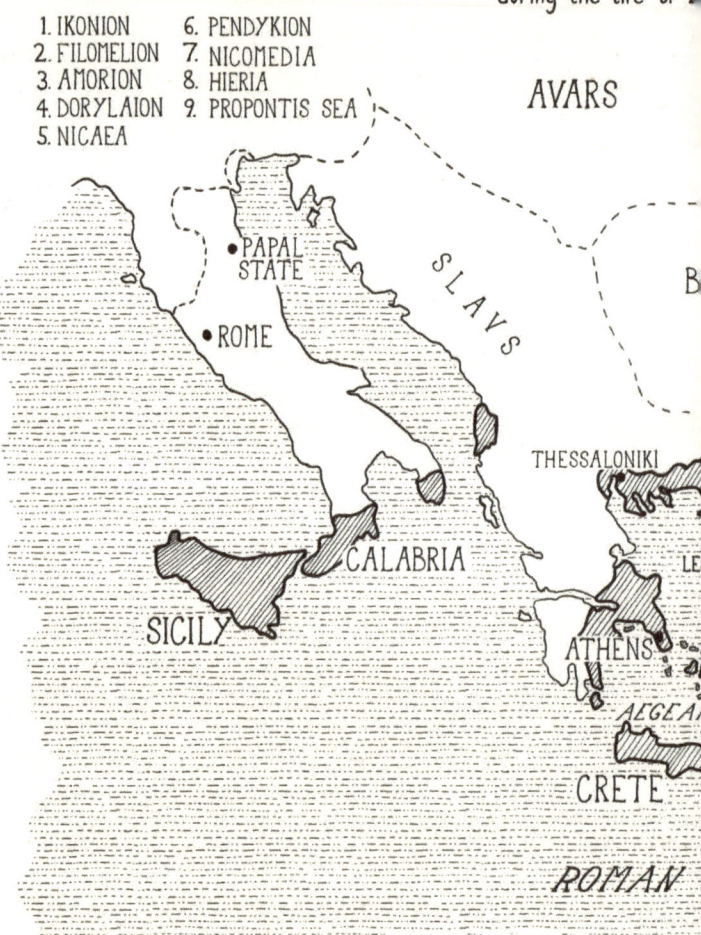

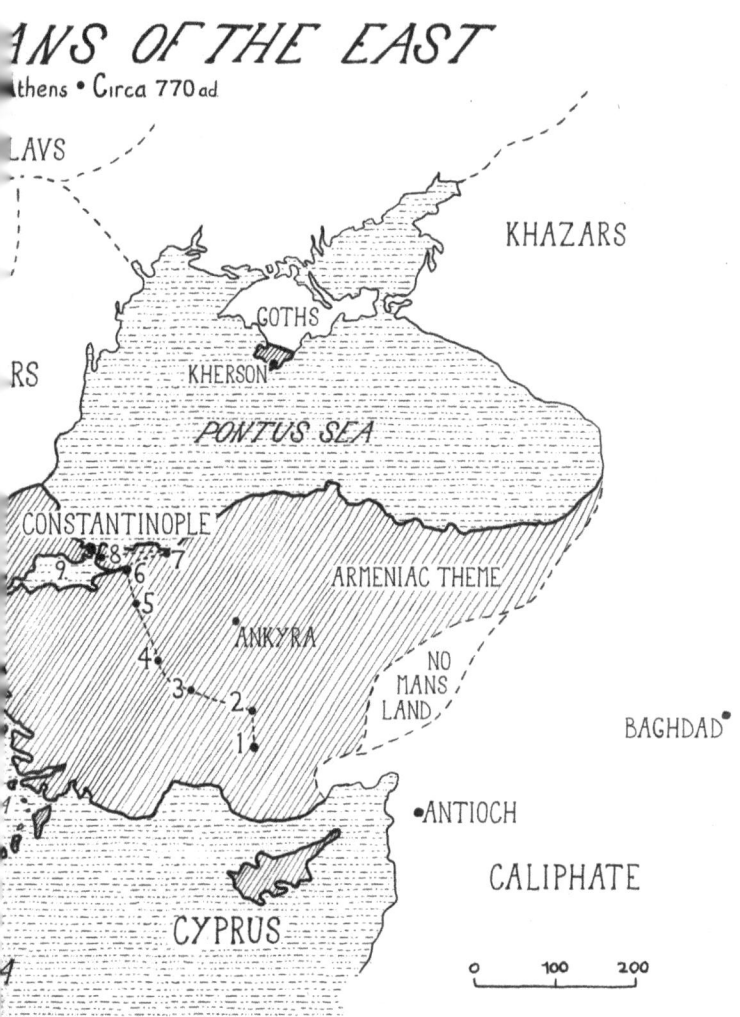

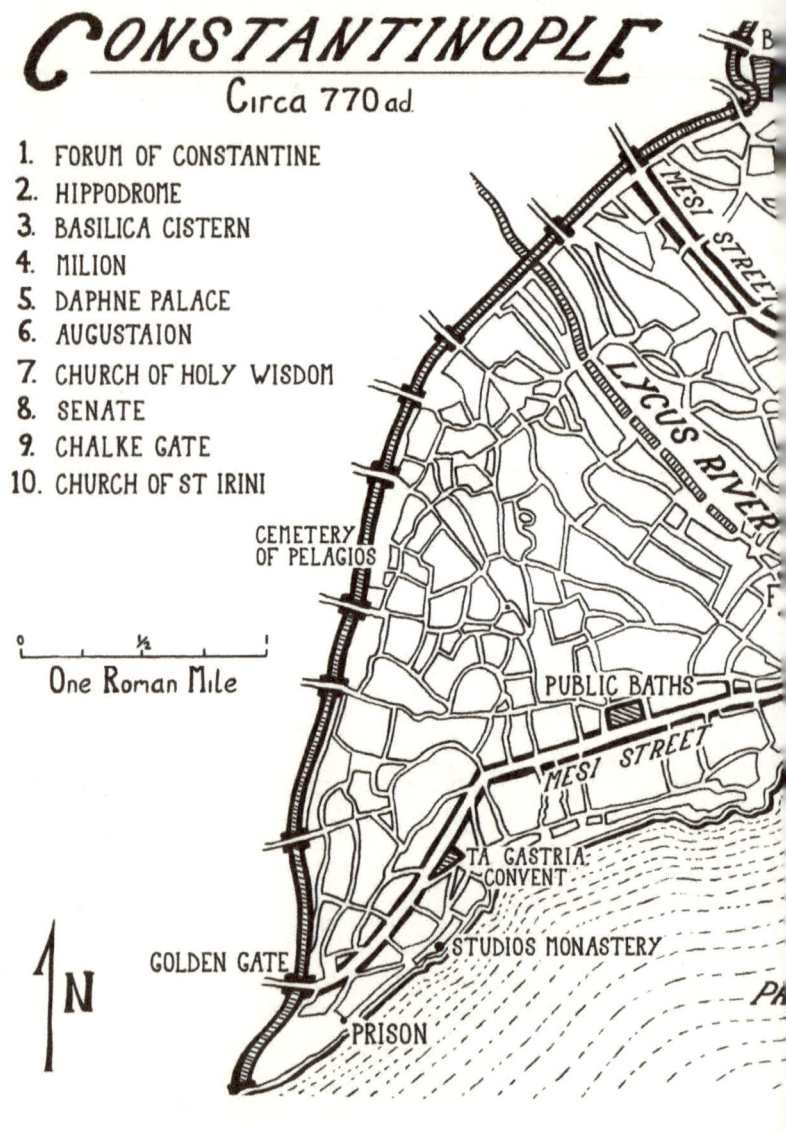

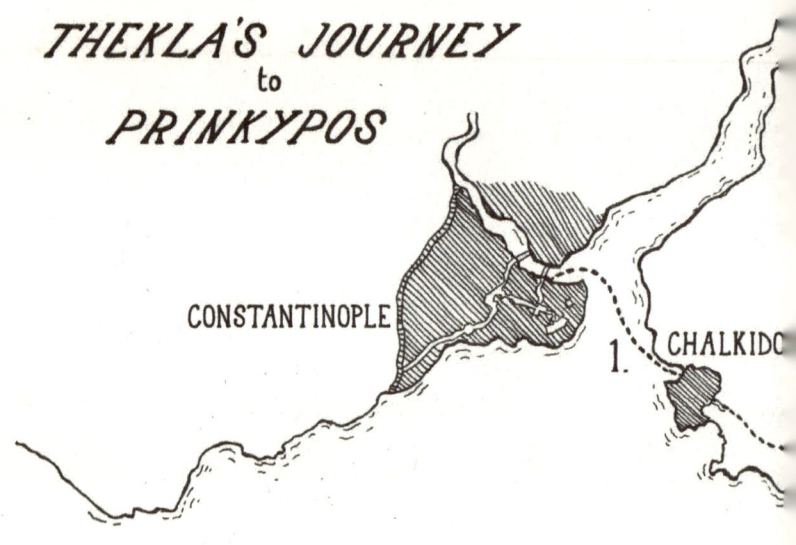

1. Ferry to Chalkidon
2. Twenty mile walk to Pendykion
3. Fishing boat to Prinkypos

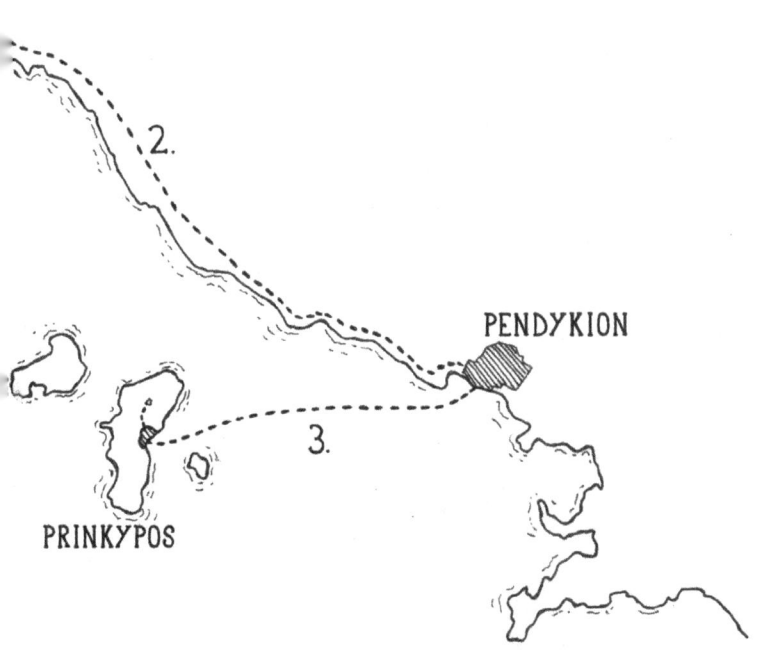

Chapter I

The week that I ran away from home, a soothsayer along the road to Constantinople told me that I would rise as high as an empress. Soothsayers will say anything to separate you from your coin, but this one had a reputation as a real seer. He was just a boy, a postulant monk living in a monastery in Filomelion, and he seemed genuinely puzzled by what he saw in the lines of my hand. Then I met Princess Irini of Athens when she visited Prinkypos Island. She was the pregnant wife of Co-emperor Leon and she got me appointed as abbess of the imperial convent she was sponsoring on Prinkypos. So I decided that the soothsayer had mixed up the empress part, and I forgot him until twenty-three years later when I was milking the convent goat. His words came into my ears and I realised that my life was now filled with Empress Irini's demands. They crowded into my duties as abbess of the Convent of the Theotokos and my meetings with my secret lover, Elias. He was now postmaster in the seaside fortress of Pendykion across the narrow strip of the Propontis Sea. Whenever Empress Irini summoned me to Constantinople, I passed through Pendykion and stayed with Elias.

I was on my way home from Constantinople and having supper with Elias in the kapelarion just inside the Pendykion town gates. He was as handsome as when we had walked from Ikonion to Constantinople twenty-three years before, just a sprinkle of grey in his dark hair to show the years. I was delaying giving him the news about my visit to Empress Irini, who was still locked in her private palace in Constantinople where her son, Emperor Constantine, had put her. It was punishment for locking him under house arrest so he couldn't be crowned Emperor. That was the good news. The bad news was that Constantine was planning to let her go free.

The kapelarios plunked a jug of wine on the table and took our order of fried sardines and lamb shoulder baked with eggplant. We pulled our knives, spoons, and tin cups from our satchels. I had caught the early morning ferry from Constantinople to Chalkidon and walked the twenty miles to Pendykion. I was hungry, tired, and sore of heart. Elias filled our cups and I took a long thirsty drink.

"How is Irini enjoying house arrest?" he joked. "Any attempt to escape?" Elias had helped put Irini under house arrest a year ago. He wanted her to stay there.

"She was so thin that I thought she was dying. She was seeing ghosts. So I fetched Doctor Moses.

"Let me guess. He said she was perfectly healthy."

"He said she was too much alone. So Irini ordered

me to write to Abbott Theodore and say that she was ill from lack of companionship. She wanted him to visit and bring her an attendant to be her companion."

Elias raised his eyebrows. "Theodore hasn't visited her for a year. Why would he come now?"

I didn't ask how Elias knew Abbott Theodore's movements. Elias disappeared from time to time and returned with the shaven face and short hair of a monk. He had been a spy for Emperor Leon. He was still spying for someone, but I didn't know whom.

"He has been Irini's friend since she came to Constantinople," I said. "He used to go to her reception in the Great Palace nearly every day, at least until he went to Bithynia to be a monk."

"So Theodore came," Elias frowned.

I nodded glumly. "And he brought his beautiful niece, Tula." I drew a breath. "Then Irini told him to go to the Great Palace and persuade Constantine to visit his poor sick mother."

The waiter banged down two laden platters between us but Elias didn't move. He kept looking at me. "Constantine has refused to visit his mother since the day he had her locked up. Why would Theodore even ask him to come?"

"Because Irini promised him that when Constantine let her out, she would appoint Theodore as abbott of the imperial monastery of Studdios in Constantinople."

Elias picked up a fried sardine while he thought that over. "Did Constantine succumb to Theodore's very persuasive arguments?"

I nodded. "Irini immediately introduced him to Tula.

She is extraordinarily beautiful, Elias. And seductive. Constantine took one look at her and had eyes for no one else. The next day, he moved her into his quarters in Daphne Palace, where she remains."

"Well, well, well. Constantine finally has a concubine." Elias smiled, to my surprise. "Following his grandfather's footsteps. Good for him."

All my frustration and anger spilled out. "But his grandfather didn't keep his concubines in the Palace. He showed respect for Empress Evdokia. Constantine has moved Maria and his two little daughters to a small suite on the far side of Daphne Palace. He plans to divorce her and wed Tula. The child is only twelve years old, Elias. She's isn't old enough to legally wed."

Elias stabbed a chunk of lamb with his knife. "This was inevitable, I suppose. Constantine never liked Maria. Irini forced the marriage. The boy was underage and Irini was Regent. Now he is choosing the wife he wants. He only has to get the Patriarch's permission to divorce Maria."

"Worse, Elias. Constantine is letting Empress Irini go free."

Elias dropped his knife with a clatter. "Has the boy lost his mind? He isn't solid enough on the throne yet. He will lose the support of the armies if he puts her back on her throne. The soldiers cheered when Commander Alexios placed the crown on his head but they were cheering because Irini was being marched to prison. The defeats that happened under her Regency, the idiots she named to head battalions. . ."

"I'll go back to Constantinople and make Constantine

change his mind," I said resolutely. "I'll tell Constantine that he needs to be a stronger emperor before he lets his mother out."

"He should have revoked her title of empress when he locked her under house arrest," Elias muttered through his teeth.

"If only he could win some battles," I sighed. "The soldiers will love him if he has victories. Constantine told me he wants to be as great a general as his grandfather."

Elias scowled. "He is too eager for victory. It shows his youth and lack of battle experience. Caliph Harun al-Rashid will give him the fight he wants soon enough."

I looked at him sharply. Elias always knew more about the army than would a postmaster of a small postal waystation. "Are you planning to disappear on one of your mysterious trips?" I demanded, without expecting an answer. Elias never answered my questions about his other lives.

I stabbed a chunk of lamb. "Irini was so beautiful and exotic when she came from Athens," I said, feeling nostalgic. "You remember, Elias. She would ride her white mare through the streets and smile at the crowds and they would shout her name. No wonder Emperor Constantine brought her to marry his son."

"Poor Leon didn't have a chance to be the emperor he wanted to be," Elias said. His voice was harsh with bitterness. "Five years was all she gave him after his father died. Then she poisoned him." Elias had been Emperor Leon's friend from childhood. He had tried to protect Leon, and failed.

"Hush. We don't know that." I glanced warily around,

but the noisy talk and clatter of platters had hidden his words.

"You're afraid of her," he accused.

"She gave me a secure life," I said, feeling defensive. "She named me abbess of the convent she was sponsoring and she didn't care that I had never taken the vows. For that, she has my loyalty."

"For that, and because when you were only eighteen, she demanded that you vow loyalty to her and protect her with your life," he added harshly.

I glared at him. "I made that vow before God and I won't go back on it, Elias, no matter what you say."

"You told me once that your greater loyalty was to Constantine."

He was right. My head was loyal to Irini but my heart belonged to Constantine. Elias touched my hand. "Don't try to convince Constantine to keep Irini locked up. The cat is out of the bag. But take care, Thekla. When Irini gets back in the Great Palace, she will take revenge on everyone who didn't help her get out of house arrest. Remember what she did when Emperor Constantine died and Leon became Emperor? She kicked Empress Evdokia and Princess Anthusa out with only the clothes on their backs. She tried to do the same to Emperor Constantine's three older sisters but Leon intervened. So she moved them into cramped quarters and took away their attendants. I fear what she will do to Commander Alexios. He put her in prison." He lowered his voice. "And I fear what she will do to Constantine. He locked her up and cut off her allowance. And to you, my loyal Thekla. You refused to go to prison with her."

I felt cold all over. I could still hear Irini's voice when we stood at the gate to Phiale prison. "Are you coming with me, Thekla?" she had asked, and I had let her go down those dark steps alone. Instead, I had gone to Magnavra Palace to watch Constantine be crowned Emperor.

We ate in silence after that, then made our way through the dark narrow lanes of the walled seaport fortress, our footsteps blending with the gentle slap of waves against the sea walls and the tramp of the guards atop the walls. The September night wasn't cold but I was chilled from fatigue and glad to climb the stairs to his room above the wheelwright. I crawled under the quilts with a contented groan and watched Elias pull off his clothes.

Don't you miss your rich house in Constantinople and your wealthy family and servants?" I inquired as he got into bed beside me and slid his arms around me.

"What do you know about my wealthy family?" he growled, but I could feel him smiling.

"Nothing. After twenty-three years of knowing you, I only know that you have one."

"And I only know that you jumped in my coach, escaping a wedding to an old grave-digger. What fun we had travelling to Constantinople. Those nights in the hay lofts. . ." His breath tickled my ear.

"I have never felt so free."

"Have you ever felt guilty pretending you're a nun?"

I was startled. "What an odd question, Elias. No, I don't feel guilty. A woman doesn't have to be a nun to head a convent; she only has to be devout. That's what the patriarch told Irini at the time. Irini only lied to Emperor Constantine that I was a nun so that Empress Evdokia couldn't stop him from naming me as abbess and letting Irini sponsor the convent."

"You could take the vows now."

I sat up and looked at him. "What has got into you, Elias? If I were a nun, I wouldn't break my vow of chastity and be here in your bed. And if I asked Father Dimitrios to hear my vows now, my nuns would know that I have lied to them all these years. No-one would trust me. The situation is fine as is. Everyone thinks that I'm your cousin."

"You could stop being an abbess. You could come live with me in my rich house in Constantinople."

I couldn't believe my ears. "What are you saying?"

"Marry me."

My thoughts tumbled and slid. "I cannot, Elias," I whispered. "My convent needs me. Irini needs me. Besides, I'm too old. I'm forty."

He pulled me back down beside him, tightened his arms, and said nothing until later, when we lay warm against each other. "Go home to your island convent. Devote yourself to your nuns and your vegetable garden. Harvest your grapes and your apples and tend to your sheep and goats. We will weather this latest storm together, with me here and you there. One day we will live together without this strip of sea separating us."

"We will be too old to enjoy it," I smiled and fell asleep.

The next morning, we climbed onto Elias's mail boat and crossed the narrow band of water to Prinkypos Island.

Autumn passed with the Feast of Saint Dimitrios. Then came Nativity when Father Dimitrios wafted incense and chanted blessings over the fishing boats bobbing in the harbour. Elias came with news that lovely Tula was still in Constantine's bed, Empress Maria and their two little daughters were in cramped quarters, and Empress Irini remained under house arrest. I began to hope that Constantine had decided to keep his mother locked up.

Then one cold morning in early January, Megalo came rushing into the kitchen, scattering snow over those of us crowded around the hearth. We had pulled our mattresses and looms into the warm room and were living there until warmer weather.

"The imperial yacht is coming—flying the imperial banner!"

"Constantine!" I jumped up but Sister Matrona put a hand on my arm. As my ekonomis, second-in-command, she could argue with me.

"Abbess Thekla, think! Why would Emperor Constantine come out in this weather? Or Empress Maria and the two little girls? Only one person could be on that yacht—Empress Irini."

I sat down hard on the hearth. "Constantine has let her out."

"What did you expect, my dear? How long could Constantine resist his mother? Bundle up. The wind is whistling like the devil himself is trying to get inside." She wrapped shawls around my head and shoulders and ordered two strong novices to do the same. "You're going to need help to get her up here."

Snow filled our footprints as we crossed the pasture

and drifts lay against the convent gates. Outside, from the top of the lane, we could see through the falling snow to waves crashing over the breakwater and a yacht moving slowly into the harbour. Fishermen were hurrying to catch the mooring lines. We struggled down the snowy lane and through the village streets and joined Father Dimitrios and his two eldest sons on the quay. The fishermen had caught the mooring lines but high waves inside the harbour were keeping them from lashing them to the bollards without scraping the yacht. A figure on deck was clinging to some sailors. Empress Irini.

"Toss her over! We'll catch her!" Father Dimitrios shouted to the sailors. The fishermen pulled the yacht as close to the quay as they dared and, with frantic strength, the sailors heaved Irini across the churning gap. Father Dimitrios and his sons caught her, and the yacht disappeared into the swirling snow.

We hustled Irini into the priest's cottage which was built against the Church of Saint Nikolaos by the harbour. We peeled off her mink hat, long lynx coat, fur boots, shawls, and scarves down to her heavy green wool tunica and wide trousers. Seated on a stool by the blazing fire, she lowered her feet into a pan of heated water. The priest's daughter brought out mugs of steaming thyme tea. Father Dimitrios and his wife had five children now, all healthy. Village priests were expected to marry and produce children. Other clergy, like monks and priests climbing the church hierarchy, were celibate or supposed to be.

"Constantine let me out of house arrest!" Irini beamed.

"I am back on the throne—as his joint ruler! Constantine never removed my title of empress. He always meant for me to return to the throne."

I choked. Constantine had sworn to me that he would never give his mother back her power. Irini looked complacent.

"Constantine wanted to let me out in September but his advisors raised all sorts of absurd objections. My dear son overruled them, finally. Goodness, what awful weather! My slave was too terrified to get on the yacht. I told my guards that I didn't need them; I am perfectly safe here."

Father Dimitrios spoke. "May I inquire how long Your Grace will bless us with your presence?"

"Until my residence is renovated. Maria has ruined it with her atrocious taste. I have ordered new rugs and curtains. Maria is being annoying. She keeps barging into my chambers and making scenes about Tula."

"So awkward," I commented.

She shot me a sharp look. "I have never liked Maria. Neither has Constantine."

I didn't like Empress Maria either. She had visited the convent once and treated my nuns and novices like servants, demanding that they bring hot water for bathing every day, and serve her meals in the imperial suite. She only came out of the suite to pray in our little church in the courtyard or watch Brother Grigorios paint icons on the church walls. I thought Maria was selfish, greedy, lazy, and slow of mind. Still, she was Constantine's wife and mother of his two little daughters. I found it shocking that Constantine had pushed her aside in favour of a concubine.

"You chose her in that phony bride show you put on, you and that eunuch, Stavrakios," I retorted.

"Maria has become intolerable," she snapped. "She visited me when I was under house arrest and was unspeakably rude. She wears my clothing and jewellery and says they are hers. They are not. They are mine."

"They belong to the Empire, as you have often told me." Then my fury poured out.

"I find it appalling that Constantine would humiliate his wife in favour of a twelve-year-old who is no better than a concubine, even if she is your attendant. There is no reason why Maria and the children had to move out of Constantine's apartments. There are plenty of suites in Daphne Palace where Constantine can visit his little toy. That's what Emperor Constantine used to do with his concubines."

A shocked silence fell over the room. Empress Irini fixed me with that frightening glare that could bring Palace officials to their knees. "How dare you. . ."

Father Dimitrios gently interrupted. "May I ask why Your Grace has honoured us with your presence during such a terrible snowstorm? There must be comfortable chambers in Daphne Palace for you during the renovations."

A satisfied smile slid over Irini's face. "I am waiting for my eunuch guards, Stavrakios and Aetios, to return from exile. Constantine has agreed to forgive their crimes and reinstate them into their previous positions. Stavrakios will again be Minister of the Imperial Post and Foreign Affairs. He will regain his title of patrikios and his seat in the Senate. Aetios will resume being Commander of the Palace Guards."

I was horrified. I wanted to rush into Constantinople and shout at Constantine to have Stavrakios and Aetios beheaded for treason. I had told him to do that the very day he was crowned Emperor.

"You must be warm by now," I snapped, standing up. "Let's get you up to the convent before it gets dark and we lose you in the woods."

The entire village must have heard that the Empress was in the priest's cottage, but no-one came out to welcome her as they had done when she had come to the island with Constantine as a child. He had grown up with their children and they adored him as one of their own. For having Empress Irini betrayed him.

So only Father Dimitrios and his two sons broke the new snow in front of us as we moved slowly up the lane, through the convent gate, and across the pasture. The men turned back when we reached the convent courtyard so as not to violate the law of religious seclusion.

In the kitchen, the nuns got us out of our snowy garments. Megalo helped Irini to a stool by the warm hearth and brought her a bowl of squash and leek soup. Megalo had been one of Irini's attendants at the Palace twenty years before and she assumed that role whenever Irini came to the convent. Irini devoured the soup and held out her hand for a cloth to wipe her mouth.

"Take me to the study." She took Megalo's arm, and we followed the wavering light of a novice's candle down the freezing passage to my large study with long glass windows that gave on to the courtyard.

Megalo settled Irini under quilts on a cushioned couch near the hearth while the novice kindled a fire and I lit the hanging oil lamps and wax candles. In the firelight and candle glow, the room shone with the wealth that Irini had brought: tapestries and heavy rugs warmed the stone walls and floor. Silver and gold vessels gleamed from the side tables.

I sat at my desk. People had to stand in the presence of the imperial family but, years before, Irini had permitted me to sit. I watched the fire crackle into flames. On normal days, I sat at my desk and looked through the long windows at the activities housed in the rooms around the courtyard: the hospice, schoolroom, scriptorium, and weaving room. My study was the heart of the convent and my sanctuary.

Which I lost when Empress Irini came. She had her own suite on the level above the study, with fireplaces and views over the Propontis Sea to the mountains of Bithynia. But she preferred my study because of the escape tunnel. When Irini was with child, she had feared that if she birthed a girl, Leon would exile her to the prison convent on the island of Lesbos. That child had been Constantine, now Emperor, but our deepest fears never leave us. So, Irini always stayed where she could get down the secret steps below the hearth and through the passage to the root cellar. From there, she could cross the kitchen garden, climb the stile over the low part of the convent wall, and follow the path down to a tiny harbour. There, an escape ship would be waiting.

Megalo and the novice left, and I poured two tiny glasses of elderberry wine. Irini drank hers down quickly and held out her glass for more. I refilled it and took my glass to my desk. She spoke quietly, as if thinking aloud.

"As soon as I am back in power, I will send Commander Mihalis the Dragon into exile. Time after time, he has defied my orders. Whenever I sent for him, he didn't come. I stripped him of his command and exiled him to his village, but Constantine has brought him back and made him commander of the Thrakian theme army."

She held out her glass again, and again I refilled it. She went on in a low voice.

"As for that traitor, Commander Alexios, he will regret that he arrested me and put me in prison. Constantine has elevated him to patrikios and made him Commander of the Palace Guards. He will not have that post for long, I swear. And I will replace every commander who ever refused my orders."

My heart went cold.

Over the following weeks, Empress Irini ate like one of our goats. She demanded hot food at all hours, and our cook, Aspasia, grew tight-lipped and irritable. Irini waded through the snowy pasture to strengthen her legs and lungs. "This year of seclusion has drained my strength. No one but you must see me so weak!" She made me keep a fire and a brazier going in my study. Sister Matrona and I grimly watched our supply of charcoal and wood dwindle.

In mid-January, Father Dimitrios and his eldest son went into Constantinople to celebrate the Veneration of the Precious Chains of the Apostle Peter at Saint Peter's Church. I took all the nuns and novices down to the harbour to wave them off on Elias's boat. We each brought Father Dimitrios some small object for him to touch to Saint Peter's chains. We also gave Elias several of our large rugs off our looms. Elias knew a good rug merchant in Constantinople who would sell them for us. Our blankets and rugs were already selling briskly in Pendykion and surrounding villages.

A week later, Megalo spotted the mail boat and we all went down to collect our objects that had touched the chains of Saint Peter and hear Father Dimitrios tell of their adventures. The novices went to visit their friends and families while Sister Matrona and Sister Evanthia and I stayed with Father Dimitrios and Elias by the priest's hearth. Elias pulled out a wax-wrapped packet for Empress Irini from his mail pouch, and a letter addressed to Megalo. I grimaced when I saw the name of the sender.

"Abbott Theodore," I scowled as I scanned the careful script. "He's writing how happy Fanis is in his new monastery." I always read the letters of the nuns and novices. I needed to know what worries they might be harbouring that could affect the peace of the convent.

Twenty years before, Megalo's husband, Fanis, had abruptly decided to become a monk and had ordered Megalo to be a nun—without giving her a divorce, which meant he kept her dowry. I had refused to let Megalo take the vows. Our founding documents, our Typikon, stated that a woman must choose to join a convent. Megalo hadn't chosen—her husband had—so Megalo lived with us as a lay person who worked to pay her board. She didn't want to be a nun, anyway. She spent hours staring over the sea, dreaming that Fanis would take her back.

"Burn it," said Sister Evanthia. "Megalo will weep for days and be more useless than ever."

I put the letter in my bag. "I want Megalo to read it. Then she will divorce Fanis and re-marry. Some elderly widower would take her."

"Megalo is thirty-five. No man will take her," retorted Sister Matrona. "Even Empress Irini won't try to find her a husband. I asked."

"How is the Empress enjoying being out of house arrest?" inquired Father Dimitrios.

"She is insufferable," snapped Sister Matrona. "She demands food day and night. She makes us wash her clothes every day. We are wasting wood and charcoal to keep her warmer than the rest of us."

I looked at him darkly. "She claims that Constantine has promised her that she will share the throne with him. She says that he is bringing Aetios and Stavrakios back from exile. And giving them their previous positions and titles."

Elias stared grimly into the fire. "Aetios and Stavrakios are already in Constantinople."

"A shocking decision, after what those evil eunuchs did to him," gasped Sister Matrona. "Constantine nearly died!"

My anger and frustration exploded. "Constantine promised me that he would never give her back her power. He promised me that he would punish those two evil eunuchs. Now he is doing whatever Irini wants!"

Elias tightened his lips. "She wants to be Empress in her own right. She wants to be alone on the throne."

Father Dimitrios looked horrified. "Surely Empress Irini knows that Constantine can put her back under house arrest any time."

Elias lifted his hands. "She knows that Constantine won't do that. She knows that he will let her take control. This cannot continue." He pulled on his cloak and left.

I kept thinking about his words as we climbed the hill to the convent. I handed the packet to Irini and warmed my hands at the fire while she unwrapped a bundle of letters.

"Aetios and Stavrakios are coming to collect me," she read with a smile. "Soon I will be back on the throne."

Sister Matrona and I walked her down to the harbour. The villagers turned their backs or stayed indoors. Father Dimitrios blessed the yacht and we waved her off. I slept soundly for the first time in weeks.

We didn't see Empress Irini again until the eighth Wednesday after Pentecost, a religious fast day when we abstained from meat, fish, oil, wine, dairy, and eggs. Seafood was permitted so we all happily tromped down to the village to join the feast in the plateia. Pots steamed with mussels, cockles, shrimp, and tiny barnacles that we speared from their casings with the tips of our knives.

The children set up a shout that the imperial yacht was coming into the harbour and Empress Irini was on deck. Sister Matrona, Father Dimitrios, and I went to greet her. She went into the church to thank Saint Nikolaos for her safe voyage while we waited with her two guards outside. The villagers were silent as we walked through the plateia—no dipped knees, no shy welcomes with flowers as when Constantine was a child. When the lane turned up the hill, Father Dimitrios returned to the feast, leaving me annoyed and frustrated that I was missing my favourite festival. Sister Matrona and two postulant nuns opened the convent gates, the guards took up their posts outside, and we crossed the pasture in silence.

Empress Irini went to sit in the big chair under the grape vine that the village carpenter had built for her years before. I went into the root cellar and filled a jug with wine from the vat sunk into the floor, and spooned soft sheep cheese and honey-lemon preserves into bowls.

"My foolish son has gone off to fight the Bulgars," Irini said as she balanced her cup on the wide arm of her chair and savoured the cheese and preserves. I sat at the long wooden table under the vines. "He plans to reinforce the fortress at Markellon. He believes that this will secure the border and honour the memory of his grandfather Constantine's battle at that same place."

"He wants to be a great general, like his grandfather."

"He's hopeless. This campaign will be a catastrophe." She was smiling.

Dispatches started arriving. Empress Irini made me wait at the top of the lane with her and her two guards until Stavrakios or Aetios had got off the yacht, crossed the plateia, and was coming up the lane. Only then could I return to my tasks, leaving her there to read the dispatch and give instructions to the eunuch. Then she would interrupt my work again by calling me into my study where I had to mark the movements of the armies by sticking pins in the wall maps while she read aloud the locations.

In mid-August, near the Feast of the Ascension of the Virgin into Heaven, Elias delivered the dispatch himself.

"Where are Stavrakios or Aetios?" I murmured while Empress Irini feverishly scanned the pages.

Elias spoke under his breath. "The cowards are afraid to leave the Palace. The final battle went to the Bulgars. It was a complete rout. They are chasing our army home; they're about two days away."

Horrified, I looked at Empress Irini. She was smiling.

"A disaster, like I predicted!" she crowed. "The Bulgars learned from their defeat at Markellon all those years ago and they built ramparts to block the roads. Constantine couldn't decide if he should breach them. Did he consult his generals? No. He consulted his astrologer. I know this stupid stargazer. He knows less of the stars than he does of the sea."

She returned to the dispatch. "While Constantine waited for favourable stars, the clever Bulgars moved their cavalry behind the hills surrounding the battlefield and attacked. They used a new weapon called an arkani. It says here that it's a long pole with a loop of rope at one end. They loop a mounted soldier out of the saddle."

She threw down the dispatch in disgust. "If we still had spies inside the Bulgar Khanate, we would have known about this weapon and used it ourselves! But no, my senile father-in-law gave the names of our spies to the lying Bulgar Khan Teleryg, and he executed them all."

She kept reading. "They raided our supplies and stole our army pay. They even stole Constantine's tent! Here are the fallen officers: Mihalis the Dragon. Good riddance. Now I don't have to exile him. A patrikios and two other commanders died. And the charlatan astrologer. He couldn't even predict his own death. The Bulgars are chasing our army back to Constantinople, what's left of them. I wouldn't be surprised if the Bulgars slaughtered them all and mounted Constantine's head on a pike."

I crossed myself with a shaking hand. "May the saints bring them safely home!"

She folded the papyrus and addressed Elias. "I will return to Constantinople this minute. You will take me and my guards on your mail boat to Pendykion. There, you will find horses for us to ride to Chalkidon; a carriage is too slow. I will commandeer a fast boat to get us across to Constantinople. You will also my order delivered to the army of the Opsikon Theme to chase off the Bulgars when they arrive, before they strip the countryside."

Elias bowed. "May I suggest that Bulgars might reach Constantinople ahead of you. Would you not be safer here until you know the fate of Emperor Constantine?"

"Certainly not. Give us fast horses in Pendykion and we will reach Constantinople by nightfall. If the Khan does capture my stupid son, there will be a ransom demand. I will have to negotiate it."

The following days were so filled with fear, I don't know how we fed the animals or ourselves; we kept staring over the sea at the golden haze of Constantinople and praying for Constantine to reach those safe walls before the Bulgar army caught him. We went down to the village every day for news but heard only a rumour that Caliph Harun al-Rashid was bringing his armies to join the Bulgars.

Each night, I sat at the window of my dormitory room clasping Saint Thekla and praying for her to protect my beloved Constantine and that great city that bore his name. My thoughts swam with horrible visions of Constantine stabbed, sliced apart, dismembered, and his head mounted on a spike.

Finally, Megalo spotted the mail boat and we all ran down to the harbour.

"Constantine and our army are safely inside Constantinople," Elias shouted as he tossed out his mooring line. "The Opsikon and Thrakian theme armies are driving the Bulgars back over the border."

But Elias wasn't through, and the news was bad. "Emperor Constantine's defeat lost him the loyalty of the Palace Guards. They tried to seize the throne. Constantine's friends warned him in time. Rumour says that his two uncles, Christoforos and Nikiforos, were behind it. Constantine has thrown them and the Palace Guards in prison. He has ordered that the tongues of Christoforos and the three younger uncles be slit."

I gasped in horror. "Christoforos is a young man, and the three younger brothers are but boys!"

"Time has passed, Thekla. Nikiforos and Christoforos are in their mid-thirties and the three younger brothers are in their twenties." He drew a deep breath. "Constantine has ordered that Nikiforos be blinded as their leader. When he is disfigured, he cannot be emperor. So says the law in the Ekloga."

"Constantine would never have anyone blinded—even

the worst of criminals!" I cried.

"Empress Irini wrote the order but Constantine signed it," Elias said grimly. "Irini has ordered that the uncles be locked in a monastery to await punishment."

"Pray that the imperial doctors do the blinding," I said fervently, "not Stavrakios or Aetios. The doctors will follow the law and only nick the skin by the eye so there is still sight. And slit the tongue a bit so there is still speech. The law in the Ekloga only says they cannot be perfect."

But that was not the worst news. "Empress Irini claims that Alexios took part in this conspiracy," said Elias.

I sat down, bewildered and confused. "That cannot be! Alexios freed Constantine from house arrest. With my own ears, I heard Alexios order his soldiers to raise Constantine on their shields and proclaim him their commander. With my own eyes, I saw Alexios kneel before Constantine and proclaim him emperor. Alexios would never take the crown for himself."

"Constantine believes that Alexios is guilty. He has had Alexios flogged and tonsured. And blinded—not by the imperial doctors. Alexios is in Phiale prison. He will surely die."

A great calm came over me, like when the wind drops before a storm. "Irini is taking revenge on Alexios for arresting her and putting Constantine on the throne."

He nodded soberly. "It is a grave mistake. Alexios was revered by the army of the Armeniakon theme. They will rise against her as they did when they arrested her and placed the crown on Constantine's head. But this time they won't put Irini in prison. They will execute her by the sword."

Chapter II

Elias was half right. The army of the Armeniakon theme did rise up when they learned that their beloved Commander Alexios had been blinded. But they didn't go after Irini. They went after Constantine. These brave soldiers had freed Constantine, raised him on their shields, and vowed their loyalty to Constantine only because of their love for Alexios. Now they vowed revenge. No fury is more powerful than that of a soldier whose loyalty has been betrayed.

First, they threw in prison the commander whom Constantine had appointed to replace Alexios as head of the Armeniakon theme army. Poor unlucky Theodoros. He had helped Constantine try to arrest Stavrakios and Aetios and failed. Empress Irini had stripped Theodore of his title and sent him into exile. Constantine brought him home but now poor Theodore lay in prison because of his loyalty to Constantine.

Constantine lost his senses. He ordered the armies of two other themes to attack the Armeniakon army and free Theodoros. They failed. By the time we got the bad news from Elias, the Armeniakon army had blinded both those commanders.

"Now we have civil war," Elias concluded grimly.

I wrote to Constantine. I told him that, long ago, his grandfather had warned Irini against setting citizen against citizen. I wrote that cousins would die on opposite sides, fields would lie untilled or burnt, and wages go unpaid. Our enemies would invade from all sides. Constantine didn't reply. He was busy building a joint army from the other themes to attack the Armeniakon army. Six months later, he led them himself.

"The outcome was simply numbers," Elias told us in the plateia after it was over. "The Armeniakon army had superb commanders but the joint armies under Constantine crushed them. Then our misguided young Emperor staged a Triumph to proclaim his victory over his own army. He tried to make it a blessed day by holding it the day after the procession when the Veil of the Virgin is carried through the streets. He had three soldiers beheaded and the rest sent into exile."

Caliph Harun al-Rashid, the young leader of the Abbasid Caliphate, took the opportunity to raid and plunder. He was only a few years older than Constantine but already was being called a military genius. He captured a fortress in Kappadokia, then a border garrison, then a town near Ikonion, in the middle of the Empire.

"Commander Elpidios was spotted fighting in the Caliph's army," Elias reported. "Stavrakios had accused Elpidios of conspiring against Irini. Elpidios fled. Irini promptly confiscated his property and sent his wife and young children to a convent."

Shortly after the raid by the Caliph's army, Empress Irini arrived in Prinkypos harbour on the imperial yacht with Empress Maria and the two little girls. The children bounced down the gangplank followed sullenly by Maria. Irini stayed on board.

"I'll be back in a week," Irini waved as the yacht sped away.

"She's going to the hot springs in Proussa," spat Maria. "Constantine is there with his concubine."

I nodded without looking at her. We both knew that they would stay all summer. Maria didn't speak as we climbed the hill behind the excited children and their servant. Efrosini was five and Irinoula was six. They had never been to the island because Maria had refused to bring them. She had been once when she was betrothed and pronounced us to be primitive.

I summoned Aspasia, Sister Matrona, and Sister Evanthia to my study and we discussed how to help the trio feel at home. "Maria's future as Empress is shaky and no one can lift a finger to help her," I explained. "She's frightened."

"Maria is spoiled and lazy and she'll train the children to be the same," retorted Aspasia. She had not forgotten Maria's demanding visit seven years before. "I won't be making separate meals for her or heating any bath water."

"She can eat in the refectory with us and bathe in the kitchen with the nuns once a week," snapped Sister Matrona.

"Or swim in the sea," added Sister Evanthia. "And no

daily laundry."

"She's still Empress Maria and we have to obey her orders," I said, feeling helpless.

"Even an empress must occupy herself," said Sister Matrona firmly. "Maria cannot sit in her room all day or pray in the church as she did before."

"It's going to be a long summer," concluded Aspasia.

The first day, Maria shouted at the girls to put their shoes back on and stop climbing the fruit trees. When they hid from her, she went into the church. She was still there when we filed in for Ninth Hour services. After our prayers, she stopped me as we were moving into the refectory.

"I will be taking my meals in the imperial suite, Abbess Thekla."

"We take our meals in the refectory, Empress. You are welcome to join us." My tone was less than gentle, for which I was immediately ashamed. I knew how abandoned Maria felt. Still, I couldn't let her disrupt the flow of convent life.

"I was served in the imperial suite when I came before." Her voice quavered.

I replied more gently. "You brought three servants. The nuns and novices have their tasks and no time to serve you. Come eat with us. Everyone is waiting."

"I'm not hungry."

"Suit yourself. This is our second meal of the day and our only heavy meal. We have bread and cheese after Esperinos services at dusk."

I went to the kitchen, irritated at Maria for treating me like a slave and at myself for being curt with her.

The little girls were perched at the kitchen table with their servant, stuffing themselves with warm flatbread loaded with honey. I picked up a platter of fried fish and followed the novices carrying platters of carrots and beans into the refectory. Maria was standing at the table with the nuns, staring hungrily at the food.

I stopped Maria as she was going up to the imperial suite with the little girls for their afternoon rest. "Will you join Sister Matrona and me for a glass of elderberry wine?" I motioned towards my study.

Her eyes slid sullenly between me and Sister Matrona. Then she preceded us into my study, sat in the chair by the long window, and stared out at the courtyard. I placed a glass filled with our elderberry wine on a tray and held it out to her. She looked at the gold-rimmed vessel as if it held poison, then slowly took it. I poured two more for Sister Matrona and me and we seated ourselves.

She glared at us. "You cannot sit before I tell you."

"May the Lord grant us health." I raised my glass to my lips. Sister Matrona did the same.

Her face flushed. We had drunk before her! But she said nothing and moistened her lips with the sweet wine.

"I understand how wretched you must feel over your husband's behaviour," I said gently.

Maria's head drooped and her shoulders began to shake. I lifted the glass from her fingers and placed it and ours on the tray. Then Sister Matrona and I folded our hands and waited.

"Constantine is fornicating with that slut!" Maria sobbed through fingers wet with tears. "Everyone is laughing at me. Wherever I go, I hear whispers. I begged Constantine to keep that girl in Heireia Palace, where his grandfather kept his concubines. I begged him to stop shaming me. He told me to go home to my mother. I went to Irini. I said that his behaviour is improper, that a concubine cannot take my place. She said that he is Emperor, he can do what he pleases."

Maria raised her eyes, red with weeping. "Irini wants me out. She brought in that concubine deliberately. When Irini was under house arrest, Constantine came to my bed. We were husband and wife. He invited me to Magnavra Palace. The foreign envoys and the ambassadors bowed to me. I brought our daughters at the end of the day and he took them on his lap and kissed them." Tears dripped onto her clenched fists.

I wanted to reassure her, but I could not.

Misery poured from her. "My attendants told me that she is with child, that Constantine will divorce me, that I will be tonsured and sent to that convent on Lesbos to die!"

Maria fell into sobs so violent that I feared she would choke. Finally, she collapsed against the cushions. Sister Matrona placed a handkerchief between her limp hands. I handed her back her elderberry wine and she took a shaky sip. Sister Matrona and I sipped ours.

"I will write to Constantine," I said gently.

"Meanwhile, you must occupy yourself," said Sister Matrona. "Otherwise, despair will take you over and you will not be able to mother your daughters. Will you copy a scroll or sit at a loom?"

Her voice was thick with despair. "Scroll."

I wrote to Constantine. I asked him when he would make his summer visit to Prinkypos. He didn't reply. Empress Maria went every day to the scriptorium and slumped over a desk, slowly copying the history of Saint Eufemia who had been martyred by Roman soldiers at Chalkidon for refusing to sacrifice to the god Ares.

The little girls were our pleasure and joy. Efrosini means joyfulness and the five-year-old lived up to her name. She was fearless and full of excitement. She demanded to know why the goats followed her but the sheep ran away, how the water got into the cisterns, why it was cool in the root cellar. She ventured alone down the broken steps to the spidery dungeon and peered through the rusted iron bars. She tried to milk a goat and got kicked. Irini was calm and sweet-tempered. She sat at the kitchen table and helped Aspasia roll out flat bread. Her light voice chanted our prayer services. Megalo and the novices took them down to the village every day to play with the village children, just as I had taken their father when he was a child. Efrosini threw herself into the sea and fought it, choking and spitting until one day she swam as fast as anyone.

Brother Grigorios had nearly finished his work on the inside walls and pillars of our small church in the courtyard and the girls loved to tell me the stories of the icons of the saints: Saint Anysia who was killed by the Romans because she wouldn't sacrifice to the old gods, Saint Vereniki who gave her veil to Jesus to wipe his forehead as he carried the cross, Saint Makrina the Righteous who was the sister of Saint Basil and taught him about community, Saint Maria Magdalene who was the Holy Myrrh Bearer and Equal to the Apostles. The girls' favourite was virtuous Saint Anastasia who fled jealous Empress Theodora by dressing as a man and living in a cave. Brother Grigorios had also painted scenes of Prinkypos and fishermen mending nets, farmers scything barley, and women stirring dye vats.

Empress Irini returned in September. Efrosini spotted the yacht. She was walking on the walls, strictly forbidden, and she and her sister raced to the convent gate while Maria and the servant frantically threw their few belongings into satchels. The girls had worn short tunicas all summer that we had sewn for them, to save their silk ones. Maria determinedly wore her silk tunicas and they had become shredded by our rough chairs. All the nuns and novices walked them down to the harbour to say goodbye.

Empress Irini was standing on the quay. Maria barely bent a knee to her before stalking up the gangplank. The little girls dutifully kissed their grandmother's cheek, raced up the gangplank, then began wailing when they realised they were leaving their paradise. Empress Irini called to the captain to return for her in a few days. She chatted cheerfully as we climbed the lane to the convent. I wasn't listening; my heart was so full of the children.

That afternoon, I remember it clearly, Irini came with me to the pasture. She carried a basket of chicken eggs that she had collected from the hen house. I had my sling and a few stones. My target was a hawk making lazy circles just out of what he knew was my range. He was watching a hen and chicks scratching at the earth.

He could drop onto a chick as swiftly and silently as a falling star and I had lost many to his talons. Irini sat in the grass and chewed on a blade of grass.

"The Synod of Frankfurt—the Frankish church—has condemned my Ecumenical Council at Nicaea. I convened it at great expense and effort and they refused to send delegates to discuss the issue of bringing back icons. Now—years later—they condemn us for voting to bring them back. They even criticised the Pope for voting for it."

I kept my eyes on the hawk and my hand on my sling, waiting for her to tell me what she wanted.

"Constantine needs sons. Maria gives him only daughters."

I put a stone in my sling. The hawk floated higher. "Maria is fertile. Two children in three years," I noted.

"And none for four years."

"She has had little opportunity." I kept my eyes on the hawk so Irini could not see my anger.

"Constantine never liked Maria. Seven years of marriage and he never bestowed upon her the title of Augusta. He intends to divorce her." She chewed on a grass blade.

I kept my voice even. "It is true that Constantine never liked Maria. The day that he learned of his betrothal, he told me that he would divorce her. But when you were under house arrest, he treated her with respect and even affection. I will go to Constantinople and speak to him."

"You will not. I forbid it!"

Startled, I returned my gaze to the circling hawk. "You are taking revenge on Maria because she told Constantine to keep you under house arrest."

Her voice grew hard. "She has come between me and my son. She sides with Constantine whenever we disagree. She stands next to him in the Consistory meetings and asks questions of his advisors. In Magnavra Palace, she addresses the ambassadors and foreign envoys before I do. Constantine said I would rule jointly with him. Me—not Maria!"

"So you exiled the poor woman here for the summer and kept Constantine for yourself—you and the little seductress."

"Watch yourself, Thekla!"

I returned my eyes to the hawk. If she wanted an apology, I wasn't giving one. After a minute, she went on.

"Tula suits him better than Maria. Tula comes from a wealthy Constantinople family. Her aunt Tisti was my attendant. If Constantine wants to divorce Maria and marry Tula, I see nothing wrong with it." Her voice rang with satisfaction.

"And you think that Tula will let you have Constantine all to yourself?"

"She is with child. She will have enough to occupy herself."

I gaped at her. My heart ached for Maria. The hawk was closing his wings to drop. I put a stone in my sling and let fly. A feather drifted down. "What does Patriarch Tarasios say about a divorce?"

She spat out the grass blade. "The Patriarch is being tiresome. He claims that under canon law, Maria cannot be divorced without cause. Failure to produce a son after producing two healthy daughters is not grounds for divorce, he claims. He took it upon himself to bring the bishops who had represented the Patriarchs of Jerusalem, Antioch, and Alexandria at the Council in Nicaea. They gave Constantine their arguments against his divorce and remarriage. He threw them out."

"What does Abbott Theodore say? Tula is his niece. He must have an opinion."

She ripped a blade of grass into shreds. "Theodore is being even more tiresome. He and that pontificating uncle of his are writing letters to bishops and abbotts saying that Maria has given Constantine no reason for divorce. What do celibate men know about procreation? Maria could produce a string of girls. But Theodore won't listen to reason. He and Platon are turning the clergy against Constantine with their moralizing."

Irini left a few days later. I asked if I could come with her. I wanted to talk to Constantine. She refused. A bitter, discontented feeling took over me as I watched the yacht leave the harbour. I lost my temper with Megalo for staring over the wall. I quarrelled with Aspasia about what she paid for fish. Our usual cheerful mealtime chatter went quiet.

Chapter III

A dizzying, stinging snowstorm sealed us in that January. Wind whistled through every crack in the walls and numbed our faces and hands when we went out to feed the beasts. We brought our wool mattresses into the kitchen and hung blankets over the door and window to block the draft. It was cosy and warm with the kettle hanging over a low fire. We carded wool, twirled it into yarn on our spindles, and knotted sweaters and stockings.

Two Sundays after Nativity, a fierce hammering came on the kitchen door. We forced it open against the blowing snow to find the stone mason's two sons. They had climbed the snowdrifts to get over the wall. We pulled them inside.

"Empress Maria and the two little girls are in Father Dimitrios's cottage," they panted, warming their hands at the hearth. "An imperial vessel dumped them on the quay late last night. Father Dimitrios heard them crying for help."

"They cannot be Maria and the girls," I reassured the worried nuns as they wrapped me and two strong novices in shawls and cloaks. "Perhaps a ship went down, and the survivors are a mother and her daughters," I speculated.

I was wrong. There they were, the three of them, huddled in blankets by the priest's fire. Maria had dragged her shawl over her head and was rocking back and forth, moaning. Alarmed and frightened, I dropped to my knees beside her. "Empress, what has happened?"

She lifted a face swollen with weeping. "He has sent us here to die."

"Who has sent you? Have Constantine's uncles taken the throne? Where is Constantine?"

"My husband has sent us. We are condemned to exile on this Godawful island!"

"Constantine would never send away his children!" I burst out.

Her moans became a scream of rage. "He has divorced me, you stupid nun! Patriarch Tarasios signed the divorce with his own hand. And he made me a nun!" She yanked off her shawl.

I clapped my hands over my mouth to stifle my cry. Maria's heavy dark hair was gone. She was completely bald. Red bleeding scrapes from an unskilled razor crisscrossed her scalp. She looked monstrous, a terrified creature with desperate eyes.

"Holy Mother of God!" Whispers filled the room like dark smoke. Efrosini and Irinoula began wailing louder. Father Dimitrios put his hands over his youngest child's eyes.

"You took the vows?" He was aghast.

"Am I mad? Patriarch Tarasios took my vows for me! His hand held the razor cutting off my hair. He looked me in the eye and pronounced me a nun. The next minute we were dragged through the snow to the boat. The Palace eunuchs wouldn't let us take anything, even the children's clothing. They said it belonged to the Empire."

"What have you done to make Constantine do this?" I blurted, then covered my mouth. How deep is the belief of women that we are to blame for the abuse done to us.

Maria's voice shook with hatred. "My duty is what I have done. I stood beside his throne for hours with an aching back when I was great with child so he could show off his manly prowess. I bore him two children. I walked in processions to every church to celebrate every saint's day. I handed out alms to orphans and poor people. Constantine was happy with me. When Irini was gone, he came to my chambers, he sat me beside him at banquets. Then Abbott Theodore begged Constantine to visit his mother. Then that witch, that she-devil, baited Constantine with that harlot. My husband forgot me and his children. He only saw those young breasts. 'Let your mother go free,' she whispered to him. Now Irini is back in the Palace and I am in exile with his children!"

I covered my eyes with shame for Constantine. "He will tire of her," I stammered. "Your hair will grow back. You will again be Empress."

"This is a tonsure, not a haircut, you stupid fool!" she shrieked. "A nun cannot be an empress!" She drew her shawl over her head and began rocking and moaning.

I reached for Efrosini but she beat at me with her fists

and clung to her mother. "Where is Papa? Bring Papa!" she screamed.

We wrapped them in cloaks and shawls and struggled through the deep snow to the convent. Maria clung to Father Dimitrios. Her tears froze on her cheeks and left white patches of frostbite. The novices carried the few bundles that Maria's attendants had managed to snatch. The stone mason's son carried seven-year-old Irini.

Efrosini screamed. She threw herself onto the snow and beat her feet and her fists, a terrified and furious five-year-old. She kicked whoever tried to lift her. When I gave up coaxing her and started walking with the others, she trailed us, screaming. Only when she was exhausted and coated in snow did she allow the priest's eldest son to carry her. We took them straight to our kitchen where the nuns' frightened faces sent Maria into a rage.

"Why are we here? Take us to the imperial suite!" she shrieked.

"It's freezing up there, Highness. We sleep by the warm fire." I kept my voice calm.

"I will not sleep in a kitchen!" Her voice rose to hysteria. "Irinoula! Efrosini! Come with me!" She yanked open the door to the passage.

Irinoula, usually so compliant, threw her arms around my legs. Efrosini crawled into the warm place behind the oven where the cats sleep. I closed the door and drew a breath. "She'll come back when she gets cold."

She didn't. Sister Matrona and I found her lying under an open window, mounded with snow. We lifted her arms over our shoulders and dragged her into the kitchen. We propped her on a chair before the fire with her bare feet in a pan of hot water and we spooned warm soup into her mouth. We held her jaw closed to make her swallow. Slowly, colour returned to her cheeks.

"Pray that she lives," I murmured to Aspasia.

"What does she have to live for?" she muttered.

That night, I slept with my arm over Maria to keep her warm. Irinoula curled up with Aspasia but Efrosini refused to come out from behind the oven. We pushed in blankets and a bowl of vegetable stew and bread which she grabbed with quick hands. During the night, I felt her small body creep next to mine.

In the morning, I opened my eyes to Maria's unblinking stare. She spoke in a monotonous stream. "She poisoned Emperor Constantine, she killed his babies that he put inside her, she poisoned the crown that Leon wore, she poisoned Patriarch Nikitas the Slav and Patriarch Pavlos. Everyone knows, everybody whispers."

My soul trembled. My eyes saw Irini gathering spring hyacinths on Prinkypos. She had hung them to dry in our kitchen to use later in a poultice for the sores on Constantine's grandfather's arms and neck. "Take care to avoid the poisonous hyacinths," I had warned her, and she had smiled. "Poison is a woman's weapon," she had replied. Then I remembered how Emperor Leon had died after wearing a crown that had raised terrible boils on his head. Irini had ordered the crown to be mounted on the wall of the Church of Holy Wisdom, never to be used again. Then Patriarch Nikitas had died, and Patriarch Pavlos had died, and Irini had appointed Tarasios, her advisor, as Patriarch, even though Tarasios wasn't a cleric and had to be swiftly ordained. Irini herself had placed the mitre of Patriarch on his head. All these memories flooded me as Maria spewed her stream of deadly words over our kitchen.

I forced my thoughts away. A person needs a pillar to lean against and Irini was mine. She had got me out of prison. She had appointed me Abbess of an imperial convent. Because of her, I slept with a full stomach in a comfortable bed. I had pledged my loyalty to her. We believe what we need to believe about those to whom we have pledged our loyalty.

The nuns were crossing themselves. Megalo knelt beside Irini and spoke in the subservient murmur of a Palace attendant. "Empress Maria, your breakfast is ready."

Maria's voice went sharp. "Where have you been, worthless servant? I have been waiting for hours in these filthy sheets. I will have you whipped."

"Empress, it won't happen again, I promise. Time for prayers. Then breakfast."

"Why is it so cold? Have you let the fire die? I will have you whipped." Maria sat up and her scarf slid off her bald head. The nuns gasped and crossed themselves. Megalo quickly wrapped her scarf around her head and drew a shawl around her shoulders. We watched in silence as she pulled on Maria's boots and led her to the commode in the hall.

From that moment, we watched Maria slide into madness. She chatted with people only she could see. She complained about food that only she could taste. She combed her bald head with nothing in her hand. Abruptly, she would join our conversation like a sane woman, only suddenly to look terrified and retreat into a world of her own.

For three days, heavy snowfall sealed us in with her madness. Finally, sunshine sparkled on the snow and we rushed outside, desperate to escape. Efrosini came out from behind the oven and went with Sister Evanthia to feed the chickens. Aspasia drew me aside.

"Trouble, Thekla. The nuns are whispering that the devil has entered Maria. They say that the devil will jump from her lips and enter our souls."

"Such foolishness!" I snapped.

"My dear, they're frightened. They cross themselves when Maria looks into a mirror that isn't there. They glance at each other when she draws a line of kohl around her eyes with no brush between her fingers. Do something or they will run to Father Dimitrios and tell him that Maria is possessed by the devil. The villagers will shun us. The fishermen won't sell us fish."

I made a face. "The poor woman is terrified. Can you blame her for losing her wits? She was betrayed by her husband and Patriarch Tarasios. And me. She thought I was a lowly abbess under her thumb and suddenly I am her prison guard."

"Do something, Thekla, or there will be trouble."

That dusk, during Esperinos services in the refectory where we prayed because the little church was too cold, I prayed aloud in a calm voice, "Mother of God, please hold Maria's spirit safe in your hands and lift her despair so that she may join our blessed community in peace."

I added that to our prayers before and after every meal and the nuns became calmer. The snow melted, the village girls came for their lessons, and their sweet voices chanting their lessons eased our minds.

Irinoula joined their lessons. These were her friends from the previous summer. Efrosini came to the classroom door but wouldn't go inside. She kicked the door and screamed at Irinoula to come out. I dragged her to the kitchen. She ran back and threw snowballs at the classroom door until she was cold and tired. Then she crawled behind the oven. We could hear her talking to the cats.

"We are going to see Papa today. We're putting on our prettiest dresses for Papa."

"She adored her father," I murmured to Aspasia and Sister Matrona. "She used to run into his arms in Magnavra Palace at the end of the day. She would sit in his lap and make him kiss her dolls and kiss her last so she could feel his kiss when she went to bed."

I admired her strength even as I abhorred the ear-splitting screams that shattered our peace. But as days passed and her screaming got her nothing, she started helping Aspasia roll out the flatbread and cook it on the iron plate over the coals. She followed me around the convent as she had the previous summer. One day she went with Irinoula to lessons.

February brought warmer weather and our return to the dormitory. Maria and the little girls moved up to the imperial suite. Sister Evanthia and I had removed the tall polished steel mirror so Maria wouldn't see the stubble of her hair. I hoped that normal life would draw Maria back from madness, that she would dress herself and the girls. But the next morning, Efrosini and Irinoula appeared in the kitchen alone.

"Mama won't get up," Efrosini said. "She stinks."

Aspasia rolled her eyes. "Heaven help us if she's soiled the bedding. It cannot be washed until warmer weather."

Sister Matrona, Megalo, and I went up and found Maria in bed staring at the ceiling. "Get her up," I said to Megalo. "Even if she is mad, she has to dress and use the commode."

"I'll get her a nun's winter habit and undergarments," said Sister Matrona. "Her Palace clothing, I will put away for when she goes home—if she ever does."

I felt ill. I went outside to feed the chickens. The sky was blue and the sea sparkled. The clean sharpness made me feel better, but when I came back into the kitchen, I stifled a cry. Maria was sitting at the table eating porridge. Sunlight glistened on her red, scraped scalp. She smiled at me and smoothed the nun's rough wool tunica she was wearing.

"My attendant has found my clothing. I had this woven exclusively for me."

I went to my study, sat at my desk, and took out a sheet of papyrus and a pen.

"My dear Constantine," I wrote. "Are you aware that your wife and daughters are here against their will? Your children cry every night because you have not kissed them. Can you send them to her parents in Paphlagonia?"

I took another sheet of papyrus. "Esteemed Empress Irini. Maria and your two granddaughters arrived in a snowstorm with no clothing except what they were wearing. Please be so kind as to send their winter clothing. I beg you to send them to Maria's parents in Paphlagonia."

Then I wrote to Maria's parents and asked them to send clothing for the three of them. I took the letters down to the harbour the next day when Megalo shouted that the mail boat was coming, but the postal carrier who sailed in was not Elias. Disappointment struck my heart like a blow. I needed to talk to Elias and unburden my shock and grief over this awful situation.

"Where is the postmaster? When is he coming back?" I inquired, trying to sound casual.

"He went off somewhere," he shrugged, taking my letters and my coin. Some weeks later, Megalo banged on my study door.

"Mail boat coming. Looks like Elias at the helm."

I hurried down to the village and found him warming himself by the priest's fire. His dark hair was cut short like a monk's, and he was clean-shaven. This meant he had been disguised as a monk and was spying for someone. But whom? He never spoke of his other life. Father Dimitrios went to get mugs of hot tea and Elias put his arms around me.

"Thekla, poor thing. How are you handling this imperial invasion?"

His embrace broke my control and I sobbed into the rough wool of his tunica. "Maria says that Constantine ordered Patriarch Tarasios to sign the divorce decree. She says that Patriarch Tarasios tonsured her with his own hand! Her scalp was bleeding! I wrote to Constantine but he hasn't answered. The children need warm clothes, Elias. An imperial boat dumped them on the quay at night in a snowstorm with nothing but what they were wearing. Where have you been? I needed to talk to you and find out the truth. Surely Constantine can't know what has happened to them."

Father Dimitrios returned with a mug of thyme tea and Elias let me go. I sank onto a stool by the fire.

Elias took another stool. "Our Emperor knows exactly where his wife and children are," he said gently. "He signed the order exiling them here. He is besotted with beautiful Tula."

"I wrote to Empress Irini but she hasn't answered. I don't even know if she got my letter."

"Why are you surprised at Maria's plight?" Elias asked. "Irini is taking revenge on Maria for persuading Constantine to keep her under house arrest. Maria got between Constantine and Irini. She became the wife and empress she was meant to be. No one was surprised when Irini returned, and Maria was forcibly tonsured and exiled. Scandalised, yes. Surprised, no."

"That poor woman," said Father Dimitrios. "I hear that she is acting strangely."

"She is going mad," I replied bluntly. "She calls Megalo her attendant and orders her to pack because the yacht is taking her back to the Palace. She combs her bald head with no comb in her fingers. Then the truth of her awful situation comes over her and she wails for her parents to come and save her. The nuns and novices whisper that the devil has taken her and will come out her lips and enter our souls. I'm worried that they will leave."

"I will come up with you today and tell them that the devil is nowhere on the island and that Maria is simply frightened," said Father Dimitrios. "Give the poor woman something to do. Wasn't she copying a scroll last summer?"

"I suggested it. She shrieked that she will have me whipped."

"Her mail may distract her." Elias drew from his pouch a waxed packet sealed with an impressive blob of red wax. "From Abbott Theodore."

"That sanctimonious snob!" I snapped. "He thinks only of his own opinions. I knew him when he was ten and he came to Irini's reception with his mother, who was her attendant. He was already full of himself. His mother was the same. I heard that she would beat her servants, then make them kneel beside her while she begged God's forgiveness."

I cracked the seal and scanned the neat writing. "Abbott Theodore and his uncle Abbott Platon oppose the divorce. They say it is not legal because there are no grounds. Maria birthed two healthy daughters and would likely produce a son. He is calling this 'mehia'—adultery. He says that if Constantine marries Tula, the marriage will be bigamy."

Father Dimitrios nodded soberly. "Worse. If Constantine breaks the marriage vow that he made before God, he is denying the existence of God. This is punishable by excommunication under canon law and possibly death under civil law."

"Constantine is Emperor. He can do whatever he wants," pointed out Elias.

I put the letter in my bag. "I don't know whether his letter will give Maria hope that she will again be the Empress or push her further into madness."

"She needs to know what Abbott Theodore is doing on her behalf," counselled Father Dimitrios. "His faith in her returning to the Palace may restore her sanity. Or Emperor Constantine will come to his senses and bring his family home," he added.

Elias shook his head. "The betrothal ceremony is set for August. The wedding is in September."

"Will Patriarch Tarasios officiate?" Father Dimitrios asked.

"The good Patriarch has refused," said Elias sarcastically. "He has issued a statement saying that the divorce might not be legal and the remarriage perhaps not entirely moral."

"But he approved the divorce!" I burst out. "He tonsured the poor woman. He even said her vows for her!"

Elias made a face. "Patriarch Tarasios is Irini's puppet. He has appointed Abbott Joseph of the Kathari Monastery to perform the wedding. He himself will attend as a guest."

"Such a hypocrite!" Father Dimitrios muttered.

Elias handed me a large and lavishly sealed letter. "For Megalo."

I scowled as I opened the letter and read the elegant sloping script. "It's from her husband, Fanis, another hypocrite. As usual, in this letter, Fanis praises Megalo for devoting herself to God. She is only here because he ordered her to become a nun. For twenty years, Megalo has received these letters and she still believes that one day Fanis will come and take her back to Constantinople to be his wife." I threw down the letter in disgust.

"Why doesn't she take the vows? I would be happy to hear them," Father Dimitrios offered.

"I won't let her," I said bluntly. "Our typikon states that a woman has to enter our convent of her own will and Megalo is here because of the will of Fanis."

"Abbott Fanis has built himself quite a monastery," noted Elias. "I've been there. It's in a forest. Cool in summer. Heated with wood in winter—no goat dung fires like on this island."

"And built with Megalo's dowry money," I snarled.

I gave the letter from Abbott Theodore to Maria and watched her read it, worried that she would start screaming. She read every line, then carefully laid it on the kitchen fire and crouched before it, muttering what sounded ominously like curses. Her had scarf slipped, and her stubbled pate gleamed in the firelight. Aspasia crossed herself and hissed at me.

"Get her out of here. I can't look at that head another minute."

I coaxed Maria into my study and used up some of our precious apple wood to kindle a fire. I gave her a small glass of our elderberry wine and joined her. Then I waded through the snow to the scriptorium and brought back the scroll of the story of Saint Makrina. I placed it on my desk and brought out my box of quills, bottle of ink, and some pages of papyrus.

"You cannot live here and do nothing," I told Maria firmly. "We all work. So will you." When I came back an hour later, she was copying the scroll.

There, Maria found peace. Concentrating on another woman's wise words edged aside her own fearful thoughts. As the weeks passed and the Lenten sun warmed the scriptorium, we moved her there. Sometimes, when I walked by the doorway, she would lift her head and greet me quietly. But other times, a terrified expression would cross her face and she would throw down her quill and run to the low place in the convent wall by the kitchen. She would throw herself over the style and down the hill, frantically trying to escape the terror inside her.

"She eats almost nothing," Aspasia murmured to Sister Matrona and me one March day as we watched Maria's skinny arms and legs flailing down the steep slope. "I fear she will starve herself to death."

"Or throw herself into the sea and drown," said Sister Matrona.

Chapter IV

Maria spotted the imperial yacht first. She would, of course. All she did besides copy scrolls was watch for ships that she believed were coming to take her to the Palace. As Easter grew nearer, she sat at the window of the imperial suite or paced the path outside the convent walls keeping her eyes fixed on the golden haze of Constantinople floating between sea and sky. Finally, her scream of joy ripped our peace.

"Papa is coming for us! The yacht is flying the imperial banner! Girls! Run to meet Papa!"

I grabbed the big iron key to the convent gate and chased them across the pasture, heart pounding. Had Constantine really come for his family? I shouldered Maria aside to get the key into the lock and watched the three of them run full tilt down the lane, bare feet flying. They owned sandals; the shoemaker in Pendykion had come out and measured the feet of everyone on the island who needed sandals. But with the warm days of spring, the little girls happily copied the nuns and went barefoot. Maria had given up shoes from indifference—the mad do not feel the cold. Her hair was growing out in uneven patches and she resembled a hedgehog. I had tried to even it out after her weekly bath, but she had screamed hysterically when I reached for the scissors.

I followed them more slowly and the imperial yacht was pulling into the harbour when I joined Father Dimitrios on the quay. The girls were jumping up and down and shrieking, "Papa, Papa!" Their eyes were fixed on the cabin door. Maria was biting her fingers.

"Constantine," she was whimpering with desperate hope.

But the passenger who stepped from the cabin was not their father. A strangled cry came from Maria's throat as Irini marched down the gangplank. Four guards followed, then Irini's mute slave staggering under bundles.

Terror and fury fought for Maria's face. "Papa is coming next," she choked, eyes on the cabin door.

Irini bent so the girls could kiss her cheek.

"Grandmama, is Papa coming out now?" demanded Efrosini.

"Papa didn't come today, sweetheart."

Maria slapped her hands over her mouth.

Efrosini's big eyes filled with tears. "Are you taking us home to Papa?"

"No, dear. You are staying here."

Efrosini crumpled to the quay in a pool of sobs. I knelt beside the distraught child and whispered in her ear. "Show Grandmama your goat and your doll that Sister Efthia made for you. Then ask her again to take you to

Papa."

Efrosini didn't move but she stopped sobbing. I kissed her wet cheek and rose.

"Good that you have come, Empress Irini." I spoke the traditional greeting and bent my knees.

Irini ran her eyes over Maria who was still staring fixedly at the yacht, hands over her mouth. "No shoes? Whatever is that garment she is wearing?"

"A nun's habit, Empress. We are saving her silk tunica for when she returns to the Palace. How long will we be blessed with your presence?"

"Until Holy Week. Everyone important in Constantinople has gone to their country houses for Lent. Constantine and Tula are staying at the Palace of Saint Mamas."

"Surely he has tired of her by now." I had said this to Aspasia that morning and she had told me not to be stupid. Sister Matrona had told me to face facts.

Irini laughed lightly. "Constantine never tires of her. They are always together. The betrothal will be in August with the wedding in September. You will attend." She nodded to Father Dimitrios and went into the church to thank Saint Nikolaos for her safe arrival.

"Auntie Thekla, what is 'betrothal'?" asked Irinoula, taking my hand.

Maria hissed the answer. "Betrothal means that you will have sisters. Papa only makes girls." When Irini came out, Maria trailed us up the hill at a distance, savagely whipping the trees with a switch she had ripped off a bush. Empress Irini glanced back at her.

"Has she lost her senses?"

"No more than her husband," I muttered.

The novices served Irini her mid-day meal at the table under the grape arbour, where tiny leaves greened the vines. The green tips of spring onions and coriander sprinkled the kitchen garden. Maria and I stood, hands folded, watching Irini eat Lenten fare: calamari baked with aubergine, boiled wild greens spiced with thyme and oregano, barley bread moistened with olive oil. Warm breezes mingled with the gentle piping of a shepherd's pipes and the perfume of our pink flowering apricot tree. It was so quiet that I could hear our goats and sheep chewing their cuds. Finally, Irini sat back and dabbed her lips with her handkerchief. "I have been indoors too long," she smiled. "In Athens, I would be having all my meals under the olive trees by now. Where are the little girls?"

They threw themselves out of the kitchen and rushed to tell her about the goats and kittens and their lessons. "Will you take us home to Papa, please, Grandmama?" Efrosini begged.

"No, sweetheart. You will stay here."

Efrosini's scream split the air. She threw herself on the ground, kicked her feet, and pounded her fists. Sister Evanthia and Megalo dragged her away screaming. Maria spoke in a sharp hiss.

"How can you be so cruel as to separate two little girls from their father?"

Irini sipped her lemon and honey drink. "Constantine sent you here, not me."

"You exiled us—not Constantine. You chose me to be his wife because you thought I was weak. You thought you could order me around like you order Constantine. When you found that I was strong, you got rid of me."

Empress Irini glanced at me. "Take her away, Thekla."

Maria slapped away my hand. "From the first day that you came to Constantinople, you planned to be Empress in your own right. You put Constantine under house arrest so you could have all the power. The army freed him and he became the emperor that he was born to be. The commanding generals respected him. The senators and ambassadors bowed to him. I told him to keep you away."

"Thekla, remove her!"

"So you put that concubine in his bed."

"I will have your tongue slit. You will never speak again."

"You cannot slit every tongue in the Empire."

"Thekla, put her in the dungeon. Ten lashes."

I nearly laughed. The dungeon door was rusted shut. And I had no whip. I called Sister Matrona and between us and a strong novice, we dragged Maria, fighting and screaming, through the courtyard, out the doors to the convent enclave and into the basilica. We got her down the steps into the crypt and I slammed the barred door. The walls echoed her curses as I turned the key. We staggered up the steps and collapsed on the church floor, panting. After a while, the screaming stopped. I could hear the soothing coos of the doves in the cupola. I returned cautiously down the steps. Maria lay in a sobbing heap on the stone floor. I searched for words that might ease her suffering.

"Maria, you have been wronged. What Constantine

and Empress Irini have done to you and the children is unforgivable. But you will not drag this convent into your misery. You will not destroy our peace."

"She is a bitch, a sorceress, a cruel tyrant!" she screamed.

I stood up. "You will stay here until she is gone."

"No! Not here." Maria crawled to the door and gripped the bars. Her face was a mess of tears and despair. "I need a window so I can watch for Constantine."

I went up and discussed the situation with the others.

"She does need light and fresh air," Sister Matrona pointed out.

"The village carpenter could install a bar over a door in the dormitory," suggested the novice.

I nodded, resigned. "Now I am truly a jailor," I muttered.

The novice went to bring blankets and food and Sister Matrona and I returned to the crypt. Maria was clinging to the bars.

"Maria, you can choose," I told her. "You can be locked in here until Empress Irini leaves or you can be locked in a dormitory room. Either way, you will be locked in. And if you scream or curse, we won't feed you."

She laughed, a frightening, maniacal shriek. "You won't let me starve. I am Empress Maria."

"Hermit monks live on water," noted Sister Matrona.

Maria's voice came so low and intense that it raised the hair on my arms. "She poisoned Emperor Constantine. She poisoned Emperor Leon. She poisoned Patriarch Nikitas and Patriarch Pavlos. She will poison

Constantine. And you."

Sister Matrona and I left. I was shaking. Sister Matrona took my arm. "You might consider finding a food tester when the Empress is in residence," she murmured.

I glanced at her, thinking she was joking, but her face was serious.

After Esperinos services at dusk, I brought supper to Irini in my study, then joined the nuns and novices in the refectory for our light meal of bread and cheese. I put some in a bowl for Maria and Sister Matrona filled a jug with watered wine. Maria was huddled in a corner of the crypt wrapped in blankets. She got up when we placed the food on the floor and came quietly with us to the latrines and the wash basins. She remained silent as we walked her back to the crypt and locked her in.

Empress Irini joined me for evening rounds, when I checked that all outside gates and doors were locked. The stars were so bright and the black sea so still that I could not discern where the stars left off and their reflections began. We walked slowly through the softly sleeping fruit trees.

"I have a few things to put in the secret room," she murmured. "Is the trapdoor in working order?"

"Yes, Highness. I grease the hinges every Friday."

"I have a mind to send Maria to the prison convent on Lesbos."

For a moment, I couldn't breathe. I forced calm into my voice. "You won't see or hear Maria again, Empress. The little girls miss their father terribly. Can they visit the Palace?"

"Efrosini is the more intelligent of the two, is she not?"

I replied cautiously, wondering what Irini was plotting. "Efrosini is only five. She reads a few words but she is quick to learn. Her sister is six and she reads well."

"Irinoula is passive. She will make a good nun."

This startled me. Was I passive? Was that why Irini had appointed me as abbess twenty years ago? The thought shook me. We went to my study where Irini's mute slave was preparing the bed. I locked the door, pulled the heavy wool curtains over the long windows, and held the candle near the hearth floor. Irini picked up the poker and placed the tip in the small hole in the stones. She pressed down. The hearth floor dropped silently, revealing the steps to the secret room and the escape passage out of the convent.

Irini took my candle and went smoothly down the steep steps, leaving the slave and me alone.

Except that we weren't alone. A shadow moved under a table. I spoke softly. "Come out, Efrosini!"

She appeared quickly, her eyes on the faint light coming from the steps. I held out my hand and led her to the top step. We could hear clinking. Irini was counting the coins and jewels that she and I had brought from the Palace over the last twenty years. The light grew dim. She was moving down the tunnel and checking the secret door into the root cellar.

"I will take you down there later," I whispered. "You must tell no one about this, not even your dolls. Promise?"

She nodded. We waited silently holding hands. The light grew brighter. Irini appeared and her eyes fell on Efrosini. She nodded thoughtfully.

"The child knows. Good. One day that will prove useful."

I took her candle and set it beside a parchment I had placed on my desk. "This is a list of every object and coin that I have brought here for you and hid inside the chest below. It does not include what you have brought. You need to read it, so that you know everything that is down there."

"In the morning," she yawned from the couch. Her slave began unlacing her boots.

"Best that you read it now." My hard tone must have caught her attention for she sat at the desk and slid her slim fingers down the page as she read the entries.

"You are a good accountant. Are you writing an account of me in your convent log?"

"Good night, Empress." I took Efrosini's hand, and we closed the door behind us.

At dawn, Sister Matrona and I took Maria to the latrines and the wash basin, then to Orthros prayers in the little church where the nuns' light chanting seemed to ease Maria's dejection. Afterwards, she walked obediently to the refectory with us and ate quietly. For once, I was glad that Empress Irini never attended services and took her meals in my study. Maria did not resist when we walked her back to the crypt. I locked her in and she wrapped herself in her blankets in the corner.

I sent a novice down to the village to tell the carpenter we needed a bar installed over a door in the dormitory. Then I went to the weaving room where Sister Filothei was supervising the nuns at the looms.

"Maria needs something to do," I said. "Inactivity

will send her into permanent madness. I would prefer that she continue copying a scroll, but we cannot move a lectern and all the copying materials into the crypt or the dormitory room. Besides, Maria might fly into one of her mad rages and damage the scroll. She will have to weave until Irini leaves."

"Maria has been badly used but she must accept her fate," said Sister Filothei. "She has been indulged her whole life and now she indulges in madness to avoid facing reality. She is not the only woman who has been abandoned here by her husband. Megalo, for example. They are both victims of a man's whims, as are all women."

I wondered if Sister Filothei knew that I had been stood up three times at the altar. I had chased my betrothed to Constantinople and spent a year looking for him. Irini had located him and made him release me from my betrothal vows. One more thing that I owed her.

"We pay a price for having eyes that see the truth," said Sister Filothei, "The price is suffering the pain of accepting reality. Megalo doesn't have the strength to accept the reality of her husband's decision to leave her here. Maria chooses madness over accepting what Constantine has done to her. Empress Irini has courage and strength but her obsession for power blinds her to reality."

I was still thinking about that when the novice returned with the carpenter and the village girls came for their lessons with Sister Evanthia. Their soft chanting soothed my ragged nerves. But I felt uneasy, and as we crossed the courtyard carrying the loom and a basket of yarn for Maria, Sister Filothei jerked her chin at the open windows of my study. Irini was looking across the courtyard at the classroom.

"What is the Empress up to now, I wonder?" she murmured.

"We will soon find out," I muttered darkly.

Maria glared at the loom when we set it up in the crypt. "I will not weave a rug. Nor will I knot one. It will ruin my hands."

"You will make a rug or we will not feed you," I snarled.

"I am the Empress," she said coldly. "You are committing treason by keeping me imprisoned. I will have you executed." Maria turned her back. We left.

"Such arrogance!" I exploded when we were outside.

Sister Filothei put her hand on my arm. "Now is Maria's chance to become a strong woman. She needs our patience or she will continue on the easy path into madness."

"She will choose madness, no matter how much patience we have," I fumed.

"Then that is the will of God."

Lessons were over and the village girls were running past us, chattering and laughing, Efrosini and Irinoula among them. I was letting them join their friends in the village for a few hours every day. Their father had formed strong friendships at their age. Then I heard Irini call Efrosini back. The child obediently disappeared into my study. Suspicious, I followed. They were sitting together on the couch. I sat at my desk and took out a bit of papyrus to write the provisions we needed from Pendykion. I was going there with Sister Filothei and Aspasia to purchase a larger stock pot and stronger yellow dye for our wool. My pen stopped when I heard Empress Irini's words.

"Efrosini, you are the direct legitimate heir to the throne of the Roman Empire of the East. Your father is now Emperor. Your grandfather was Emperor Leon. Your great-grandfather was Emperor Constantine. Your great-great grandfather was Emperor Leon the Isaurian who founded the Isaurian dynasty. You were born in the Purple Chamber as are all imperial children. Your Papa does not have a son. That means that you will be Empress Efrosini."

"Like you, Grandmama?" asked the five-year-old with quiet intensity.

"Yes, my sweet, and I will teach you everything you need to know."

This was lunacy. Constantine and Tula could produce a string of sons. Irini was putting impossible thoughts in the child's head, just as she had done with Constantine, telling him that he would marry the daughter of Charles of the Franks and rule both the Frankish Empire and the Empire of the Romans of the East. I put down my quill.

"Empress Irini, begging your pardon, but Constantine will very likely have a son. It is not wise to put impossible ideas in a child's head. Efrosini has been exiled to my convent and she is under my care, as are my nuns and novices. It is my duty to teach her the truth and not allow her to succumb to wild dreams." I held Irini's gaze. I didn't care that she could send me into exile for arguing with her. Efrosini's mind and spirit were my responsibility.

Irini arched her eyebrows. "Can you predict the future, Abbess Thekla? Did you predict that you would be governing an imperial convent and giving unwanted advice to an empress? Let Efrosini learn about the Empire. Her destiny is my concern, not yours."

"Irinoula is older. She is the next in line to the throne," I snapped.

"Irinoula lacks the strong will that I will need in my co-empress. I choose Efrosini."

What could I say? So, I stilled my mouth but not my ears or eyes. Every morning until Saturday before Holy Week when Irini departed, Efrosini went to Sister Efthia's class and learned to read, write, and do sums while Irini answered any dispatches that Elias had brought. Then Efrosini and Irini sat in my study under my watchful eye while Irini pointed to the maps on my wall and taught Efrosini the names of the towns, rivers, and seas. She taught her the locations of the fortresses and the duties of their commanders. Efrosini was cheerful and compliant. She had a quick mind and wanted to please her grandmother. After Ninth Hour prayers and our mid-afternoon meal, they went for a walk. I knew Irini would be drilling Efrosini on the day's lesson.

As much as I disapproved of what Irini was doing, I was glad of their daily walk because I could let Maria out and set her to weeding the garden and sweeping the courtyard. She needed outdoor exercise. Once, she tried to climb the stile over the wall, but Aspasia spotted her, and the novices and I dragged her to the crypt where I left her overnight with no food. She never tried again. When Megalo or one of the nuns shouted that Empress Irini and Efrosini were returning from their walk, we locked Maria in her barred dormitory room. At dusk, we took her to the latrines and wash basins, to prayer services, and to the refectory. Then back in her barred dormitory cell.

Every evening after my rounds, I sat at the table in my dormitory cell and, by splintered starlight or wavery candlelight, wrote my reflections in the convent log. Sometimes my fury at Constantine and Irini was so great that it was a wonder that my words didn't burst into flames.

By the time Holy Week arrived and Irini left, Efrosini could rattle off the names of the themes, fortified cities, market towns, and military bases. She could recite the seas, rivers, empires at our borders, and name all the Palace officials and their duties. She could even read a few words in Latin. She was a bright child and gobbled down the lessons like sweets. I didn't like Irini telling the child that she would become an empress, but I conceded that the lessons were showing Efrosini how to use her mind and it was clear to everyone that she had become a happier child.

The day the imperial yacht came for Empress Irini, the two little girls and I walked her to the quay. The lanes were empty; the villagers continued to shun the Empress for her treatment of Constantine. Now they also blamed her for exiling Maria and the children to the island.

At the gangplank, Efrosini fastened her piercing gaze on her grandmother. "Can we go with you today to see

Papa, Grandmama?"

"No, sweetheart. Not today."

The girls must have talked it over, because they silently held hands and watched their grandmother stride up the gangplank. Only after the yacht had sailed away did they press their little faces into my shoulder and sob.

Maria was waiting for them in the plateia. Sister Matrona had let her out when she saw the yacht leave the harbour. The girls flung themselves into Maria's lap in a tangle of arms and legs and kissing cheeks. As I watched them run out of the village and along the sea path, the heaviness in my heart lightened. Still, I felt that Saint Thekla was sending me a message in that joyful reunion of mother and daughters. She was warning me of dark times to come.

We are who we are and we suffer the consequences of our actions. If only Irini had not been so determined to sit alone on the throne; if only Constantine had not been such a gentle soul and wanted to please his mother; if only he had more of his grandfather and less of his father; if only the eunuchs whom Irini had appointed to high positions had not been so greedy. If only, if only. I saw the beginning and the middle and I tried to warn them of the end, but they didn't listen. All I could do was watch the consequences unfold.

The day Irini left, I brought Efrosini into my study and locked the door. I showed her how to open the trapdoor in the hearth with the poker. I took her down the steps, through the passage, and through the secret door into the root cellar. "This is our secret, just for you, Grandmama Irini, and me. You must promise not even to tell your dolls."

She nodded solemnly and I knew she would keep her promise.

In September, Maria shouted that the imperial yacht was entering the harbour. My heart sank. I had persuaded myself that this day would never come, that Constantine would not wed Tula but rather come to his senses and summon Maria and his children home. I dragged myself to my study, took my tiny icon of Saint Thekla from my desk, and tied her in the corner of my scarf. Then I folded my hands and waited.

Maria burst into my study. She had put on the yellow silk tunica that she had been wearing when she arrived nine months before. The delicate fabric was ripped and soiled with food stains and earth. Maria smoothed the battered garment with careful hands.

"Constantine has sent the yacht for me. There is a banquet tonight. I must be at his side."

Sister Matrona and two novices blocked the doorway. The mad are strong. It took all four of us to drag her to the crypt.

"Let her out when the yacht leaves the harbour," I told Sister Matrona. She looked at me sideways. This is what happens with madness. After a while, even the kindest soul will take the practical route. And I had another problem—Efrosini. When I returned to my study for my shawl and cloak, she was waiting, holding the doll that Sister Efthia had made.

"I'm coming with you. Papa wants me."

I knelt in front of her. "I am so sorry, my sweet. I cannot take you."

The agony in her eyes cut me like a knife. She fought for control, a small six-year-old, trying to grow up fast. "Papa came last night and told me to come."

"Papa meant next time, dear heart."

She collapsed on the floor and her body shook in silent sobs of despair. I sat cross-legged and gathered the limp child into my lap. "Next time the yacht takes me to the Palace, you will come with me. I promise before my icon of Saint Thekla." I untied Saint Thekla from my scarf and laid her on my heart.

What madness to make such a promise! Promises must be kept, no matter how foolish. But it was all I could offer a desperate child. Efrosini sat up and looked at me with her straight, piercing gaze.

"Write your promise in front of Saint Thekla."

So I sat at my desk and propped Saint Thekla against my heavy brass candlestick so that the saint could see me writing on the bit of papyrus. I read it aloud: "Abbess Thekla of Ikonion promises to take Efrosini, daughter of Emperor Constantine and Empress Maria, to Constantinople when Abbess Thekla goes on the imperial yacht next time. My promise is witnessed by Saint Thekla of Ikonion."

I signed it. I showed it to Efrosini. Then I showed it to Saint Thekla. Efrosini took the note and showed it to her doll. Then she tucked it inside her doll's underclothes. She and Irinoula walked me to the quay. As I waved goodbye from the deck, Efrosini lifted up the doll's tunica to show her underclothes, a reminder of my promise.

Constantine had me admitted to his chambers immediately and led me to a couch. I had not seen him for a year. His arms were more muscled and his shoulders wider. He held himself as a soldier accustomed to carrying a sword and shield. Even more, he moved with the easy, satisfied grace of the young men in my village who slept with their wives every night. Still, to say that he was not ashamed would give his sweet face the lie.

"Maria only gave me girls," were his first words.

"She is fertile. She would give you boys eventually."

He held up his hand just like his mother did to stop me from saying something she didn't want to hear. "My mother chose Maria. I choose Tula."

I drew a breath. "When you locked your mother under house arrest, people said that you became the leader you were born to be. The generals respected your decisions. You brought Maria to the Consistory and Magnavra Palace. You went to her bed. Then you let your mother out of house arrest. Now you sleep with a concubine and your wife and children are abandoned on an island. Why did you let Empress Irini out?"

He put his hands over his face. "The truth is, I felt lost. I have never known a day without my mother. I learned to read from her maps. She knows the Empire. She can recite the laws of the Ekloga. She sat in meetings in the Consistory and Magnavra Palace when she was younger than I. She speaks easily with the advisors and ambassadors and foreign envoys. The monks in the monasteries trust her. Most of all, Auntie Thekla, she is my mother and she gave me life. I could not sleep knowing I had locked her away."

I stared at his handsome face but what I saw was the little boy with round cheeks and chubby fingers who had brought me seashells and wriggling beetles. He had been a sweet, gentle child. He had sobbed in despair when his grandfather had died. He had wept at his father's death four years later. What had happened to that sensitive child that he could abandon his two daughters who adored him? I tried to speak calmly.

"Dino," I said, using the name we called him when he was a child. "I vowed my loyalty to Irini but she had you arrested and beaten until you nearly died. She locked you in your suite for nine months. You were the legitimate Emperor, made Co-emperor by your father, and she denied you the throne. The army had to march on Constantinople to name you as Emperor. Every day my heart feels the pain of her lies and deceit."

He went to the window and stared at the sea. "She apologized. She admitted she was wrong to keep me from the throne. She told me that we had ruled together when she was Regent and we could rule jointly again."

I threw up my hands. "Dino, she never allowed you to do anything when she was Regent. Do not let her persuade you that she did."

He didn't meet my eyes. "She gives money to poor houses and orphanages. She visits hospitals. She prays at a different church every day and gives them money. She organized the Council at Nicaea and brought icons back into the church."

"Which you protested at the time. You didn't want to sign the Declaration of Faith."

"I was young. Now I see her wisdom."

I glared at him, feeling helpless. They attacked each other and came to me for comfort—now they were allied against me. "Abbott Theodore and Abbott Platon are sending letters all over the Empire condemning you as an adulterer. They say your marriage to Tula will be bigamy."

He turned on me in anger. "Do you think I don't know?" He snatched up two letters and thrust them at me. "Read what these sanctimonious, pompous censors write to me. They sit in their quiet monastery in Bithynia and pass judgment on me who lives in a hornet's nest! I make sure that our army and navy keep the Caliph's army from raiding their monastery lands and they malign me with their letters. Theodore viciously condemns my marriage to Tula, then—listen to this—he finishes with, 'I deplore any censoriousness or bitter animosity. All I want is for myself and those with me to be left in our penitential seclusion. By your kindness and skill straighten what is crooked and make the rough places plain.'"

He flung down the letters. "Penitential seclusion? I have seen the luxuries that he enjoys in his monastery. When he tires of his responsibilities, he goes to his personal estate where servants wait on him. Now I understand why my grandfather got fed up with the monks and burnt down their monasteries."

I tried to use reason. "Constantine, the Empire is being divided by your divorce and remarriage. Is this young woman worth all this turmoil?"

He answered with a fury that I had never seen before. "Show respect to my betrothed, Auntie Thekla. I will not hear you speak ill of her."

I drew a breath. "Please let me bring your children

to visit you. They miss you terribly. They cry every night because you aren't there to kiss them."

His anger vanished and he dropped to the couch with his face in his hands. "If only I could see them again! I miss them more than you can imagine. But my mother says it is unwise to bring them here. Abbott Theodore and Abbott Platon will use them as ammunition in their letters. They will say that I am denying the law of inheritance."

"Then let them live with Maria's family in Paphlagonia. They are princesses. They need a better education than they are getting on the island." I didn't mention what Empress Irini was teaching Efrosini.

He lifted his hands helplessly. "I want to, but my mother says there are army factions in Paphlagonia who will use them to start a rebellion." He hesitated, not meeting my eyes. "How is Maria? My mother says she is well."

"Maria has gone mad," I replied bluntly. "She wears the rags of her Palace clothing and believes she is in the Palace. She roams the island, talking to herself. The village people whisper that the devil has entered her and they stone her. She comes home with blood running down her arms."

He covered his eyes. "God forgive me; I didn't know. My mother told me she was happy and occupied copying scrolls."

"We lock her up when your mother comes. If we didn't, she will scream in her face."

He sighed. "I feel sympathy for her. But you surely remember when Stavrakios beat me and threw me in prison for trying to arrest him. You went to Maria and begged her to come. Maria refused. When I was under house arrest, Maria went to live with her parents. She didn't share my solitude."

"She stayed long enough for you to put another child inside her," I flared.

He held up his hand. "Say no more. Do what you can for her. She is your responsibility now, not mine."

The second wedding of Constantine, fourth emperor of the Isaurian dynasty, was a simple affair in the Church of Saint Mamas, high on Galata Hill across the narrow waters of the Golden Horn from Constantinople. Irini took me with her in her carriage. We left Chalke Gate buffeted by crowds of monks shouting "Mihia! Adultery!" and transferred to the imperial barge to cross the Golden Horn. Then we entered another carriage and were pulled up the hill by straining oxen.

Neither of us spoke, partly because of the monks shouting outside our curtained windows and, on my side, because I was angry with her and Constantine. Safely inside the lovely Palace of Saint Mamas, I cooled my anger with sweetened lemon drink and pastries while Empress Irini unloaded her grievances onto my shoulders.

"Abbott Theodore isn't coming to the wedding. Or his mother, Tisti. Traitors! Tisti was my attendant when I was first married. She saw Constantine be born in the Purple Chamber. Tula is her niece! Her husband and her other children aren't coming either—too busy occupying the high moral ground."

Patriarch Tarasios had no moral difficulty attending

the wedding. He stood apart, wearing his usual lack of expression, while Abbott Joseph chanted the service. Tula's wealthy family filled the church wearing brilliantly coloured silk tunicas. Constantine was exultantly happy—his face shone with it—and his thirteen-year-old bride was radiant.

But Empress Irini's exotic beauty outshone them all. Her tunica was woven of gold and silver thread, and sapphires and rubies sparkled at her ears and throat. The bride and groom placed the nuptial crowns on each other's heads. Then Constantine immediately crowned Tula as Empress Augusta—normally bestowed only after the birth of a son. I left, nauseated. Eight years before, when Constantine had married Maria, I had felt equally ill, but that was because Constantine was miserable.

Outside the church, a familiar voice in my ear broke into my thoughts. "Not going to the banquet, as I see by your gloomy face."

"Elias!" I looked him over. He was decked out in a red silk tunica and sleeveless skaramaggion of green silk. He even wore green leggings and red shoes. "You're among the guests, as I see by your glorious attire," I retorted sourly.

"A family obligation, not my choice. I suggest you remove yourself before there is trouble. I would join you if I could."

Indeed, the plateia was packed with monks in their dark garb, oppressive and disquieting, a mirror of the storm clouds darkening the sky. I hurried down side streets to the Golden Horn and crossed on a barge carrying pigs destined for the swine market. My feet found their way to Ta Gastria convent and Abbess Pulkeria's study.

When I first came to Constantinople, I had sought shelter at Ta Gastria convent, lining up outside the gate with other poor women needing a meal and a bed. Abbess Pulkeria had found me employment as a kitchen maid in the wealthy home of Megalo's parents. Then the Abbess had hired me as her bookkeeper as I was good at sums. Now I always visited Abbess Pulkeria whenever I came to Constantinople. I was comforted by the shelter of those familiar walls and Abbess Pulkeria's wise counsel.

Abbess Pulkeria was getting stiff in her joints, as I saw when she rose from her desk to greet me. We sat on a couch and drank elderberry wine while she listened intently to my description of the wedding and the shouting monks. She shook her head soberly.

"Abbott Theodore has sent three letters to me and many other abbesses. He is calling this marriage bigamy. He accuses Emperor Constantine of denying the existence of God by breaking his marriage vows that he made in God's name. He is calling for Abbott Joseph to be defrocked for officiating at the wedding of a bigamist. I cannot argue with his reasoning."

"Nor can I," I said, feeling miserable. "Particularly since I am the prison guard for Constantine's too-swiftly divorced wife."

Abbess Pulkeria lowered her voice. "There is a rumour that Empress Irini has manipulated this divorce and remarriage. She did it to discredit Constantine and weaken his popularity. Then her eunuchs and Palace

Guards will crown her as sole ruler."

The thought made me dizzy. "The army chooses a new emperor and the army hates Irini," I fumbled. "So do the priests. Only the monks like her."

"The army is not as happy with Constantine as think," she countered quietly.

"Constantine used to be popular, and he will be again," I said stubbornly. But I knew that Stavrakios and Aetios would stop at nothing to get rid of him.

I ate supper with the poor women at the two long tables rather than suffer the prying questions of the rich paying guests in their private dining room. However, I gratefully accepted Abbess Pulkeria's offer of a private guest room. I slept fitfully, worried about Constantine, and left at dawn when the novice opened the convent gate. The enormous gold angels who gazed down upon me from the Golden Gate towers also seemed worried. I caught the first ferry to Chalkidon. As I bought bread and cheese in the Chalkidon market for my twenty-mile walk, I prayed that I could find a fisherman in Pendykion who would take me across to Prinkypos Island that evening. Otherwise, I would have to sleep in the cold convent in Pendykion. Elias was in Constantinople celebrating the imperial wedding. I would not be sharing his bed.

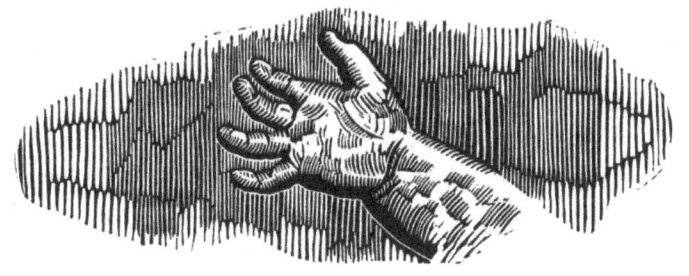

Chapter V

Maria's scream yanked me out of my account books. I jumped up from my desk and ran out to find her standing on the convent wall staring down at the sea far below. The mad have no sense of danger or death. I held my breath until she jumped down and ran for the gate with her daughters right behind her. Her shorn hair had grown out and Sister Matrona had trimmed it to her jaw, like her daughters. They were all barefoot, even though the early spring was chilly. I climbed up the ladder to look over the wall to see why she had screamed. The imperial yacht was coming but without the imperial banner, so no Irini or Constantine. I hadn't seen either of them for a year and I didn't want to. Efrosini and Irinoula held my heart. They were bright and cheerful girls of six and seven and we all loved them.

A tall thin figure came out on deck and raised an arm in greeting. I returned the wave with a smile, recognizing Irini's cousin, Theo. I liked him and had trusted him from the moment I met him, which was the same day that

I met Irini. But there was something hidden in Theo—like why he never went back to Athens. He had come with Irini when Emperor Constantine brought her from Athens but he had never married and continued to live alone in a suite at Daphne Palace. He and Emperor Leon had become close friends and were always together eating and drinking in the kapelaria of Constantinople. Theo struggled with deep melancholy after Leon died. He found some solace as a father to Constantine but his melancholy returned when Constantine was under house arrest. Theo loved the little girls and he came often to the island bringing dolls and fabric for tunicas. I stored the bolts of silk and linen in a stone vat sealed with wax for when the children were allowed to leave. On the island, they wore rough woven tunicas like the village girls, wool in winter and linen in summer. Theo could spend a whole day on the island chatting with Father Dimitrios and the villagers. Maria and the little girls always went down when he was there. After he left, Maria seemed calmer.

I splashed water on my face and arms in the kitchen and downed a mug of cool mint tea. In the early years of the convent when I was young and eager to prove my worth, I hurried to the quay whenever the imperial yacht came. Now I took my time.

Maria and the two girls were climbing on the gate when I got there with the key. They raced down the lane and I found them with Theo and Father Dimitrios on the bench by the church. The girls were holding their new dolls. They owned many now, which they shared with the village girls and also left around the convent. I came upon them perched on the latrine or sleeping with the goats. I even found one on an icon stand in the church. Theo handed me a satchel.

"Gifts from Irini. Sandals for the children and summer dresses."

I narrowed my eyes. "She has never sent anything before. What does she want?" I held up the dresses so Maria could see them. She was perched on a boulder near the quay, feet dangling in the water. Theo was watching her.

"Maria is descending further into madness," he murmured.

I felt the sadness and anger that came whenever I really looked at Maria. "Mothers pull their children indoors when she comes through the village. Sometimes Maria comes back with bruises on her arms and back. People are throwing stones at her."

Father Dimitrios sighed. "I cannot stop them. They believe she is possessed by the devil, no matter what I say. One day, I fear that someone will push her into the sea."

"Then she will drown," I said flatly. "I can only protect her by locking her up and I won't do that unless Empress Irini is at the convent and Maria becomes a menace. Maria does have her moments of sanity. I keep hoping that she will find her way back to clarity."

Theo looked at Father Dimitrios. "Can you perform an exorcism? You had great success exorcising the ghost of Patriarch Constantine."

I looked at him sharply to see if he was joking but his handsome face was serious.

Father Dimitrios shook his head. "The devil has not entered her soul. Maria escapes accepting that she is a prisoner here. Now she is a prisoner of her own mind."

We watched Maria as she jumped off the boulder and began prying mussels off the rocks with her knife. She pulled up her tunica to make a basket and was piling them in. Her bare legs were bruised and cut. Theo looked away.

"I have come to bring you to Constantinople, Abbess Thekla," he said.

I made a face. "Theo, tell the Empress that I'm busy."

"You may enjoy yourself," he smiled. "Irini has discovered the finger bone of Saint Eufemia. It was lost years ago and Patriarch Tarasios is reinstating it in the Church of Saint Eufemia by the Hippodrome. Irini wants you at the ceremony as her spiritual advisor."

Father Dimitrios crossed himself. "Praised be to God! A miracle that it was found!"

I laughed. "Another phony relic? Remember the coffin with the inscription that was supposedly written before the birth of Christ? The one that named her and Constantine as rulers?"

Father Dimitrios looked alarmed. "That wasn't genuine?"

Theo smiled kindly at him. "Perhaps it was, who knows? But this one might well be the real article. Patriarch Tarasios has recognised the casket that held the bone."

"I saw it when I was a boy," mused Father Dimitrios. "Then Emperor Constantine threw it in the sea because the bone exuded sweet myrrh and people were praying before it. He stored weapons in the church."

Theo shrugged. "Oh, I doubt if Emperor Constantine threw it in the sea. He never destroyed relics—only icons. Every church in Constantinople has always had some relic of a saint—a bone or scrap of clothing. That's why the Council of Nicaea could rule that all churches must have a relic—they were already there. Emperor Constantine confiscated this one because the priests were taking money from people to pray before it."

"Where did Empress Irini find this so-called relic? This sounds like another of her ploys," I said.

Theo smiled. "A bishop discovered it in a chapel on an island that he had just inherited from his father. Emperor Constantine had probably told a Palace Guards to get rid of the bone and the guard had sold it."

"Now tell me the real reason that she wants me at this ceremony?" I demanded sharply. "She prays before hundreds of relics in churches every year and never wanted me before."

"You are to bring the little girls with you."

I narrowed my eyes at him. "I have begged her to let the children visit their father and she has always refused. Why now?"

He lifted his hands and shrugged.

I thought that over. Then it came to me. "People are whispering that Irini exiled the children out here—not Constantine. She wants to show herself as a loving grandmother. Well, I'm not playing that game."

Theo gave me his sweetest smile. "Let the little girls see their father, dear Abbess. Besides, it's an order from the Empress. You don't have a choice."

The captain whistled and Theo got to his feet. "Come on, girls. Time to see your father."

I grabbed the girls. "Tell Empress Irini that we have the plague. Come, girls. We're going back to the convent."

But Efrosini sat down and I couldn't drag her. "Auntie Thekla, you promised I could go see Papa."

"I promised that you could go when I go. And I'm not going."

Suddenly Maria flung away the mussels and began splashing towards the yacht. "I'm going to the Palace to live with Constantine!" she screamed.

"Run, girls!" Theo shouted and the three of them sprinted down the quay and up the gangplank.

"Stop! Come back here!" I shouted, chasing them down the quay, furious at Theo and Irini both. But before I knew what was happening, two guards grabbed me and dragged me up the gangplank and onto the yacht. The crew quickly hauled up the gangplank and the fishermen threw back the mooring lines. The sail caught the wind as Theo and I hustled the girls into the cabin so they could not see their mother running back and forth on the quay, screaming.

Tears of joy flowed down Constantine's cheeks when his daughters ran into his arms. "I didn't want to send you away," he wept as they wriggled with happiness. "So many times, I told my mother that I wanted to bring you home."

"Then why didn't you?" I snarled.

"She said that Maria would come with them and cause trouble." He tightened his embrace around his children. "You are home now, my children, and you will stay as long as you want. I promise."

He sent them with servants to retrieve their toys and clothing from the storeroom. My heart warmed to hear their bright cries pointing out familiar places, showing each other that they were home.

"They weep for your kisses every night," I reproached him. "Can't you bring them back, just them? Leave Maria with me."

He set his jaw, just like his mother. "Abbott Theodore and Abbott Platon are making that impossible. They continue to blanket the Empire with letters saying that my divorce is not legal and that I have committed bigamy. This is treason. I cannot ignore it or they will undermine my authority as Emperor. Neither can I provoke the issue. If I bring my daughters back here, Abbott Theodore will say I am acknowledging that my marriage to Maria is legal. I have tried to reason with them. I sent one of Theodore's relatives, a bishop, to talk sense into them. He gave up. He says that Theodore enjoys his own words too much to stop spreading them around the Empire."

"I could have told him that," I said sourly.

"I sent another cleric who also gave up. Theodore quoted him from Job, Moses, Saint Basil." Constantine threw up his hands. "Now Theodore is writing letters saying that Abbott Joseph should be defrocked for carrying out the wedding ceremony. And that I should annul Maria's vows as a nun and take her back as my wife! I cannot! I am legally wed to Tula and she is with child! Our first!"

"Her first. Your third," I snapped.

He scowled at me. "Auntie Thekla, I was willing to

pardon Abbott Theodore and Abbott Platon when they defamed us before I married Tula. But they continue! Whenever we leave the Palace, people shout 'Adulterer'! I cannot allow this disrespect to continue. I have sent Commander Bardanes Tourkos to bring Abbott Platon to Constantinople. Platon will stand before me and recant—or go to prison. Platon is old and infirm but he cannot accuse me without consequences."

"And Theodore?" I asked cautiously.

"He will be scourged, along with three of his monks. Bardanes Tourkos will force-march him and ten of his monks into exile in Thessaloniki. This will stop the monks of Constantinople from shouting 'Bigamist' from their monastery walls when I pass."

He slumped then, and looked worn and haggard. He glanced around to make sure we were alone, then covered his mouth with his hand so that no one peeping through the many spy holes in the walls could read his lips. I had learned that trick when I stayed with Irini here over the years.

"Stavrakios and Aetios are again plotting to seize the throne. My friends Petros and Antonios and other army officers came secretly to tell me. They urge me to arrest those two eunuchs and send them into exile. The army will help me, they promise."

"Put the heads of those eunuchs on spikes!" I burst out.

He covered his face with his hands and groaned. "Even if I could bring myself to do such a thing, my mother will block me. What a fool I was to bring her eunuchs back from exile—all of them!" He looked at me with desperate eyes. "Petros claims that my mother is part of this plot. What has she told you?"

"Nothing!" I was aghast. "Dino, you must put your mother back under house arrest before she and her eunuchs start a Palace revolt!"

He shook his head miserably. "Aetios is head of the Palace Guards, and they surround her day and night. My mother appointed most of the Palace administrators and they are loyal to her. I cannot speak privately with my advisors without her learning of it. Patriarch Tarasios will say nothing against her. Only Nikiforos in the Finance Ministry argues against her decisions. I feel powerless. I have written to Charles of the Franks and asked if she has sent envoys to his court and what they are telling him."

"Has he replied?" I tried not to show my panic.

Again he shook his head. "Protocol forced me to send the letter through our consul in Sicily and he is my mother's appointee. He will inform her and probably destroy the letter."

I drew a long breath. "Petros and your loyal army friends must sleep across your doorway—even inside your bedchamber."

"If only Alexios were here," he said, tears wetting his cheeks. "But my dear friend is blinded and exiled—probably dead—and by my own foolish order! My mother told me that he had conspired against me and I believed her."

The little girls were running back waving their toys. I watched him gather them into his arms. "Why is Irini holding this Saint Eufemia relic ceremony?" I asked.

Constantine shrugged. "I know nothing about it."

His advisors came then and I took the girls to play with their toys in the Palace gardens. I didn't see Constantine until the following day when we were all gathered inside the tiny Church of Saint Eufemia near the Hippodrome.

Constantine stood on the men's side and I stood on the women's side behind Empress Irini who was holding the girls' hands. Around me grouped Princess Anthusa, Empress Tula with her mother and sisters, and every wealthy society woman who could smash themselves into the tiny church. In the centre stood a low table with a purple velvet cushion bearing a tiny jewelled box. Whispers came from around me: "Such a cruel father, to exile his daughters so he could marry that harlot. How wonderful that Empress Irini cares for them."

I felt ill. Irini was now a loving grandmother and Constantine a cruel father.

After much chanting, Patriarch Tarasios lifted the cushion and held it towards Princess Anthusa. She took the jewelled box reverently in both hands, kissed it, and placed it inside a niche in the stone wall. She closed the barred door and locked it with a key. I leaned down and whispered in the girls' ears.

"Go to Papa! Hug Papa."

Against all protocol, Efrosini and Irini flung themselves across the church and wrapped their arms around their father's legs. Constantine dropped to his knees and pulled them into his arms. Tears ran into his trim beard. The sly smiles around me became nods of approval. "Loving father. Adores his children."

Tula stared stiffly ahead, red dots flaming her cheeks.

I smiled. The little marriage-wrecker was now the harlot who had separated the Emperor from his adoring daughters. Then, with a gentle smile, Tula slid a protective hand over her abdomen. The whispers changed to, "A son to inherit the throne?" The little girls were forgotten.

Empress Irini led the procession out and Constantine followed holding the girls' hands. Tula leaned on her mother's arm, feigning fatigue. I slipped out a side door. I wanted to make sure that the girls got into Constantine's carriage and he took them to the Palace. But Princess Anthusa stood in my way.

"Patriarch Tarasios has agreed to hear my vows," she murmured in her low harsh voice. "I'm going into seclusion as a contemplative nun at the Convent of Saint Ammonia."

"May God grant you peace." I tried to move on.

She glanced around. "Tell Constantine to watch his back."

"What do you mean?"

"People are saying that Empress Irini is using this bigamy issue to make Constantine lose favour with the army. If they rise against him, Irini will claim the throne for herself alone."

"That's absurd!" I said. "Why would the army care who Constantine weds?"

But she had moved away. Her words had slowed me and Empress Irini was already putting the girls inside her own carriage. Theo and I climbed in after them.

"What did Princess Anthusa want?" Empress Irini demanded as we lurched forward.

"She rejoices that you have restored the relic of Saint

Eufemia to her church. Are you taking the children back to their father? He promised them that they could stay as long as they want."

She looked at me coldly. "You are taking the girls back to Prinkypos now. Patriarch Tarasios has offered the use of his yacht."

What could I do but glare at her? Another carriage waited farther on and Empress Irini practically shoved the four of us out. As her carriage clattered away, I glared at Theo. He was lifting the wailing children into the new carriage.

"Why didn't you get the girls into Constantine's carriage? He promised them that they could stay for a long time. Now they won't trust him."

"It's out of my hands," he muttered.

I grabbed his arm, furious. "Can't you help Constantine make good decisions? The monks don't trust him because of what he is doing to Abbott Theodore and Abbott Platon. Did you know that Constantine has ordered Platon to recant in front of him, and Theodore will be force-marched into exile in Thessaloniki!"

"Don't waste your sympathy on those two abbotts," Theo snapped. "They will gain more followers as martyrs."

"This is Irini's doing," I hissed at him. "She brought Constantine together with Tula. Princess Anthusa just told me that Irini did it to discredit Constantine so that the army will lose confidence in him. Irini is creating a civil war over this issue!" I stormed.

He looked at me hard. "Irini is terrified that Constantine will exile her to that convent on Lesbos. She is trying to save herself. Can you blame her?"

"But she is destroying her son to save herself. Theo! After all that you have seen her do, after all you know about her, how can you continue to be loyal?"

His gaze hardened. "Thekla, you see what I see. You know what I know. Yet you come when she calls. You take care of her when she comes to Prinkypos. You vowed to give your life for her and you will do that, won't you?"

"I have no choice. I made the vow before God."

"We have many choices and many loyalties—to God, to our Empire, to our friends, our family, and ourselves. But loyalties can conflict. You must choose which of your loyalties to follow. You can refuse to do what Irini wants and still be loyal to her by keeping her on the right path."

"And that's what you are doing?"

"We are trying."

"Who is 'we'?" I demanded. He shook his head.

"At least, will you stop Irini from creating a civil war over Constantine's marriage?"

Theo removed my hand from his arm. "It's too late. Constantine is married. And he won't help himself. He could call on his many loyal friends in the army to rise against his mother and put her and those two eunuchs in prison. But he won't lift a finger against her."

I thought about that as I climbed into the carriage and we rattled through the Golden Gate to Rymin harbour. If I understood what Theo was saying, he was loyal to Irini but would not let her harm Constantine. I had to be satisfied with that.

I helped the girls onto the luxurious yacht of Patriarch Tarasios and thought about Theo's many kinds of loyalty. I was loyal to Irini, but I was also loyal to my nuns, protecting and nourishing them, and to Constantine, doing whatever he needed. But Theo had said that I also owed loyalty to myself. I had never considered that. I didn't even know what he meant.

Empress Irini came to the island shortly after the ceremony. Maria shouted her arrival, as always. I don't know why. We always dragged her to the crypt or locked her in the dormitory room. The mad have no practical memory, I suppose. Sister Matrona, Efrosini, and I went down to meet the yacht. Irinoula stayed with her mother in the crypt.

The Empress made quick work of her prayer in the church while we waited silently outside with her mute slave, Father Dimitrios, and her guards. Up in my study, Irini downed two glasses of elderberry wine and restlessly paced the room.

"Constantine has stopped paying tribute to the Bulgars. He says he needs the money to repair the sea wall. Mistake. The wall was broken during his great-grandfather's reign when an iceberg crashed into it. No enemy navy has ever tried to breach it. So why repair it?"

"Constantine told me that people will feel more secure inside solid walls." He had often spoken of the need to repair the wall, even as a child.

"Nonsense. People feel secure when they have peace, and we have it because we are paying tribute to the Bulgars so they won't attack us. We wouldn't be paying if Constantine hadn't bungled the battle at Markellon.

Now the idiot is planning a spring offensive against the Bulgars. Another mistake." She threw up her hands. "We know nothing about the Bulgar army. We used to have spies in that godforsaken place until Constantine's grandfather went senile and gave their names to that trickster general Teleryg who murdered our spies."

I couldn't stop my retort. "You yourself stopped paying tribute to Caliph Harun, even though your advisors—and Constantine—warned you that he would attack. And he did." Constantine had been in his early teens then and well informed about the Empire.

"Harun crossed our eastern border and marched overland. But when he reached Chrysopolis, he had no barges to cross the Propontis. So he couldn't attack the walls of Constantinople. This is a very different situation. The Bulgars will march straight from their border to the Golden Gate. They will set up camp with their filthy beasts and their campfire smoke and launch their excrement over our walls. Harun will bring the army of the Caliphate to join the Bulgars and that will be the end of us."

"No army has ever breached the walls of Constantinople, as you just said."

"They will starve us out. Like Constantine's grandfather starved Artavasdos out of Constantinople and ended two years of civil war."

She dropped into the big cushioned chair by the fire and stared into the flames. "Constantine is trying to get rid of me. Stavrakios says he is talking to his advisors about sending me to that convent on Lesbos to die. What has he told you?" She turned on me suddenly to catch my expression before I could change it.

"Nothing!" I tried to appear surprised.

She gave me a suspicious look, then held out her glass for me to refill. "Every day is another battle with that child. I am weary of it. I gave him birth under difficult circumstances. I kept him from being killed by his murderous uncles. I was Regent for him. Everything I did was for his benefit and he repaid me by putting me under house arrest for over a year. I nearly starved and froze. Now he is plotting to put me away. A male emperor in my position would have thrown him in Phiale prison by now."

My heart went cold. I didn't move, like a rabbit facing a fox.

"Do you remember the ancient Greek story of Medea?" she went on.

I forced myself to speak calmly. "You told me long ago, Highness," I managed. "Medea's husband abandoned her for another woman. Medea poisoned the new wife. Then she killed her children to punish her husband."

Irini waved that away. "Nonsense. That's what the scholars say. They are wrong. Medea killed her children so that they couldn't grow up and kill her first." She put down her empty glass. "Call my slave. I'm going to bed."

Two months later, on the seventh of October, Empress Tula, barely fourteen, gave birth in the Purple Chamber to Baby Leon, heir to the throne of the Empire of the Romans of the East. Constantine did not send the yacht for me. I learned about the birth when Elias brought the official announcement. Father Dimitrios banged the semantron to summon everyone on the island to the plateia to hear the happy news.

"Many lives, Baby Leon," we shouted and dipped our tin cups into a vat of wine to toast the baby and his parents. I took only a sip. I could not bear to look at Maria and the two girls silently standing apart. I was as silent as they, sick with broken pride that Constantine had not sent for me to be present when his son was born. Afterwards, Elias took me to walk along the sea path.

"I'll take you into Constantinople so you can hold Constantine's first son," he offered gently.

But my pride would not let me go to hold the first grandson I would never have. I should have gone. It would have been the last time I saw Constantine happy.

Chapter VI

My conscience still bothers me about Maria. I forced myself to be patient but I never could help her accept her fate. My ears still hear her screams of rage every time Empress Irini came to the convent and we dragged poor Maria screaming to the basilica crypt or the barred dormitory room. God knows how many times I begged Irini and Constantine to send her and the girls to Maria's parents who lived far from Constantinople. Always I got the same answer: ambitious army officers could use them to denounce Constantine as an adulterer and denier of God. We could have another civil war.

Even the patience of Sister Filothei could not help Maria accept that she was no longer Empress Maria, married to Constantine. On Maria's mad days, she would comb her hair without a comb in her hand or order Megalo to pack her things because her holiday on Prinkypos was over and she was going back to Constantinople. Finally, we stopped trying to talk her back to reality because the truth of her life would send her into a panic. She would climb the stile at the low part of the wall and throw herself down the steep path to the tiny harbour by the ruins of the old monastery, wailing for her mother to come and get her. At first, she returned by herself, exhausted and hungry, but as the years of exile wore on, she retreated more into her own world and days would pass without her presence inside the convent. We stopped searching for her, knowing that some goatherd would hammer on the convent gate and lead us to the cave where Maria was sleeping. We would coax her up to the convent, bathe her, feed her, and put her in bed where she would lie motionless for long dark days staring at the beams in the ceiling.

Maria did have good days when she would dress herself and the children, attend prayer services, and join us for meals in the refectory. She worked in the kitchen and copied scrolls loaned by the monasteries on the other islands. Our library grew under her hand. More than once, though, Sister Evanthia brought me a page of Maria's work and showed me where she had written "Lord help Maria here against her will".

"Do not rebuke her or make her re-copy the page," I always told Sister Evanthia. "I want others to hear Maria's silent scream of despair."

The fifth Saturday of Lent was a lovely day, I remember distinctly. The apricot trees were all pink blossoms, scenting the breeze. Tiny lambs bounced in the green pastures. Maria had trailed Aspasia and me to the harbour. She was wearing her yellow silk tunica which had become so shredded that we made her wear it over a nun's tunica. She had pushed thistles into the tangles of her hair to keep it off her face and stuck red poppies into the tangles. She was carrying a convent cat. At the harbour, it spotted the harbour cats and clawed Maria until she cursed it and threw it down. She settled on the boulders near the quay.

Elias was sitting with the fishermen. His thick dark hair was grey at the temples but his lean body had not softened. My hands could feel his body. I looked away but my hands still felt the muscles of his back and shoulders. Some memories are too powerful to fade. Elias was running his eyes over me. Perhaps he was thinking the same. My body also had not thickened. How could it, working a convent farm at the top of a steep hill?

The fishermen had spread their nets out to mend but their hands were idle. They were looking soberly across the flat sea to Pendykion. The sea and wind were so still that I could hear the faraway tramp of soldiers' boots on the coastal road, along with faint shouts, the clatter of mules' hooves, and the creak of wagons. Fluttering banners made it look festive. It wasn't. Our armies were marching to push Caliph Harun al-Rashid back over our eastern border.

"The latest news is that Harun's armies have reached Ikonion," said Elias. "They are headed for Amorion, a much richer town."

I felt ill. Ikonion was my birthplace, a month's walk from Constantinople. My family lived in a nearby farming village, if they still lived. I had not heard from them since the day I ran away from home.

"Is Constantine over there leading those soldiers?" A fisherman jerked his chin at the mainland.

Elias shook his head. "He's at Proussa hot springs in Bithynia meeting his commanders. Empress Tula and Empress Irini are with him. In a few days, he will leave to join the other theme armies at the Malagina horse farms."

"Will he lead the campaign?" I ventured. I was bursting with pride imagining Constantine bravely leading that column of soldiers to Amorion, yet I wanted him to stay back in the column, safe from ambush.

Elias scowled. "Stavrakios is commanding the campaign."

"Stavrakios?" I was shocked. "Constantine told me that many army officers want him arrested and exiled. Why ever would Constantine appoint him as commanding general?"

"Empress Irini insisted," he said grimly.

"Another losing campaign against the great Harun," a fisherman muttered.

"Maybe not," Elias shrugged. "The officers at the kapelaria in Pendykion told me that Constantine has become a real leader. The soldiers are in good spirits. They spoke of victory."

"She will take his victory and fling it into the cesspool." Maria's calm voice startled us. She had a frightening way of slipping between sane and mad. Elias nodded.

"There is an odd tension in Constantinople. Wealthy people are spending more time in their estates far from the city. Some are taking up residence in monasteries and convents. A monk from Medikion monastery in

Bithynia told me that they have admitted many new monks. I heard the same about Pelekiti Monastery and the monasteries of Pavlopetrion and Dalmatiou."

Father Dimitrios nodded, "Commander Bardanes Tourkos has founded a monastery over there on Proti Island, and some Palace official has founded a monastery on Chalki Island. What strange times we live in. Empress Irini has rebuilt monasteries and convents that were torched by the Constantine's grandfather, and now people are leaving Constantinople to live in them."

Elias handed me a letter with Empress Irini's seal sunk into the red wax. I cracked it open reluctantly, dreading what was inside. I sighed.

"Empress Irini still won't allow Maria and the girls to go to her parents' home. The usual excuse: some discontented army commander could say that the little girls are heirs to the throne and could start a civil war." I kept my voice low and my hand over my mouth so Maria couldn't hear me or read my lips. But she picked up a rock and slammed it into the sea. The mad can read your minds.

By the next afternoon, the line of soldiers was gone, leaving me feeling uneasy and isolated. When Empress Irini stayed on Prinkypos during campaigns, she received regular dispatches from the front, so we knew what was happening. Now we had to rely on Elias to report what the couriers from the front were saying. The fishermen picked up a bit of news in the seaside villages where they sold their catch, so we heard that Constantine's unit had left Proussa to join his battalion at Malagina, a two-day march. Then, some days later, Maria shouted that the imperial yacht was coming from the southeast, the direction of Proussa, imperial banner flying. I joined the nuns looking over the wall. The yacht passed us and continued on to Constantinople. I frowned, puzzled.

"That has to be Empress Irini and Empress Tula returning to Constantinople from Proussa. But why? Proussa is two days closer to the battle front than Constantinople. If Irini stayed, she would get the dispatches sooner."

"With Constantine gone, Irini has to lead the ceremonies of Holy Week, which starts on Sunday," Sister Matrona reminded me.

But two days later, Elias brought us the real reason. Maria shouted that the mail boat was coming so I put down my hoe and hurried with the nuns to the top of the lane where we could see the harbour. Elias spotted us and beckoned with a wave. He was waiting by the church with Father Dimitrios. He looked exhausted.

"Was there a battle?" I demanded. "Was Constantine victorious?"

Elias shook his head. "No battle. Emperor Constantine had just started out for Malagina with Stavrakios and Aetios when Empress Irini sent a message with two of Constantine's officers. She wrote that word had come by signal tower that Caliph Harun was retreating. Irini told Constantine in her message to go to Constantinople with Aetios and Stavrakios. Irini and Tula would meet him there."

"But Caliph Harun never retreats," frowned Father Dimitrios.

Elias nodded, grim. "The message was false—a complete lie. Empress Irini had promised Constantine's two officers that she would give them command of the campaign if they delivered this false message to him. She also promised to recall Stavrakios. And she promised to leave the throne and resign to private life."

I gasped. "I don't believe it! Irini would never give up the throne. Constantine's commanders would never lie to him. They are loyal."

Elias tightened his lips. "The officers hate Stavrakios and Aetios and they hate Empress Irini. If they did what she wanted, they could get rid of all three of them and lead the campaign. Also, Irini is Empress, remember? They had to obey."

I felt ill. "So they lied to Constantine."

He nodded. "Constantine obeyed Irini. He turned towards Constantinople with Aetios and Stavrakios. I know because they came through Pendykion to change horses. If I had only known, I would have stopped them." He choked and stared at his hands. Then he continued. "Constantine was well on his way when the two officers got back to Proussa. They told Empress Irini that Constantine was headed for Constantinople. They expected her to give them command of the campaign and write orders to recall Stavrakios."

"Fools!" I exploded. "Of course, she laughed at them."

"She called them traitors. They threatened to tell Constantine that she had lied. She said she would tell Constantine to have them blinded and exiled. Then she and Tula went by yacht to Constantinople."

Sister Matrona nodded. "We saw the yacht passing."

"Now you will tell us that Constantine is in prison," said Father Dimitrios through tight lips.

Elias nodded grimly. "The officers raced after Constantine to stop him from falling into the trap. But they failed. When Constantine reached the Palace of Saint Mamas where he had married Tula, across the Golden Horn from Constantinople, Aetios and Stavrakios seized him. He escaped into the church and took sanctuary behind the altar. But they dragged him out. Constantine is in Phiale Prison inside the Great Palace."

My body went quiet. I felt like a wind had been beating against me and suddenly stopped. In that calm, I felt the line of time passing through me and I saw the future as clearly as I saw the past. "Now Empress Irini will declare herself Empress in her own right. But she needs a legitimate claim to the crown. She will crown Efrosini Co-empress and announce it on Easter Day."

"The army will rise against her," said Elias. "They will execute both of them.

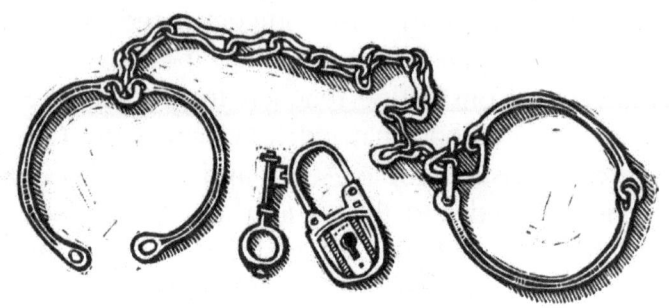

Chapter VII

Two days before Easter, Aetios arrived to take Efrosini away. I was prepared. When Maria shouted that the imperial yacht was in the harbour with Aetios on deck, I called Efrosini, Aspasia, Sister Matrona, and Sister Evanthia into my study.

"Aetios has probably come to take Efrosini so that Irini can crown her as Co-empress. I am going with her. Sister Matrona is in charge until I return—if I do return. Empress Irini may accuse me of being loyal to Constantine and not to her. This is treason now that she holds the throne. If you hear that I am in prison or sent into exile, pay all the nuns and novices their stipends and tell everyone to go home or find another convent. Irini will close the convent out of anger at me."

Sister Matrona snorted. "She won't close the convent. That woman is a deer surrounded by wolves. When the army rises against her, she needs you here to hide her and help her escape."

"She has Stavrakios and Aetios."

"They will be the first to sink their knives into her back."

I had not seen Aetios since before Constantine had exiled him and Stavrakios. When I opened the convent gate, I looked him over. The stocky eunuch was bald, short, and muscled like a wrestler, unlike Stavrakios who was tall and broad-shouldered with thick hair. Today, Aetios wore a gold chain around his neck and jewelled bands on his wrists. They glittered in the sunlight.

"I'm coming with Efrosini," I said without a greeting and he shrugged.

Everyone in the convent walked us to the harbour. Seven-year-old Efrosini smiled calmly at the villagers who crowded the plateia and the quay, calling out blessings. I took Aspasia's arm.

"Do you remember how to get into the secret room?" I murmured.

"From the root cellar, yes."

"When you are certain that I am not coming back, take my purses from the hole under the steps. My savings are yours, my dear friend. We have been together since the first day I came to Constantinople."

She squeezed my arm. "What about the chest with all the purses and plate that Empress Irini has been stashing down there?"

"Leave it. It belongs to the Treasury. One day some official will come for it."

I sat close to Efrosini in the yacht cabin with my hand on the hilt of my knife and did not speak to Aetios on the opposite bench. He didn't address us either until we had reached Constantinople and climbed the hill to Irini's reception room in Daphne Palace.

"Wait here," he grunted.

Theo came in, looking pale. He didn't meet my eyes. Patriarch Tarasios followed with Aetios and Stavrakios who took up guard positions at the door. Then I heard the quick click of Irini's shoes and she strode into the room. Emeralds and rubies glittered at her ears and throat. Her long tunica and sleeveless skaramaggion over it shone with gold and silver thread. But my eyes were fixed on the gold band across her brow.

She lifted her arms in triumph. "Abbess Thekla, Efrosini, you see before you the sole ruler of the Roman Empire of the East! I have just crowned myself Empress in my own right!"

"Where is Constantine?" I demanded harshly.

Irini ignored me and addressed Efrosini. "Efrosini, dear heart, today in Magnavra Palace, I will crown you my Co-empress. I will place on your head the same crown that your grandfather placed on your father's head when he was nine, only two years older than you. These men are our witnesses. Come, child. Let us walk together to Magnavra Palace where all emperors are crowned." She held out her hand.

Efrosini did not move. A measured, watchful quiet had replaced the wild energy that had exploded into tantrums when she was five. "Papa is Emperor, not you, Grandmama. Only Papa can name his Co-emperor."

"I earned this crown through hard work, my child," Irini snapped. "Your father forfeited it through incompetence and cowardice."

My voice shook with anger. "Constantine was no

coward. He turned back from fighting Harun because he obeyed your lies. You can throw him in prison but the army will come to release him, as they did before. This time, they will execute you and the traitors who put you on the throne."

"Still your mouth!" Irini shouted. "I will have you blinded and exiled! Aetios, take her away!"

But Nikiforos the Finance Minister burst into the room. His normally calm face was agitated and pale. "Empress, a message has come from Amorion by signal tower. Our army cannot stop Harun's assault. He is demanding tribute or he will burn Amorion to the ground. You must send a delegation immediately to sue for peace and negotiate the tribute. If you don't, Harun will continue on to Ankyra and even reach Constantinople."

She waved her hand. "Then arrange it. Why are you standing there? Send negotiators. When Harun starts back towards his border, Aetios and Stavrakios will attack and take back what they have stolen. I have declared Aetios my second-in-command. Aetios, you can overcome Harun easily when he is in retreat, can you not?"

"Of course, Empress," he bowed.

I could not hold my tongue. "Invading armies do not wait for negotiators. You can be sure that Harun's soldiers are already burning crops and dragging people away as slaves. Constantine would be there with his army if you had not stopped him. You are a traitor to your people."

"Still your mouth, Thekla! Efrosini, come here."

I drew Efrosini tightly against me. "Can you bring the dead soldiers of Amorion back to life? Can you turn burnt crops green again and raise slaughtered sheep from the dead? May God punish you for your shameful deeds." I pulled Efrosini towards the door.

"Where are you going?" Irini shrilled.

"To take Efrosini to her father."

Irini forced calm into her voice. "Aetios, take them to Constantine. Then bring Efrosini back quickly. I will name her Co-empress this very day."

I had been to Phiale prison when my beloved Constantine lay in that filthy hole after he had tried and failed to arrest Stavrakios for his greed and plunder of the Treasury. Now my poor boy sat slumped on the wet floor of a dark cell, his head wrapped in his arms. He jumped to his feet when the guard unlocked the door.

"Auntie Thekla, have you learned the horror of my mother's treachery? She sent my own officers to lie to me that Harun had withdrawn. I believed them and I obeyed her, fool that I was. I fell into her trap. Now I cannot stop Harun from attacking Amorion. Alexios would have saved me but I had him blinded! She will blind me, Auntie Thekla. I will die in this dreadful place."

The anger that had given me strength left me. I clasped him in my arms and sobbed. "I will get you out, my Dino."

"Leave me here," he replied miserably. "I do not deserve the crown of the Isaurians if I can be fooled so easily. All I want is to see Tula and my son. They are at her parents' house in the neighbourhood behind the Church of Holy Wisdom. I beg you, bring them here so that my eyes can behold them one last time before I lose my sight."

"What of Charles of the Franks?" I asked frantically. "You wrote to him. He could save you."

"He never answered my letter. My mother surely had it destroyed. Listen, Auntie Thekla, there are jewels and gold hidden in Daphne Palace. You know the place, under the Sigma where I used to leave secret messages for you when I was a child. This is all I can leave my children; I cannot leave them my good name because I have dishonoured my name. I have failed to follow the brave paths of my father and my grandfather."

Efrosini and I hurried out of the prison and ran to Chalke Gate. We would have slipped out before it closed at dusk, but that devil Aetios blocked us. He sneered and reached for Efrosini.

"Have you forgotten that Empress Irini ordered me to bring Efrosini back?"

I thrust her behind me and put my hand on my knife. "Let us pass. We are taking a message to Empress Tula at her parents' home."

Aetios slid his arm around my waist and pushed his stinking breath in my face. "I have never had a nun. After I have had you, I will take you to the house. I know the place."

My knife jumped into my hand and the blade pressed into his throat. "Say your prayers, eunuch. You lost your balls to the knife. Now you will lose your throat."

"You will not kill me in front of the guards," he said, but his voice was strained.

I pressed harder. "I know this guard. He will look the other way."

"There is a curfew. The night watch will drag you and

the child to prison."

"You will persuade him otherwise." I stepped back, holding my knife ready. With a scowl at the guard who was deliberately looking away, Aetios led us through the dark streets to the house of Tula's parents. No lamp burned at the gate.

"They've left for their estate outside Constantinople," Aetios smirked.

But I pounded on the gate and shouted until it opened a crack. "I have a message for Empress Tula from her husband," I told a frightened servant and I pushed open the door.

We followed her candle through dark rooms to a chamber where a kandilli with six candles showed Tula lying on a couch. Her mother sat by her side holding baby Leon. Suddenly I was thrust into the past. On a similar dark night, Constantine had lain in a pool of blood, beaten nearly to death by Stavrakios. I had come to the house of Empress Maria's parents in this same wealthy neighbourhood. Maria was there, big with child. I had begged Maria to come to the Palace prison and help me persuade Irini to let Constantine go free. Maria had refused.

Tula's young face was thin and frightened. I spoke urgently.

"Your husband lies in Phiale prison, Empress. He is unharmed but we fear for his life. He begs you to come and bring his son. He wants to see you before. . ." I could not speak the words.

Her mother cut in, just as Empress Maria's mother had done. "Tula isn't leaving her bed. She is again with child. And baby Leon is ill."

I could hear the harsh rasping breath of a very sick child but I kept my eyes on Tula and pressed on. "Years ago, when Empress Maria was big with child, she refused to come to Constantine in prison. Now she is exiled and Constantine is your husband who needs you."

I watched her. When I was only three years older than she, I had crossed half the Empire on foot. I had worked as a kitchen maid and a bookkeeper and survived prison.

"I cannot," Tula whispered.

Bitter disappointment filled my mouth. I gripped Efrosini's hand and we hurried outside and through the dark streets to the medical compound of Doctor Moses. I pounded on the gate, desperately looking over my shoulder for the night guards. The cover of the peep hole slid open. "It's Thekla and Efrosini," I hissed into the faint candlelight inside.

The door opened a slit and I pushed through, pulling Efrosini behind me. Andreas, the doctor's assistant, held his candle to my face. Tears came to my eyes and I blinked them away. So many years had passed since I had met Andreas! I had been a young woman living at Ta Gastria convent. I had cut my leg badly and gone to Sampson Hospital where Andreas and Doctor Moses had cured my infection. Andreas had asked me to marry him, but I had chosen to be an abbess. Andreas had married someone else. He had hardly changed, I saw in the wavering candlelight, still had his calm gaze and the suggestion of a sweet smile. He motioned for us to follow him across the courtyard where I smelled the aroma of chicken and vegetable soup. Despite my fear, my mouth watered.

Doctor Moses was sitting at the kitchen table with a bowl of soup in front of him. I had not seen him in many years, but he had scarcely changed from the handsome, dark-haired man with a kind face and an easy smile. Grey sprinkled his dark hair now and lines of worry lay etched across his brow. He half rose and waved me to a stool at the table.

"Bring Abbess Thekla a bowl of soup, if you would," he said to a woman stirring the soup kettle over the hearth.

"There is no time!" I said with shaking voice. "Empress Irini has betrayed Constantine with her lies! She has sent him to Phiale prison. I just saw him. He is certain that he will be blinded. You must stop Irini, Doctor; I beg you. She will not listen to me."

Doctor Moses put down his spoon and shook his head. "Aetios was just here. Irini has ordered me to perform the official blinding mutilation. Aetios said that if I refuse, he will do it himself."

The room tilted and I would have fallen if Andreas had not guided me to a stool. "You cannot disfigure Constantine!" I choked. "He is the true Emperor!"

"Never would I do such a thing," Doctor Moses said grimly. "I told Aetios that I would not even nick the skin of Constantine's face. Tomorrow I will tell Empress Irini myself."

I groaned and put my face in my hands. "She has just named herself Empress and sole ruler. She plans to name Efrosini as Co-empress this very night. Patriarch Tarasios and her cousin Theo will be her witnesses. And

Stavrakios and Aetios."

He shook his head sadly. "The army will not tolerate a woman ruling in her own right, much less two women. They will rise against her. Neither she nor Efrosini will survive. You must hide the child, but not here. Aetios will come looking for you. Take her where Aetios can't find her. And Abbess Thekla, I have little hope that I can stop Empress Irini from having Constantine mutilated. She is doing exactly what any emperor would do to stay in power."

Andreas let us out through the back gate and we kept to the dark side streets until we reached the Forum of Constantine. My eyes anxiously scanned the shadowy figures of the prostitutes sitting on the library steps waiting for customers. At last, I spotted a familiar figure and we hurried towards her. "Eleni?" I called softly.

A woman rose to meet us. She grasped my arms. "Thekla, my dear! What are you doing out past curfew? And who is this child?"

"The daughter of Constantine." The grief I had been choking back burst out in sobs, muffled in Eleni's strong shoulder. She was my first friend in Constantinople. We had met in the dormitory at Ta Gastria convent where she went whenever she needed a rest.

"Follow me," she said briskly and we hurried down narrow lanes to the familiar dark door at the end of an alley—the brothel. One quick tap and we were inside and climbing the steep stairs to the room where Elias met people he didn't want to meet in public, or so Eleni had told me. I had slept there one winter night when I got locked out of Ta Gastria convent after returning late from work at the home of Megalo's parents. Elias had found me searching for Aspasia's apartment and brought me to the brothel.

The room was as I remembered, warm with thick rugs and a wide bed. A servant appeared with carrot soup thickened with chunks of bread. Efrosini ate quickly and slipped into sleep like a fox into its burrow. I looked at her innocent face and whispered into the darkness. "No matter what happens in the war between Irini and Constantine, I will keep Efrosini alive—do you hear my vow, Saint Thekla? I will give my life to keep hers."

With that, I dropped into a sleep so deep that when a familiar voice came into my ears, I thought I was dreaming. But a strong hand shook me and I opened my eyes to see Elias standing over me. He was wearing a monk's shabby tunica. I threw myself into his arms.

"How did you know we were here?" I said into his shoulder.

He smiled. "Do not question the ways of the angels who live in this place. Come quickly. Our boat is waiting."

At the brothel door, Efrosini and I pulled our scarves over our faces, then we stuck like leeches to Elias and blended into the crowds pushing out the Golden Gate. A fishing boat was waiting at Rymin harbour. Elias boosted us aboard and jumped in himself. As the fisherman raised his sail, I squinted through the faint dawn light. A tall, thin figure was standing on the beach. He lifted an arm in farewell. Was that Theo?

Strong winds took us swiftly to Prinkypos and, by mid-day, we were climbing out of the boat into the arms of Father Dimitrios and Sister Matrona.

"We escaped," announced Efrosini cheerfully. "I am not yet Co-empress." She went over to greet Maria who was watching us from a boulder.

"Maria has been sleeping in a cave," Father Dimitrios murmured. "I fear that her wits have completely gone."

"She is sane compared to Empress Irini," I said grimly. "Irini has declared herself Empress in her own right. She has locked Constantine in Phiale prison and ordered Doctor Moses to mutilate his eyes. She intends to name Efrosini as her Co-empress."

"Keep the child hidden until we get Constantine out of prison," warned Elias as he climbed back into the boat.

Father Dimitrios put his hand on my shoulder. "You and I have lived through a great deal these twenty-odd years, haven't we, Abbess Thekla?"

I smiled as I felt the comfort of his words. Father Dimitrios had been my friend and confidant ever since I was eighteen, thrown on the pier by imperial soldiers when I was transferred from a prison in Constantinople. I was guilty of living in a convent where the nuns were painting icons. I had lost my icon of Saint Thekla and had fallen into despair. Father Dimitrios had coaxed my heart back to life. Now the priest's long beard was more grey than black, he had five children and his eldest son was a priest with him.

In the plateia, I told the bewildered villagers that their beloved Constantine was again in prison on his mother's orders. Maria held her daughters' hands and listened quietly. Then we silently climbed the lane to the convent. Again she listened quietly as I told the nuns. That evening, as I made my rounds, I found her sitting in the dark scriptorium. As I gathered my strength to remind her that it was time for bed, a small shadow passed me. Irinoula took her mother's hand and they crossed the silent courtyard to their beds.

I, too, found my bed. But safe within its familiar bounds, my thoughts tumbled and swirled. Had Irini forced Doctor Moses to mutilate Constantine's eyes? Would Aetios come and drag Efrosini away to become Co-empress? If I hid her, would Empress Irini crown Irinoula as Co-empress? I could flee with them to Ikonion and say they were my daughters, I thought wildly, but as I gazed at the stars through my open window, I knew we could not escape Irini if we remained in the Empire. In the Caliphate, we might be safe. Elias had said that there was a Christian community in Antioch. Elias would take us there. With that fragile plan, I fell asleep.

The next morning, I let our two geese out into the pasture. Geese are vicious fowls with loud raucous calls. They will attack a stranger with their sharp stabbing beaks. If Aetios or Stavrakios came to take Efrosini or Irinoula, the geese would delay the eunuchs until I had hidden the children inside the secret room under my study.

Easter passed. I gathered my courage and went into Constantinople to the Great Palace but the prison guards wouldn't let me see Constantine. I went to Empress Irini and begged her to release him. "You are risking the anger of the army by keeping him in prison. They will execute you if he dies!" I shouted at her, losing my temper.

"Take her to the harbour and throw her in the sea," Irini ordered Stavrakios and turned her back on me.

I didn't struggle as Stavrakios dragged me down through the terraces and gardens of the Great Palace and threw me in the deep water outside the imperial harbour. I could swim. A fisherman pulled me out and I dried out in his cottage in Rymin. I got on the ferry to Chalkidon and spent the night in the convent. In the morning, I climbed on the coach to Pendykion.

"Stop visiting Constantine," Elias said. We were in the kapelarion having fish soup. "You can't help the poor boy. We are doing what we can."

"Who is 'we'?" I demanded. Theo had said the same.

He shook his head and didn't answer.

April passed and May brought the early flowering plum trees and a carpet of red poppies across the fields. Elias had no news of Constantine except that he was still in prison. He handed me a letter from his pouch. Theo's seal was sunk into the red sealing wax. "Baby Leon, the first child of Constantine and Tula, has died. He was seven months old," I read.

Maria had followed to the harbour. I gave the letter to her and watched her read it. After Esperinos services and our evening meal, I found her sitting on the church steps. She was cradling a bundle of blankets and weeping.

Chapter VIII

The fifteenth of August is the Feast of the Ascension of the Virgin into Heaven, the most important and joyful day of the year. Yet I awoke at dawn with a sense of foreboding. I lay breathing in the scented dew, listening to Father Dimitrios bang the semantron announcing the blessed day. I should be at peace, I thought. We had fasted for fifteen days. Nothing with blood had passed our lips, nor had eggs, milk, or red wine. After morning prayers, we would go down to the village and join the feast celebrating the day when the Mother of God rose into Heaven, leaving behind only her veil and her belt.

I had seen both those holy items when Empress Irini took me to the Church of the Virgin of the Copper Market and to Blachernae Church. She had laid a purse of coins in the priest's hands and introduced me as Abbess of the Convent of the Theotokos on Prinkypos Island. How proud I had felt. Now I felt bewildered. I was a prison guard for mad Maria and her two daughters who were growing up with a future as empty as the sky. At least,

I thought, Constantine would be safe today. Irini would not risk the wrath of God and everyone in the Empire by ordering Doctor Moses to mutilate the eyes of the legitimate Emperor on this most holy day.

One of my failings is that I am not naturally suspicious. So I paid no attention when Elias arrived looking sombre. Then children began shouting that the imperial yacht was coming into the harbour.

"Empress Irini has let Constantine out of prison!" I cried. "He's home!"

Elias grabbed my arm. "Thekla, don't be an idiot! The yacht has come for Efrosini. Irini will crown Efrosini as Co-empress. Every important announcement is made on a major holy day."

Father Dimitrios rushed over. "Get Efrosini into my woodshed!"

But it was too late. Stavrakios was already in the plateia. He snapped his fingers at me and pointed at Efrosini. "Get her on the yacht. The Empress wants her."

I pushed Efrosini behind me. "You must agree to first take us to Emperor Constantine," I demanded.

His smile was a cruel twist of his lips. "It will be my pleasure to unite father and daughter."

I looked around for Elias but he had gone.

The wind had changed directions and was coming from the north, as always on the day the Mother of God ascended into Heaven, so Efrosini and I were shivering with cold when we climbed out at the imperial harbour and climbed the steps. But instead of going towards the prison, Stavrakios turned towards Daphne Palace. Puzzled, we followed him up those familiar marble steps and through the long arcades.

"We're nearing the Purple Chamber," I murmured to Efrosini. "It is the room decreed by Emperor Leon as the place where all imperial children will be born. Your father entered the world in the Purple Chamber. You and Irinoula and baby Leon were born there."

I should have known better. I should have gone in first and kept Efrosini behind me instead of letting her run ahead, excited to see her beloved father. She screamed.

The horror that lay on that bed will never leave my eyes. I flung my scarf around Efrosini's face so she could not look again. With my shawl, I tried to staunch the blood pouring from Constantine's eyes.

"Oh Dino, my poor Dino," I cried, my voice shaking in horror.

"Auntie Thekla?" Constantine reached out with blood-wet fingers.

"I'm here, Dino, my heart. I will take care of you." But how could I stop the river of blood soaking into the pillow? I looked around, frantic for help. Aetios was slouched against the wall; Patriarch Tarasios was standing in the doorway, his face white.

"Get help, Patriarch!" I screamed at him. "Get a doctor!"

He pointed at a man kneeling in a corner, rinsing a bloody cloth in a bucket of water.

"Doctor Moses!" I cried in disbelief. "You said you would not touch Constantine's face!"

"Aetios did this." He glared with hatred at the sneering eunuch. "I went to the prison this morning to pray with Constantine on this most holy day and the guards said that Aetios had taken him here. I was too late. That butcher had already gouged out his eyes. And now those two monsters won't let me send for opium to stop the pain."

My knife jumped into my hand and I went for Aetios but Stavrakios twisted it away and pressed the point into my throat.

"Tell your dear Dino to admit where he has hidden the gold and jewels. Then we will give him all the opium he wants. 'It's under the Sigma' is all he says. What Sigma? You know, don't you, Abbess?"

I wrenched away and turned back to Constantine. But my beloved boy had gone limp. "Doctor Moses!" I gasped frantically. "He has died!"

Doctor Moses hurried over and laid his ear on Constantine's chest. "He is alive, but barely. Go to Empress Irini. Tell her that I must take Constantine to my clinic or he will die."

I grabbed Efrosini's hand and we stumbled out of that awful room. My legs were shaking so much that I could hardly walk. I could not have found Irini's suite if seven-year-old Efrosini had not kept her wits and guided us through that maze of halls. The eunuch guarding Irini's door blocked us.

"Let me in!" I screamed and kept screaming until Theo flung open the door. His face was ashen. He pulled us in. Empress Irini was pacing the map room. She turned to me eagerly, her face half frightened, half excited.

"You have brought Efrosini to become Co-empress! I knew you would come!"

"Liar! Murderer!" I shouted at her. "You sent Aetios to

gouge out Constantine's eyes!"

"No! Thekla, I did not," she protested. "I told Aetios to take Constantine to the Purple Chamber and to crease one eye. Constantine has suffered no harm to his sight."

I grabbed her arms and shook her. "When will you stop lying! You well know that your son is bleeding to death from his eyes. Aetios has gouged out both of them, just as you ordered."

She pushed me away angrily. "You are the liar! From the moment that Constantine was born, you have been loyal to him, not to me."

I flung my blood-wet scarf around her wrists and swiftly bound them together. "This blood on my scarf is from Constantine's eyes. Long ago, he told me that you would kill him to get the throne. He was right. You have murdered your own son."

She tried to wrench her hands away but I twisted the scarf tighter. Holding it with one hand, I lifted my right hand, palm towards her, in the time-honoured way we lay a curse. "Irini of Athens, I curse you in the name of . . ."

"Stop!" Irini pulled free and flung the bloody scarf on the floor. "Listen to me! Constantine told me he was going to ban icons by imperial edict. He said they were idols and that people were worshipping them. He said that God was punishing him by causing his defeats in battle. I told him that he couldn't ban icons; the edict was passed by the Council at Nicaea. He said that he was Emperor and he could do whatever he wanted. He was going to have Aetios and Stavrakios executed in the Hippodrome and have their heads mounted on spikes over the Milion. He was going to send me to Lesbos to die in that convent. I had to stop him, Thekla. I had no choice."

"So you sent Aetios to kill him in the most horrible way."

"No! I told Aetios to cut the skin beside his eye so he couldn't be Emperor. That's all. Constantine isn't injured, Thekla." She looked wildly at Theo who was standing at the window looking at the sea. "Theo, tell me he can see."

Theo didn't move, just kept staring at the sea.

I answered with a steady voice. "Constantine lives, but only barely. You must allow Doctor Moses to take Constantine to his clinic. And you must pray that your son survives. Because if he dies, the army will come after you. And if you run to my convent to escape their swords, I will open the gate to them myself and watch your blood water the earth."

Irini grabbed Theo's arm. "Go with Thekla. Tell Aetios that Doctor Moses can take him to his clinic." She reached for Efrosini. "The child stays with me."

"Never." I pulled Efrosini from her grasp and the three of us ran.

When we were nearly to the Purple Chamber, I heard footsteps behind us. Terrified, I looked over my shoulder, then stumbled with relief. Elias caught me before I fell.

"Tell me I am not too late!" he panted. "I bribed the guards to let me take Constantine from the prison at dawn this morning, but when I got through Chalke Gate, Aetios was waiting. He locked me in the dungeon under Chalke Gate. The guards just now let me out."

"We are too late," I wept. "Aetios has gouged out his eyes."

"Dear God!" Elias grabbed Theo and slammed him against the wall. "Could you not have stopped your cousin from sending that monster?"

"You know I could not," Theo wept.

I pulled Elias away. "Empress Irini says we can take him to Doctor Moses's clinic. Hurry before she changes her mind."

But again, we were too late. Aetios laughed when we burst in the door. "It is dusk. Chalke Gate is locked for the night."

"Then we will take him out in the morning," said Doctor Moses.

So we stayed with Constantine all night in the room where he had been born—Doctor Moses, Theo, Elias, Efrosini, and me. The Palace doctors brought bandages, opium for pain, valerian for sleep, and drugs to stop the bleeding. The Palace kitchen sent food. I choked down a mouthful, then exhaustion took me. I awoke at dawn when two frightened Palace bearers arrived with a litter. It was dawn, they said, and a carriage was waiting.

The sky was still dark when we emerged from Daphne Palace. It felt as if a storm were brewing but there was no scent of rain. We laid Constantine in the carriage and Efrosini held his bandaged head in her lap. Doctor Moses and Theo climbed in with them and I sat up with the coachman and Elias so I could direct the driver to the house of Tula's parents. When we reached Chalke Gate, the guards were staring at the strangely dark sky. The captain of the guards shouted that they could not open the gate.

"They need the order of the Emperor to open Chalke Gate in the morning," muttered Elias. He swung down and pulled the captain over to the carriage.

"Look inside," Elias pointed. "Emperor Constantine would order the gate to be opened if he could. We are taking him to the clinic of Doctor Moses."

One glance and the captain's face went white. He shouted and Chalke Gate swung open. In that strange, dark dawn, we rumbled through the cobbled streets to the home of Tula's parents. I remained with the coachmen while Elias, Theo, and Doctor Moses pounded on the door. They returned quickly, supporting Tula between them. When she saw Constantine, her eyes rolled back and she fainted. They laid her on the floor of the carriage and Elias climbed up by me and the coachman.

"Rymin harbour," he ordered.

"What are you saying?" I snapped. "We are going to Doctor Moses's clinic."

"Aetios and Stavrakios will be waiting there. They will murder Constantine. Aetios is planning to put his brother on the throne and he can do that only when Constantine is dead. On Prinkypos, Constantine will be safe."

Dawn should have been brightening Rymin harbour but sky and sea remained dark. Elias shouted for help to some fishermen who were gazing at the grey horizon. They wrapped canvas around oars to make a stretcher and carried Constantine to a fishing boat. They set the stretcher down on the sand so Doctor Moses could change the bandage over his eyes.

That's when I saw Aetios creeping out of the darkness,

knife in hand. In an instant, I was behind him with a rock in my hand. I hit his head with all my strength and he slumped onto the sand.

Elias and the fishermen carried Constantine into the boat. Elias helped Efrosini and me into the boat. Theo helped Tula. The fishermen pushed us out and a light breeze filled our sails. My eyes stayed on Theo and Doctor Moses until that strange darkness took us and we were alone on an inky sea.

My fingers found Saint Thekla tied in the corner of my scarf and I pressed her to my heart. "Who do I pray for first?" I asked. "Do I pray for Constantine to live even though his eyes will never again see? Do I pray for his daughter who must carry the memory of her father's blinded eyes and her grandmother's treachery? Do I pray for this pregnant wife to have the strength to raise her child without a father? Or do I pray for Empress Irini to find her lost soul?"

Elias held my hand while our eyes searched the dark sky for the morning star to guide us, but no familiar spark pierced the gloom. Carried on a flutter of breeze, we drifted along a flat sea with no sun to mark the hours. Angels must have pulled us to Prinkypos Island because, after unknown time, we heard the deep chanting of Father Dimitrios and smelled the fragrance of thyme incense.

Father Dimitrios and the villagers were standing on the quay. He stopped swinging his censor and they stared in shock at Constantine and the blood-soaked bandage over his eyes. "Heaven has taken away our sun in horror at what Empress Irini has done," Father

Dimitrios whispered.

In that strange darkness, the village men made a stretcher of oars and canvas and carried Constantine up the lane to the convent. They laid him on the couch in my study and Sister Efthia brought bandages, opium, and valerian from the hospice. Aspasia brought warm stones from the kitchen hearth to warm him. Tula and Efrosini held his hands while Father Dimitrios chanted last rites.

Me? I went to the cistern in the kitchen garden. In that strange, grey light, Aspasia poured buckets of water over my hands but no matter how I scrubbed, I saw the water running red onto the earth. I tore off my clothes and scrubbed myself with a rough sponge while Aspasia poured water over me but still I saw the water running red. I fell to my knees and pounded my forehead on the earth. "I couldn't save him. I was too late," I whispered.

Aspasia and Sister Evanthia wrapped me in blankets and laid me on a mattress by the fire. When I awoke, it was night and Aspasia was sleeping beside me with her arm over me. I put on the clean clothes that she had left for me and went to my study.

Father Dimitrios was sitting beside Constantine, his grey head bowed over his clasped hands. Tula was sleeping over the foot of the couch and Irinoula and Efrosini were asleep on another couch. Sister Efthia was coaxing broth into Constantine's lips. The room smelled of thyme incense. I sat on a stool by the fire. A shadow came to stand by me. Maria.

Days passed and the sun rose into a grey dawn and set into night with only shadows to mark the day. Elias appeared and led me out to the courtyard. He put his arms around me and I leaned against him and closed my eyes.

"He's still alive," I whispered into his tunica. "I don't know for how long."

"I went to Pendykion," he murmured. "Mail couriers from Constantinople are saying that people have blocked Chalke Gate. They are shouting that Empress Irini is a murderer and should be pulled from the throne."

"Once, long ago," I said, "when you and I were walking to Constantinople, I told you that if I had stayed in my village, I would have died with all the same memories as everyone else. Now I wish that I had stayed there, because the memories that I have now are too much for me to bear."

He tightened his arms. "We all have painful memories, Thekla. They help us make decisions in the future. You must be strong and bear them because the memories you will make from now on will be even more painful than the memories you already have."

Boats began arriving in that strange darkness that never brightened into day. The lane up to the convent became a shadowy river of people bringing food and prayers. As Abbess, I should have stood at the convent gate to greet them but my feet wouldn't leave Constantine. Monks from the monasteries on Proti, Chalki, and the other islands camped in the ruins of the old monastery. Their deep voices floated up, chanting the prayers of Orthros, Ninth Hour, and Esperinos. Elias came every day and took me to sit at the top of the lane on the bench by the cemetery. The chain of islands at our feet were barely visible in the dark mist.

"The islands are ghost boats waiting to carry Constantine away," I said and Elias took my hand.

On the seventeenth day, my beloved Constantine sighed his last. I lost the child that I never had. I washed his body as I had bathed him when he was a child, my last act of love. Father Dimitrios anointed him with scented oil and we dressed him in his rich clothes that the nuns had scrubbed clean of blood. Sister Efthia laid a cloth over his poor eyes to hide the wounds. The monks placed him on a plank and carried him into the basilica where the icons that Brother Grigorios had painted gazed down on him. Maria sat in a low chair on one side of him and Efrosini, Irinoula, and Tula sat on the other. A stream of people laid flowers on his body until he was a hill of blooms.

Late that afternoon, the monks sewed him into a shroud, leaving his face open to that strange, dark sky, and carried him to the cemetery. The village men had opened one of the two long shafts. The bones of the nuns who had been buried there over the twenty-five years that I had been Abbess had been cleaned and laid in their ossuaries in the basilica crypt.

Father Dimitrios closed the shroud over his face and the island men whom Constantine had known all his life lowered his physical remains into the shaft. Father Dimitrios dropped in the first handful of earth, then Constantine's two wives and daughters, then me. Then everyone else dropped a handful of earth onto their beloved boy who had grown up among them whom they loved as their own.

Chapter IX

The darkness that shrouded us on the day that Constantine was blinded lifted on the day we buried him. Our blessed sun returned. But inside me, darkness remained. I could not speak. I sat in my study staring at the wall. I saw the infant Constantine slide into the midwife's hands. I saw him take his first steps into my arms. I saw him feed the chickens, pick sumac berries, gather mussels off the rocks, and splash in the sea. Our hearts had joined when his eyes met mine as he left his mother's body and our bond of love would not let him go.

Father Dimitrios and Elias came every day. They walked me through the pasture. They pointed out the sheep and goats and chickens. Efrosini sat by my bed until I slept. Finally, one morning, Sister Matrona brought a cup of mountain tea to my bed and pulled over a chair.

"It's time for you to join the world, Thekla. You are frightening the nuns. Too much grieving is self-indulgence. Get up and go to work."

With that, my visions of Constantine dissolved like salt in water. A sense of relief came over me as I stood at the window and smelled the sea. I saw apples reddening in our orchard and grapes growing heavy on our vines. I heard the click of swallows snapping up insects as they swooped past my window. I went to the kitchen and watched Aspasia's muscular hands roll out flatbread. I saw Tula big with Constantine's child and I saw Maria sitting at her window gazing at the golden haze of Constantinople. One day, feeling stronger, I went down to the harbour and greeted the villagers. I sat on the boulder with Father Dimitrios where we had sat when I was eighteen and had lost my icon of Saint Thekla. My spirit had slid into despair.

How is Tula faring?" asked Father Dimitrios. "Her husband and her first child are dead and she is exiled here with no mother to help her through the coming birth."

"She came here as a weak and vain young woman but she has gained strength through her ordeal and from our communal way of life. Or perhaps it is because we have no mirrors and she cannot dwell on her beauty. She rises at dawn for prayers and takes her meals with us in the refectory. She helps with what chores she can manage, big as she is. Every day she puts flowers on Constantine's grave."

The next time Elias sailed in, I went down to the harbour and we walked along the sea until we were far from the village. "Come away with me," Elias said, taking my hands. "We will climb the hills of Bithynia like we did long ago. We will sleep in the meadows and watch the stars cross the sky."

My eyes traced the green hills of Bithynia where we had lain in each other's arms under a blanket of stars. "Tula is about to give birth. I cannot leave her."

"Sister Efthia is an excellent midwife."

"Maria is the problem. She follows Tula. Sometimes she holds her belly as if she too is carrying a child. They have separate suites but they share the stairs. I fear what Maria might do when the baby is born. I don't want to lock her up like when Empress Irini comes—if she ever does come. I called her a traitor and accused her of ordering Aetios to murder Constantine."

"Oh, she will come." His voice was hard. "She needs you to help her escape when the army comes for her."

"I told her that if she tried to escape them by hiding in this convent, I would open the gate to them myself."

He raised his eyebrows. "But you vowed to protect her with your life."

My head felt muddled. "I don't know what I will do. Can a vow of loyalty simply become a habit?"

His voice softened. "Once you told me that Abbess Pulkeria believed that Saint Thekla brought you and Irini together to help Irini find the right path. When you bend to Irini's will against your conscience, is that following that right path?"

I could not answer.

In September, Tula delivered a healthy boy. It was an easy birth. The infant drank his fill and slept in his lambswool cocoon. Maria hovered by the door until Irinoula took her hand and led her to the scriptorium. After Ninth Hour services, I saw Maria sitting on the ground in the kitchen garden holding a bundle against her breast. For one terrifying moment, I thought she had snatched the infant. I leapt out the door but it was only a blanket.

Shortly after that, Elias arrived with a letter for Tula. We sat in the cottage of Father Dimitrios and, as always with letters, I opened it so I would know any difficult news that might cause distress. "It is from Abbott Theodore," I reported. "He offers his condolences and wishes Tula strength in her sorrow. He tells her that her virtue will be rewarded in Heaven." I put it away with distaste. "Why does Theodore continue to write these letters? His words will not cheer her. Does he have nothing else to do in exile in Thessaloniki?"

"He's back," Elias said. "Empress Irini brought him and Platon back to their monastery in Bithynia."

"Why?" I puzzled. "They covered the Empire with their letters condemning Constantine's marriage to Tula as bigamy, knowing that Irini was backing the marriage."

"The issue of bigamy is over," explained Elias. "Constantine is dead. Tula may be the legitimate wife and mother of the next emperor, but Irini has got her locked away here. Irini's present claim to the throne is through Constantine and his daughters."

"Irini manipulated Constantine into divorcing Maria and marrying Tula, and it might as well never have happened," I said bitterly.

He nodded. "Abbott Theodore never condemned Irini for her support of the divorce or the re-marriage. He has only praised her because she brought back icons."

A few weeks later, what we had been dreading happened. Empress Irini arrived. We were picking grapes and dumping them into the vat for making juice. Our grapes were particularly sweet that year and we had wasps. I heard Maria scream from atop the convent wall, "Constantine has come for me!"

Two novices caught her as she was climbing the gate and they dragged her screaming into the basilica crypt. I locked her in and sat on the floor of the nave to catch my breath. Efrosini put her arm around me and I pressed my face into her small shoulder.

"My sweet, your grandmother may have come to take you to Constantinople and name you her Co-empress. It isn't safe for you, and it isn't right."

"We will find out what she wants, Auntie Thekla. Then we will decide what to do."

Her calm answer steadied me. "You speak to her. I cannot trust myself to be civil."

So Efrosini and I walked down to the harbour to meet her while Irinoula sat with her mother behind bars. Father Dimitrios, alone, was waiting on the quay. Six guards got off first, hands on the hilts of their swords, ready to draw them against any villager who wanted revenge for the death of their beloved Constantine. Empress Irini strode down the gangplank, leaving Aetios to guard the yacht. She kissed Efrosini, nodded to Father Dimitrios and me, and went into the church to pray while her guards waited outside the church with us. As we walked through the empty streets, shouts of "Shame!" came from behind slammed shutters.

At the convent cemetery, Irini drew her shawl over her head and bowed her head before the stone slab covering Constantine's grave while Father Dimitrios chanted a prayer. I searched my heart for pity and found none.

The guards took up posts outside the convent gates, Father Dimitrios went back to the village, and we continued through the pasture. Irini gazed at the goats and sheep. A hawk circled and she looked at him too. She went inside the basilica and greeted old Brother Grigorios who was up on a ladder painting stars on a pillar. She went into the little church in the courtyard and moved slowly along the walls, looking at the scenes of the village and the women saints working alongside the village people. She said nothing about the scene of Constantine with blood dripping from his eyes and his wives and daughters weeping beside him. She ignored the scene of villagers placing flowers on his grave.

"I heard that Tula delivered a boy," she said as we left the church. "How is the child? He is heir to the throne now." Her eyes skimmed the windows of the imperial suites.

Efrosini answered. "Mother and child are both healthy, Grandmama. My mother is also well."

Empress Irini went into my study. She gazed at the maps and touched the account book on my desk. Finally she threw herself in the chair by the open window. Aspasia brought her a mug of mountain tea and Efrosini and I stood, waiting. I was shaking inside. I wanted to scream at Irini and curse her. Still, as I saw the lines of fatigue on her face, I felt a twinge of pity. It vanished with her next words.

"Constantine's uncles have again conspired to gain the throne. Their stupidity has no limit. They somehow escaped from the monastery where I had exiled them and got themselves into the sanctuary behind the altar in the Church of Holy Wisdom. Some idiot had told them that one of them would be proclaimed as emperor by general acclaim. No one came to acclaim them, of course. Aetios talked them out from behind the altar and arrested them."

"Did he drag them out, like Stavrakios dragged Constantine from sanctuary in the Church of Saint Mamas?" I had not wanted to speak but the words flew from me.

"I have exiled them to Athens. They will be under my uncle's charge."

She rose and moved restlessly to stare at the map of the Caliphate. "Caliph Harun al-Rashid has sent his uncle Abdulmalik to raid Kappadokia and Galatia. They are plundering the countryside and taking prisoners. Our army cannot drive them back. I was forced to send envoys to offer terms of peace. Abdulmalik turned them down."

"Harun will negotiate only when there is no more plunder to be had," commented Efrosini. I was impressed by her grasp of politics. Still, she was eight and Irini had been teaching her since she was five.

Empress Irini nodded. "I sent an ambassador all the way to Baghdad to offer terms of peace directly to Caliph Harun. The arrogant bastard rejected them. He wants tribute. Gold coins. Bolts of silk." She threw up her hands. "I need stronger theme armies but men keep joining monasteries to escape conscription. My father-in-law was driven into a fury by the same thing. He wrote an edict decreeing that monks were not exempt from conscription. I can't enforce it. The peasants will fill the streets with protests and the men will hide in the monasteries anyway. I would hire foreign soldiers but Nikiforos the Finance Minister claims that we lack funds. He blames me. He says I should have raised taxes on the farming villages. I had lowered them. Blood from a stone, I told him."

She dropped onto a couch. "I have sent ambassadors to Charles of the Franks with a personal letter. I told him of my son's death and my accession as sole ruler. Charles's latest wife has died, probably in childbirth. I've asked him to help us against Caliph Harun."

"Charles will not help you against Harun or the Bulgars," said Efrosini. "They are not his enemies."

Irini nodded gloomily. "Charles is even making alliances with Harun. He has asked Harun for an elephant, of all things, and Harun has sent one. Apparently, Charles is starting a wild beast menagerie. Now he wants Harun to send him a lion. Charles should be more careful. Harun is bent on expanding his empire. One day, his armies will stand at the gates of Aachen. I wrote to Charles and told him so. I also offered him a reason to help us against Harun. I have proposed that we unify our two empires through marriage. Charles to me."

I gaped at her. "You called off the marriage you arranged between your son and Charles's daughter and now you want to marry the man himself? Have you lost your senses?"

"Can you think of a better way to get Charles to send his armies to defend us?" she snapped.

"Long ago, you told me that if the Emperor died, you

would rule on your own."

"And I will. Charles will live in Aachen and rule the Franks. I will live in Constantinople and rule the Romans of the East. We will fight our enemies together."

"Has Charles answered your proposal?" asked Efrosini.

Irini made a face. "He has sent a cautious reply, offering terms. He did offer to release the brother of Patriarch Tarasios. The idiot let himself be captured by the Frankish army when Adalgisos went on that failed expedition to Sicily."

"What does Patriarch Tarasios say about your marriage?" inquired Efrosini. "Charles is not of the Eastern Church. That will cause concern."

Irini poured herself a glass of elderberry wine. "Tarasios opposes," she said coldly, drinking the wine quickly and refilling her glass. "He is a senile old man and lacking in courage. He and the bishops claim that Charles will marry me and immediately grant Pope Leo control over the liturgy of the Eastern Church. Such nonsense! Twelve years ago, Pope Adrianos wanted the Ecumenical Council at Nicaea to adopt the beliefs of the Church of Rome. I refused then, and I will refuse now. But the bishops don't trust me to stand fast."

She restlessly paced the room. "Those dim-witted clerics are nothing more than a flock of short-sighted, fearful old men. My marriage to Charles would be a simple alliance to secure our borders, yet the fools fixate on religious matters. Ungrateful morons! I let them pontificate about religious law to their hearts' content at Nicaea. I gave them back their icons. And now they block me! Curse them all! I will marry Charles, no matter what they say. Stavrakios approves. He agrees that we need help to fight Harun and the Bulgars. And the Magyars and the Goths and the Slavs and the rest of those greedy pagans who stare over our borders with covetous eyes."

"And Aetios?" Efrosini asked. "What does he advise?"

Her lips tightened. "He opposes."

"Why do you allow those eunuchs to have opinions?" My voice shook with loathing for those vile eunuchs. "They are not your advisors."

She glared at me. "They keep me informed of what goes on in the Palace behind the false smiles and lies of my advisors!" Irini snapped.

Efrosini interrupted my retort. "Why does Aetios oppose the marriage?" she asked in her quiet voice.

"Aetios claims that Charles will take us over, that he will move his army into Constantinople and replace the Palace Guards and all my commanders with his own officers. We will become a puppet state of the Franks, Aetios claims. Charles will depose me and I will die in exile."

"Who do you trust more, Stavrakios or Aetios?" Efrosini asked.

She sighed. "Aetios is my second-in-command and Chief of the Patricians. I should listen to his advice."

I exploded. "Empress, those two eunuchs are conniving against you. They give you opposite opinions to confuse you. Do not give them this power!"

"Silence!" she snapped. "You have no opinion in this or any other matter."

I raised my voice. "Everyone but you knows the wealth those thieves have stolen from the Treasury. Aetios wants to put his brother on the throne. This is common knowledge. The brother is not a eunuch and can be an emperor. You will end up in exile and dead."

"Stop your mouth!" she shouted. "You do not understand how slender is my grip on the throne. My only claim as Empress is that I am the widow of Emperor Leon. The army is against me because I am a woman. The bishops won't acknowledge me as head of the church because I am a woman. The senators and patricians watch me like wolves around a tethered goat. Only Stavrakios and Aetios are keeping me on the throne. I have to reward their loyalty."

"You are bribing them, not rewarding them," I retorted. "They will demand larger and larger bribes and turn against you anyway." I left the room without asking permission.

I didn't want to see her that evening. I sent in her meal with a novice. Then, to my dismay, she joined me as I was making my rounds. We stood at the low place in the wall and gazed at the stars dipping their sparkling fingers into the still sea. The stars were so bright that I could see my shadow by their light. Irini sighed.

"When I was a child in Athens, I used to sit at my bedroom window high on the hill of Athens and watch the constellations cross the sky. I cannot do that in Constantinople. The city walls chop up the sky."

Her words brought me back to when I was a child and gazing at the stars. I felt my heart melt. Irini could do that. She knew how to break down walls.

For the next three days, Empress Irini coached Efrosini in the ceremony that would make her Co-empress. I didn't want to hear it. Even thinking about Efrosini being Co-empress made me ill. So I devoted my days to Tula and Maria. Tula refused to leave her room while Irini was there, except for prayer services and meals, neither of which Irini attended. So I kept Tula company in her room and I watched over the infant when Tula needed the latrine or a nap. My eyes saw Constantine when he was an infant.

As for Maria, Sister Matrona and I lifted the bar off the door of her dormitory room each morning and walked her to the latrine and wash basin, then Orthros prayers and breakfast. If she remained docile, I took her to the scriptorium and locked us both inside. I stayed with her so she couldn't destroy a scroll in a mad fit. I began copying a scroll written by Theophrastus about plants. I had read that scroll to Irini when she was so uncomfortable during the difficult days just before Constantine was born. Reading about plants and their uses calmed me now as they had calmed Irini then.

On the fourth day of Irini's stay, Maria shouted from her window that an imperial warship was coming. Efrosini and I went with Irini to the top of the lane and watched a warship drop anchor outside the little harbour. Sailors splashed down a dingy and rowed a guard to the quay. He spoke to Father Dimitrios and, shortly after, I heard the bang of the semantron. The guard panted up the lane towards us.

"Abdulmalik and the army of Caliph Harun al-Rashid are marching towards Malagina," he reported to Irini.

"They are after our warhorses again," she scowled. "I will return to Constantinople."

As I watched her march down the lane without a backward look, I thought about when Elias and I had walked to Constantinople and stopped at the Malagina stud farm. I had seen the beautiful warhorses grazing in those green pastures. That night I had slept in Elias's arms for the first time. I watched Irini get into the dingy and then climb the ladder to the warship deck. Oars flashed and they were gone. Efrosini went to tell Tula that she could come out. Megalo went to free Maria. I called the nuns together in the refectory and gave them the news.

Weeks later, Elias brought more news. "Abdulmalik raided the stables at Malagina and stole many warhorses and baggage mules. He even stole the warhorses that belonged to Stavrakios. Harun's other forces raided Lydia on the south coast. They have withdrawn, after burning fields and stealing livestock. The good news is that they did not march on Constantinople."

"The other good news is that Irini did not name Efrosini as her Co-empress," I added with satisfaction.

Chapter X

Irini hid inside the Great Palace for a year, protected by the Palace Guards. The army hated her for blinding Constantine. They hated her for the disastrous defeat at Amorion when she had prevented Constantine from stopping Harun from sacking the countryside. That defeat resulted in Irini paying tribute to Harun in gold and bolts of silk just so he would stay on his side of the border. Which didn't work, because Abdulmalik raided Malagina and Lydia. The eunuchs whom Irini had named as generals were worse than useless.

The first week in Lent, I was down in the harbour with Efrosini, Sister Matrona, and Aspasia, buying fish for supper, when Elias arrived in the mail boat and helped a thin and slightly hunched man climb out of the small boat.

"That's Nikiforos the Finance Minister," I muttered, staring in disbelief. "The last time he was here was when the convent was reconsecrated after Irini had it renovated. What possibly could he be doing here now?"

To my surprise, Nikiforos came over and greeted me politely by name. I introduced Efrosini and the two nuns. He greeted them equally politely but his eyes lingered on Efrosini. She was nine then and gaining height, a quick-witted and observant child.

"What brings you to our island?" I inquired.

"I am checking on the imperial convents. A budgetary visit, you understand. And it is a lovely spring day for a sea trip."

At the top of the lane, he stopped to greet Tula who was placing flowers on Constantine's grave. Tula's son was playing in the grass. The child was just over a year old, a healthy, chubby joy to us all. We crossed the pasture and entered the basilica. Irini had built it after Nikiforos had last visited the convent. He lit a candle, placed it in the sand pit, and greeted Brother Grigorios. The monk was perched on scaffolding, painting an icon high on a wall. Brother Grigorios nodded silently, having had his tongue cut out years before as punishment for painting icons. Nikiforos toured the church and gazed at the other icons on the pillars and walls.

We continued to the tiny church in our courtyard where he studied the icons covering the walls. "Also the work of Brother Grigorios," I murmured. He nodded.

We crossed the courtyard to my study. Efrosini went for mint tea and our lemon sweets. Nikiforos looked around the room.

I confess to the sin of pride. The rich colours of the rugs shone in the sunlight that entered through the long open windows to the courtyard. The chairs and tables gleamed, polished with beeswax by the novices. Polished silver and brass plate shone from the side tables. Nikiforos moved around the room, gazing at Irini's maps of the Empire and fingering the tapestries that covered the other walls. He seated himself in the big chair by the window.

"Everything in the convent belongs to the convent," I noted. "It is written in our typikon."

He smiled. "Of course, I read your typikon when it was registered."

Efrosini brought tea and sweets which he consumed with polite appreciation. "Now I would like to review your account books," he said.

"I brought them to be reviewed when I received my last salary," I protested.

"I would like to see them again."

Puzzled, I retrieved them from Sister Matrona's storage room and he sat at my desk and read for some time, with great attention.

"I complement you on your bookkeeping," he commented as he closed the final page. "Now if you will show me through your convent."

So Efrosini and Sister Matrona and I showed him through the hospice, weaving room, and library where he examined the scrolls and codices. I pointed at the windows of the imperial suites. "Empress Maria and Empress Tula live there with their children," I explained. He nodded.

We took him through the flower gardens that Irini had the Palace gardeners put in, and the orchard, kitchen garden, and animal sheds.

"You are breaking the law of religious seclusion," I

pointed out as he went down into the root cellar but he just nodded. Efrosini and I followed and watched him warily while he looked over the array of jars on the shelves. They disguised the door that hid the passage to the secret room. For all I knew, Nikiforos had a plan of the convent from when it was built by Emperor Leon as an imperial prison monastery. Leon had built prison monasteries on nearly every island in the chain. I held my breath until he went up the steps and thanked us for the lovely afternoon.

Efrosini, Sister Matrona, and I walked him to the convent gate where Elias was waiting. We watched the two men go down the lane, cross the plateia, and climb into the mail boat.

"What was that all about?" puzzled Sister Matrona.

I shook my head, equally puzzled. "Elias once said that Nikiforos is the only Palace official who will argue with Empress Irini."

Not long after that, Maria shouted that the imperial yacht was passing by the convent and I went to look over the wall. Aetios was standing on deck. The breath went out of me and I sat heavily on the grass. Efrosini sat beside me. I took her hand.

"Aetios is probably here to take you into Constantinople for the Lenten and Easter ceremonies. Empress Irini will want you by her side, to show that you are her choice as heir. You must be brave. When your father was nine, his father died and Empress Irini made him carry out the Easter ceremonies. He cried because he feared that he would make a mistake and she would be angry."

"I'm not afraid of Grandmama, Auntie Thekla. I won't

cry."

Efrosini wasn't afraid, but I was—of what the army might do. They could capture the imperial yacht and take Efrosini. They could send her into exile and death. I was also afraid of Aetios. I was convinced that one day he would turn against Irini and claim the throne for his brother.

"I worry that Empress Irini will name you as her Co-empress on Easter," I said.

"She will name Tula's son as Co-emperor," said Efrosini. "He is the male heir."

I shook my head. "Elias says that the Senate could declare the child of Constantine and Tula to be the legitimate heir. Tula is still Empress Augusta. The Senate could name her as the boy's regent. Irini has to name you as her Co-empress before they do that. That strengthens her claim that Maria is Constantine's legitimate wife and you are his heir. I am going with you into Constantinople. Maybe I can persuade her not to name you as Co-empress."

I went to my study and tied Saint Thekla into my shawl. I wasn't going to let Efrosini out of my sight.

My fears were groundless. Aetios didn't speak to us on the yacht and took us straight to Irini's suite in Daphne Palace. Empress Irini did not name Efrosini as Co-empress, only kept the child beside her through the many ceremonies of Holy Week and Easter.

Lent, a year later, was a different story. Aetios came for Efrosini on Great Sunday of Holy Week. He led us silently to the map room where Irini was glaring at the map of the Empire. Every time I saw her, she was more richly dressed and wore more jewels.

"My army commanders are useless failures! Caliph Harun has sent Abdulmalik to invade Bithynia! They are nearing Abbott Theodore's monastery. Those defenceless monks are in real danger. I have summoned them to Constantinople and I am giving them Studios Monastery. It used to be the largest monastery in Constantinople until the monks objected to my father-in-law's ban on icons. He drove them out and took it into imperial possession. Now it's in ruins and empty except for ten of those mad Akimeti monks who chant day and night to stay awake so they can praise God without stopping. Patriarch Tarasios has approved the transfer and has named Theodore as abbott."

The monks arrived a few days before Easter. Empress Irini dragged Efrosini and me along with a herd of dignitaries to the Monastery of Studios to give them a formal welcome. As we jolted down Mesi Street inside the imperial coach, Empress Irini sang Abbott Theodore's praises. "He is a genius of organization. He has brought many small monasteries under the umbrella of his monastery and now they support each other with their harvests, their libraries—everything. The monks are required to read an hour a day. Abbott Theodore has invented a faster way of writing what he calls 'miniscule' script so his monks can copy more scrolls in less time."

Studios monastery was truly in ruins, as we saw when our coach pulled through the broken gates. Efrosini wrinkled her nose. "Even rats wouldn't live in this garbage dump."

Irini waved that away. "I have ordered Nikiforos the

Finance Minister to give Abbott Theodore an unlimited budget to restore it. This is Theodore's reward for his loyalty to me over the years. He has been my confidant and loyal friend ever since I came to Constantinople and he remains my most loyal supporter."

I didn't like Abbott Theodore and I wasn't looking forward to seeing him but I was curious to view the monastery. I had often glanced through the broken gates when I was living at Ta Gastria convent.

Abbott Theodore came rushing out to greet Irini. I had not seen him since he brought his niece Tula to be Irini's attendant when Irini was under house arrest. Now he was even more round and energetic. He greeted Empress Irini and Efrosini effusively and did the same for the senators, patricians, and wealthy dignitaries who were climbing cautiously out of their carriages. Nikiforos the Finance Minister nodded politely to me. Left to our own devices, Efrosini and I wandered off to look around.

"The Akimeti monks certainly sacrificed housekeeping to prayer," I noted as we gazed upon the shambles of the filthy kitchen. The latrines behind it were unspeakable and the huge dormitory up two flights of stone stairs stank. We retreated to the abbott's study where Abbott Theodore was expounding on his planned repairs. The massive desk was strewn with drawings and notes.

"I will administer this monastery as an independent monastic conclave that will resist imperial coercion," he proudly told the dignitaries.

I saw Minister Nikiforos raise an eyebrow. "This monastery belongs to the crown," he said quietly, making it clear that the Empress could throw Abbott Theodore and his monks out whenever she wanted. Irini remained silent—the reward for Abbott Theodore's own silence when she had sent Aetios to blind Constantine, I thought bitterly.

"Patrikios Leon is donating an icon of Christ," Abbott Theodore went on with a patronising nod at the donor who was shaking rat droppings off the hem of his long cloak. "I am commissioning wall icons of the sainted theologians." He pointed at the crumbling plaster walls as if the saints were already peering down at us: "John the Evangelist, Paul, Zacharias, Dionysios, Basil, Grigorios of Nazianzos and . . ."

"No women saints?" I interrupted loudly.

His beady eyes found me. "Ah, Abbess Thekla. You must add my Rules for Monastic Life to your typikon for your little convent."

"Our typikon was approved by the Eparch of the Monasteries." I snapped but I shouldn't have bothered. He was already moving on, waving his arms enthusiastically.

"I am restoring the monastic traditions of the Church Fathers. Communal life will replace the solitary life of the hermit. Poverty and charity will be first in importance."

"How does poverty fit into an unlimited imperial budget?" murmured Nikiforos, with a glance at Irini.

When we left, two monks loaded a heavy scroll into our carriage. Efrosini and I unrolled it in Irini's map room and I squinted hopelessly at the small, strangely-shaped letters. "Miniscule print, Theodore calls it, and rightly so," I muttered irritably.

Efrosini read aloud in her light voice: "'There will be a hierarchy of officials, each with his special work, for which he is responsible, and for which he must report to the abbott. There will be constant and diligent instruction of all members of the community in the fundamental ideas of the monastic life; everyone's mind must be quite clear as to their position and responsibilities. Officials are second in command to the abbott. First steward, sub-steward, epistemonarchs to settle disputes among the monks, observers to watch the monks . . .'"

"Spies," I noted.

She nodded. "'. . a canonarch to superintend the church music, a taxiarch to maintain order in processions and other rituals, and various caretakers of larder and table. There will be craftsmen, builders, tailors, gardeners and a porter who opens the door, and excitatores who will arouse slumbering brethren to their religious duties. During Lent, a special brother will go to all kitchens and workshops, saying, 'Fathers and Brothers: we die, we die, we die. Let us remember the Kingdom of Heaven.'"

"Abbott Theodore must never sleep to ensure that his monks complete their assigned tasks," Efrosini noted and we both laughed.

"Our nuns do their tasks in their own way and everyone is happy," I said.

That Lent and Easter, Irini was in her glory, more beautiful than ever. Even the hostile crowds restrained their angry shouts during the annual procession to the Church of Holy Apostles when four white horses pulled her carriage. I was in the crowd watching the procession and I recognized Bardanes Tourkos leading one of the horses. He had force-marched Abbott Theodore into exile in Thessaloniki. He was building a monastery on Proti Island, Father Dimitrios had said.

Irini let us go home after Easter. Efrosini and I were packing when Irini marched into our chamber. "Constantine's five uncles are plotting against me again."

"I thought they were in Athens under your uncle's eye," said Efrosini.

"They are. He locked them in a monastery. But I just got word that the leader of the Slavs in that area has hatched a plan to rescue the idiots and proclaim one of them as Emperor. Stavrakios says that some of my uncle's own soldiers are part of the plot. This is treason and my uncle is part of it."

Efrosini and I were silent, watching her flushed face. "I am ordering my uncle to blind those five traitors by his own hand. I have ordered Theo to take my message to his father, personally. I told Theo that he must watch his father carry out the blinding and report back to me."

Efrosini went white and I gasped. "Why such cruel punishment, Empress?"

Irini's voice was cold. "It is no more cruel than what I suffered in my uncle's house. I was brought there as an orphan when my parents died and I had no power against my uncle. He knew what would happen to me when he put me on that warship with Emperor Constantine. Now he will suffer for that—and all the years when I suffered as an orphan living in his house."

After she left, I sat feeling buffeted by her rage. Still, I felt a surge of admiration for her that I hadn't felt for years. She had survived through sheer determination. Efrosini and I went to Theo's suite to say goodbye. His handsome face was pale as he and his servants packed his trunks. Irini's mute slave was helping them.

Theo's eyes were bitter and angry. "I made Irini let her slave go home to Athens. She is old. As for me, I will deliver Irini's order to my father but I will not watch him blind those five men. And I will never return to Constantinople."

"Did the Slavs really plan to make one of them Emperor?" Efrosini asked.

Theo continued flinging things into a trunk. "Of course not," he snorted. "Why would a bunch of nomadic Slavs meddle in our affairs? The idea is absurd. Irini made up the whole thing so she could get rid of the five in line for the throne. You must warn her about Stavrakios. He is blatantly bribing army officers to rise against Irini—and he has found many."

"How can you leave her in this danger?" I burst out. "You are her only friend."

"I have warned Irini about Stavrakios but she won't listen. Besides, she has ordered me to go to Athens and I'm obeying orders," he snapped. "If I stay here, Stavrakios or Aetios will kill me and what good would I be to Irini then? Take care, both of you. You are their next targets."

He stood up and stretched his back. "Come with me to Athens," he said impulsively. "It is a lovely town. Peaceful. You will be safe."

I thought about his words as Efrosini and I sat on the yacht taking us to Prinkypos. "One day, let us go to Athens," I said. "Irini has said that she will never return there, yet I have heard her speak of the beauty of Athens, and with fondness."

"We will go there together, you and I," said Efrosini. "We will be safe."

Chapter XI

Once upon a time, I believed that the army had refused to vow loyalty to Empress Irini because she was a woman. I believed that the bishops wouldn't accept her as head of the Eastern Church because she was a woman. I was wrong. After Irini put Constantine under house arrest, she appointed her own army commanders and they obeyed her orders. As for the bishops, they flocked to her Ecumenical Council at Nicaea like geese to grain, knowing full well that the Council was her creation and that Patriarch Tarasios was under her thumb. Abbott Theodore and Brother Theophanes may have drafted the documents but she told them what to write. Patriarch Tarasios may have led the sessions but she told him what to say. Irini, alone, persuaded Pope Adrianos to send papal delegates—a real achievement considering the enmity that had long existed between the Eastern and the Latin churches. The bishops and monks who packed the Church of the Dormition in Nicaea were not so stupid as to believe that Patriarch Tarasios had achieved that miracle of organization without the Palace behind him. Everyone knew that Empress Irini had returned our icons to our homes and churches.

But after the Council was over, things turned sour. The problem was that Irini knew how to criticize and blame but not how to praise or trust. No man or woman had ever given her reason to trust, except me, and she didn't even trust me. She gave her trust to the Palace eunuchs. They were neither man nor woman so they couldn't have children and pass their positions to them. And eunuchs ran the Palace. They were experienced administrators and many were strong soldiers—Aetios and Stavrakios, for example. So from the day she wed Co-emperor Leon at age seventeen, she hired eunuchs for her household servants and guards. They became her allies. They taught her how to dress and behave at Palace functions. They brought her the gossip that she needed to fight the sneers of her mother-in-law, her sister-in-law, and the wives of patricians and senators who were attendants to the Empress. As the years passed, Irini filled the Palace with eunuchs. She believed they would protect her.

But most eunuchs are devious and cunning and Stavrakios and Aetios were pure evil. Finally Stavrakios showed his greedy, power-hungry nature in a manner so blatant that even Irini couldn't ignore it. Efrosini, Aspasia, and I were down at the quay buying fish when Elias sailed in with the news.

"Stavrakios got caught bribing the Palace Guards and officials to help him seize the throne. Aetios had evidence. And witnesses."

I shrugged and pointed at a sea bass for the fisherman to put in my basket. "Aetios forged the evidence and bribed the witnesses. Aetios is patrikios and second-in-command of the armed forces after Empress Irini, but he also wants the position that Irini gave Stavrakios. That would make him commander of all the armies. He won't succeed. Stavrakios will persuade Irini that Aetios has lied. She will forgive Stavrakios."

"Not this time. Irini had Stavrakios brought before the Council of Senators. Nikitas Triphillios brought more witnesses and evidence. Nikitas is a patrikios and a commander in the Palace Guards so Irini believed him. She made Stavrakios apologise to her. She exiled him to his home in Kappadokia. No one in the army or government service can have any contact with him."

"A slap on the wrist," I shrugged. "A holiday in his home town. He will return."

"He will be assassinated," stated Efrosini, whose grasp of Palace intrigue was beginning to worry me.

"Aetios is getting even more rude and arrogant," Elias added darkly. "The mail couriers say that he openly insults everyone."

I draped wet seaweed over my fish and gave the basket to Efrosini who went over to chat with her friends. Elias and I sat on a boulder by the sea. I lowered my voice.

"What I find so disturbing that I cannot sleep nights is that Empress Irini trusts me the same as she trusts Aetios. This makes me a liar or a thief, like him."

He laughed. "Don't be silly. You are not a liar and a thief. Well, except that you have never taken the vows of a nun and you let everyone think that you have. And you probably hide money and jewels here that you and the Empress steal from the Palace."

I smiled, thinking of the secret room under my study and the chest filled with gold coins, silver plate, and purses heavy with jewels. "There are also icons."

He burst out laughing. "We are a pair, aren't we, dear Thekla, each with our secrets. We suit each other."

Empress Irini came out a month later. Maria alerted us from her window, as usual, and, as usual, the novices chased her down and locked her in the basilica crypt. Irinoula stayed with her. The girl had quietly asked me if she could take the vows. She was twelve and could enter our convent. At seventeen, she could become a novice. Her even, quiet temperament made her suitable for convent life. She sang the services sweetly but not fervently, she carried out any task that was needed, and she cared for her mad mother with patience and kindness.

Efrosini and I went down to meet the yacht. To my shock, Empress Irini could barely walk down the gangplank. She clung to my arm and struggled for breath.

"They are poisoning me," she gasped as the imperial bearers assembled a chair litter. "This convent is the only place where I am safe."

Shaken, I followed the bearers through the village, wondering if people would take pity on her and come out. But no, shutters slammed and shouts of "Shame!" followed us. We settled Irini on a couch in my study and Sister Efthia brewed an herbal concoction to rinse away the poison. I sat at my desk and noted in my ledger that Empress Irini had arrived, poisoned.

Irini gazed sourly at the spring flowers blooming against the little church. Her voice was bitter. "I cannot discover who has poisoned me. Everyone I have trusted lies to me or turns against me. Theo has gone to Athens. Abbott Theodore is busy with Studios Monastery. I cannot trust my army commanders. Stavrakios was on my personal staff for thirteen years and now I see that he only wanted wealth and power. Aetios tells me he is planning a revolt from Kappadokia. I have sent Aetios to put it down."

"Aetios will murder Stavrakios," Efrosini commented.

Irini shrugged. "I have named Aetios as Commander of the theme of Anatolia."

I was unable to choke back my anger at her blindness. "This is exactly what Aetios planned," I snapped. "He accused Stavrakios of conspiracy against you, you believed him, and now Aetios has the highest military rank of the theme armies. He has done nothing to earn it, like the other army officers who rise through the ranks. Mark my words: Aetios will die with a spear in his back."

Irini scowled at me. "You sound like Nikitas Triphillios and my cousin Leon in the Palace Guards. They are jealous of Aetios and will say nothing good about him. Nikiforos the Finance Minister doesn't like Aetios either. I promoted Nikiforos to that position and now I regret it. When I go back to Constantinople, I will find someone better. A eunuch." She drank another cup of herbal infusion and dozed off.

Over the following days, she drank restorative teas, and listened to the school girls chant their lessons. Irinoula read to her in her quiet voice. Irinoula had prayed to forgive her grandmother for the death of her father," she told me. Efrosini refused to discuss her father's death. She also refused to read to her grandmother.

Tula ignored Irini. The formerly spoiled bride had become a sweet young woman and a sturdy member of our convent. Our daily prayer services had eased her grief and despair after Constantine's death. She helped Aspasia cook while her son played on a blanket on the floor. She consoled Megalo when a pontificating letter came from Abbott Theodore. The lullabies she sang to her son soothed us all to sleep.

I let Maria move freely about the convent as long as she didn't go near the window of my study where Irini lay resting. Some days after she arrived, the mail boat came and I took Maria with me. Elias had letters and dispatches for Irini, a letter for Efrosini, and one for me. Maria waded in the sea while I sat on the bench by the church with Father Dimitrios and read through the mail.

"Theo has reached Athens," I read. "He writes of a pleasant voyage and his pleasure at being home again. He says nothing about his father blinding Constantine's five uncles. Has he written to you?"

"He has," replied Elias, but said nothing more and struck up a conversation with Father Dimitrios.

I took Irini's mail up to her and she read it aloud from her couch.

"My ambassador in Rome writes that on the coming Day of Nativity, Pope Leo of Rome will name Charles of the Franks as Emperor of the Holy Roman Empire." She scowled. "That's what the Pope is calling it, even though it is neither Holy nor Roman. We are the Holy

Roman Empire. Constantine the Great proclaimed it so when he founded Constantinople." She returned to the letter. "The clergy and nobles will proclaim him Augustus." She put down the letter. "I am Empress Augusta of the Roman Empire of the East. Now that Charles has such an elevated title, surely we should join our empires through marriage. My ambassadors in Aachen tell me that Charles continues to speak of it."

"Aetios opposes, you said. And your advisors."

"My advisors have changed their minds. They want good relations with Charles. I will send the great man a gift to assure him of my interest. I am considering sending the Veil of the Virgin from the Blachernae Church. Or the belt of the Virgin from the Church of the Virgin of the Copper Market."

Dismayed, I protested. "Empress! The Mother of God left us those to show her love for us."

"Charles will appreciate the significance. He knows that possessing either one will raise him in the eyes of the Pope and the entire Christian world."

"You will lose what little love the monks have left for you." But she was asleep.

Slowly, Irini re-gained her strength. She went down to the secret room and checked the escape route. She counted her treasure. She resumed teaching Efrosini how to rule the Empire. She wrote letters. While Irini was ill, Maria had behaved herself, but as Irini began to move about the convent, Maria started peering at her around corners and hissing. We locked Maria in the crypt and didn't feed her for a day. After that, we kept her locked in her dormitory room.

By mid-June, Irini was ready to go back to Constantinople. She gave me a message for Elias to send to Aetios to come and get her. Maria spotted the mail boat and shouted. I took my time going down. I was forty-eight that year, as was Irini, and the hill felt steeper, even going down.

"Stavrakios has died," Elias told me as he handed me a pile of dispatches.

"Good riddance. May his soul never find rest," I cursed absently, sorting through the mail. I handed him Irini's letter to send to Aetios. "Irini wants to go back to Constantinople."

"The poison didn't work, apparently," Elias replied cheerfully.

I looked at him sharply. "Do you know who poisoned her?"

"Aetios, of course. Everyone knows."

Back in the convent, I gave Irini the dispatches and she read bits of them aloud. "Stavrakios coughed up blood and died. I suppose Aetios poisoned him. A pity he had to end this way."

"You never saw Stavrakios as he really was. Be careful that you aren't doing the same with Aetios," I warned. She ignored me.

The yacht took her away the next day. Efrosini and Irinoula went down with her and her guards. Her departure seemed final for some reason that I couldn't explain. Irinoula felt it too.

"Will she ever come back?" she asked.

"Where else can she go?" answered Efrosini.

Irini returned briefly in the autumn under full armed

guard. They set up camp at the top of the lane. "I have sent the Veil of the Virgin to Charles of the Franks," she said as we walked through the pasture. "He has replied with a proposal of marriage. I have refused."

I was startled. "I thought you wanted to marry the man."

"He is Charles the Great Liar," she said bitterly. "My spies in Aachen informed me that Charles had been planning to invade our lands in Sicily and Calabria. He proposed marriage instead. The liar thought he could conquer us by marriage. Aetios was right to mistrust Charles. And I was right to give Aetios the post that Stavrakios held. Now Aetios commands all the armies on the Asian side of the Empire. I have named his brother Leon as sole commander of Thrace and Makedonia to the west. At last, I have two commanders who are loyal only to me."

"Have you lost your mind?" I shouted, frightening away the sheep. "Now Aetios and his brother command enough battalions to seize the throne! Aetios will crown his brother as Emperor."

She turned on me with a snarl. "You are not my advisor. Still your mouth or I will send you to that convent on Lesbos where everyone dies in a year."

She left a few days later. "What a relief that she is gone," said Aspasia.

I couldn't agree more.

Chapter XII

Aetios's arrogance, wily ways, and his elevated power angered and frightened too many powerful people. But they didn't turn on him as I had hoped. They turned on Irini. It was October and we were down in the village trampling the grapes into juice for wine when Elias sailed in, back from one of his mysterious journeys. He had been gone some weeks and I had begun to worry. I was standing in the big vat squishing grapes with my feet. I spotted him rounding the church wearing a satisfied look, like our kitchen cat holding down a wriggling mouse. He waved a small embroidered pouch at me. I recognized it immediately and climbed out of the vat. I snatched it from him and tipped out a topaz ring.

"Irini's ring! Where did you get this?"

"A courier brought it," he said, and handed me a letter from his mail pouch.

Everyone gathered around as I scanned the lines. "She writes that this topaz ring proves this message is from her. She wants me to come to Constantinople. What has happened, Elias?"

He looked around with a grin at the villagers pushing to hear. "Yesterday the Senate arrested the Empress. She is locked inside her private palace. Deposed. The Senate has crowned Nikiforos the Finance Minister as Emperor."

I sat down hard, confused and bewildered among the cheers around me. My voice quavered. "This is so sudden! How did it come about?"

"Aetios brought her down, as you predicted. Aetios lost a major skirmish with Harun's army. Then Patriarch Tarasios brought Nikitas Triphillios before the Senate. Nikitas swore before God that Irini was intending to name Aetios' brother as Emperor. Irini's cousin Leon backed him up, saying that Empress Irini had agreed to relinquish the throne to the brother of Aetios. The Senate immediately voted to depose her. Nikiforos the Finance Minister arrested her himself. The Senate crowned him Emperor."

"Where is Aetios?" Father Dimitrios frowned.

"The devil and his brother have escaped over the Bulgar border, so I heard."

I stared at the letter, feeling bewildered. "Why does she want me to come?"

Elias sat down beside me and spoke gently. "You know why, Thekla. Irini doesn't give up. She wants you to help her escape. But it's over for her, Thekla. She stole the crown from Constantine and now Nikiforos has taken it from her. Do not go to Constantinople. Emperor Nikiforos will lock you in with her. You will die together."

Maria pushed to the front of the crowd. She smoothed her filthy tunica. "The demon is deposed. Now I am Empress. Megalo! Pack my trunks. My husband is waiting."

Tula crouched by Elias. "I can go home to my parents, can't I? Irini can't keep me here any longer. Or my son." Her soft voice ached with longing.

Elias spoke with sympathy but he shook his head. "Your son is the legitimate heir to the throne of the Isaurians. The army vowed their loyalty to the child's great-grandfather and to his grandfather and their descendants—your son. The army is backing Emperor Nikiforos at the moment, but some ambitious commander could claim that your son is the true emperor and gather support to put your son on the throne. Emperor Nikiforos can't let that happen. If you take your son from here, Emperor Nikiforos will suspect that you are joining a revolt. I couldn't guarantee your life or your son's."

He turned to Efrosini. "The same is true for you and your sister. You are possible heirs to the throne, even though your father divorced your mother. Emperor Nikiforos will be watching you. If you leave here, he will suspect that you are building support against him. I cannot assure your safety."

"Grandmama has been arrested before. She will get back on the throne," said Efrosini. "Charles of the Franks will rescue her if she agrees to marry him. Pope Leo will send his army if she tells him he can control the liturgy of the Eastern Church. Caliph Harun al-Rashid will come if she promises him Anatolia."

Even in my confused state, I marvelled at the eleven-year-old's grasp of politics. And I remembered the letters that Empress Irini had written to those faraway rulers when she was under house arrest. Irini had enough gold and jewels under my study floor to buy her way to freedom.

Tula shook her head. "No one will help a woman who blinded her own son."

"Don't go to Constantinople," Elias repeated gently.

I looked at him. "You were present in the Palace when they arrested Irini."

He nodded, watching me. "Yes, I was present."

"You helped Patriarch Tarasios bring Nikitas Trifillios before the Senate. You helped Nikiforos the Finance Minister depose Irini."

He nodded. "And I saved her life. Aetios would have killed her and put his brother on the throne. Now she is very much alive and in her private palace. And obviously plotting to escape," he added with a smile.

Anger rose in me. "All these years, you have been using me. You asked what Irini was thinking and planning and I told you. Then you took my words straight to Nikiforos and Patriarch Tarasios."

He nodded but his lips tightened. "We were trying to protect Constantine. We failed."

"Theo was part of your plotting."

"Yes, although he kept trying to protect Irini. Nikiforos was frightened of what her decisions were doing to the Empire. Theo finally gave up trying to help her make wise decisions. He went home. So should you, Thekla. Don't go to her now. She doesn't deserve your courage." He reached for my hand.

I pushed his hand away. "She is trying to stay on the throne just like every emperor before her."

"She made bad administrative and military decisions

and she wouldn't listen to anyone's advice besides Aetios and Stavrakios."

"I am going to Constantinople. I have kept my vow of loyalty all these years. I will not be disloyal now, no matter what she has done."

Efrosini took my hand. "I will go with you. She is my grandmother."

"You are risking that child's life," cautioned Father Dimitrios.

"I choose to go," said Efrosini. "Elias, please take us to Pendykion and put us on a coach."

Elias sighed, resigned. "I will take you all the way to Constantinople. At least I will know that you are safe."

Maria's screams from the locked crypt of the Church of Saint Nikolaos followed us out of the harbour. The autumn wind filled our sail and we reached Rymin fishing harbour and the Golden Gate before dusk. The guards at Irini's private palace took the coin I slipped them. As I pushed open the gate into the gardens, Elias disappeared into the shadowy lanes of the city. Irini ran to clasp us in her arms and pulled us inside the house.

Efrosini had never been to Irini's private palace and her eyes widened at the wealth and luxury—delicate tapestries, heavy rugs, tables gleaming with gold and silver dishes. The aroma of grilled meat and the clatter of pans floated from the kitchen. Irini drew us to couches near a wood fire and poured wine into silver goblets.

"Thekla, my loyal friend! And my dear granddaughter! I knew you would help me."

The words burst from me. "Your uncle in Athens, will he come for you? Will he protect you if you can reach

Athens?"

Her voice went cold. "My dear uncle handed me over to Emperor Constantine when I was seventeen, knowing what kind of womanizer he was. My dear uncle never answered my letters when I was under house arrest. When Constantine released me, my uncle sent my cousin Leon to protect me, he said, so I made Leon a guard in my residence. Leon was among those who arrested me!"

She paced the room. "So many traitors! Nikitas Triphillios and his brother Sisinnios led two of the white horses that drew my carriage to Holy Apostles last Easter. Those traitors told Patriarch Tarasios that I would proclaim the brother of Aetios as Emperor. And Tarasios—that traitor—brought Nikitas Trifillios to the Senate to condemn me. I elevated Tarasios to the highest position in the church and he betrayed me! My household eunuch from Sinope—I named him patrikios and gave him the highest position in the Palace Guards. I paid him in gold and jewels and silk! He joined the rest of them to arrest me."

"Would Charles of the Franks offer you sanctuary? Could his ambassadors help get you away?" Efrosini asked.

"Charles the Great Liar? He said publicly that a woman cannot lead an empire. His ambassadors stood there and watched Nikiforos arrest me. I called to the ambassadors for help and they turned away."

She flung herself onto the couch and gulped down her wine. Calmer, she glanced towards the kitchen, then leaned closer and spoke in a whisper. "You both will help me get back on the throne. Before the year is out, I promise you, Efrosini will be Co-empress sitting on the throne beside me in Magnavra Palace. We will rule the Empire together."

"Do you have a plan?" Efrosini asked cautiously.

Irini's smile was crafty. She lowered her voice. "Listen carefully. Emperor Nikiforos will come here to gloat over my disgrace. I will feign despair. I will ask that this palace be my prison, as when I was under house arrest. Nikiforos will refuse. He fears that I will gather support. He will tell me—gloating—that my exile will be Prinkypos where I will suffer with Tula and Maria and my grandchildren. I will bow my head obediently. But when I am there, in the dark of night, I will escape through the secret tunnel and down to the sea where a boat will be waiting."

"What if no fisherman will take you, Grandmama?" Efrosini's voice was sharp.

"Fisherman? Oh no, dear. My ally will come by boat and take me to his army. Together we will march against Nikiforos and I will be back on the throne."

She had gone mad. Tears filled my eyes and the pain of grief stabbed my throat. "Who is this ally with a ship?" I asked carefully.

Irini glanced towards the kitchen. "Bardanes Tourkos," she whispered. "He was one of the men who led the white horses pulling my carriage at Easter. He was there when Nikiforos arrested me. Everyone turned against me, but not Bardanes Tourkos."

"Why did he not stop them from arresting you?" Efrosini asked, taking her hand.

"One man against many? All he could do was keep me from harm. Yesterday, he came here secretly. He told me of his dream of being Emperor. He has the backing of many army units, he says. He promised me this: when he takes the throne, I will sit me beside him."

"Why does he need an empress?" Efrosini asked. "He could take the throne for himself."

Irini's voice grew impatient. "Because he needs my money, dear heart. He has to pay soldiers and buy horses and weapons. I have wealth hidden on Prinkypos. And here. Feel my cloak, dear child. I have sewn coins and jewels into the hem. Tonight we will sew more coins into your cloak. In the morning, the two of you will wear them to Ta Gastria convent. You and Abbess Pulkeria will unstitch them and the good Abbess will hide them." She looked at me. "She will hide them where she hid the wealth of Empress Evdokia years ago."

I nodded to myself. I knew where that was hidden. All those years ago, when I lived at Ta Gastria convent, I had seen where Abbess Pulkeria had hidden Empress Evdokia's stolen jewellery and coins. But first loyalties come first and even though I had vowed loyalty to Irini, my first loyalty was to Abbess Pulkeria. I had never told Irini of the dry cistern under the abbess's study with the trapdoor hidden under her rug. Elias was right. We have many loyalties and we must choose which loyalty is the greatest.

Efrosini interrupted my thoughts. "The guards will search us when we leave."

"Don't be silly, dear. Tell them you are nuns going to visit a convent and you will return. We must do this tonight. Nikiforos will come tomorrow and have this palace searched top to bottom."

"How will you get your treasure back from Ta Gastria convent?" I asked, but as soon as the words were out of my mouth, my heart sank because I knew what she would say.

"You will return to Constantinople and take it to Prinkypos," she said with a smug smile.

That evening, after we had eaten well and the servants had gone home, we sewed gold coins and jewels into Efrosini's cloak. I hardly slept that night, worrying that the guards would search us as we left. But Irini was right; they let us pass. I glanced behind us as we walked to Ta Gastria convent, fearing that Emperor Nikiforos knew that we were here and was having us followed. But I saw no one.

Abbess Pulkeria nodded slowly as we explained and she helped us snip out the gold and jewels and put in in a pouch. I carried it down the ladder into the dry cistern under her study. There were still hundreds of icons hidden down there, I saw, when I lifted my candle. They would stay there. Emperor Nikiforos could again ban icons. I brushed the dust off my tunica and climbed into the light.

We hid the trapdoor under the rug again and Abbess Pulkeria motioned us to the couch. She took her accustomed place at her desk, folded her hands, and looked sternly at us.

"Be very careful about where you place your loyalty. I advise you: do not follow Irini into exile, wherever that may be. You will most certainly die with her. Saint

Thekla brought you to Prinkypos to build a community of women. They need you."

She drew a breath. "I did not like Emperor Constantine, Irini's father-in-law. He banned icons and persecuted the monks who kept making them. But he was a great Emperor. His first and only loyalty was to the Empire. He cared only for the good of his people. He defended us well and with enormous courage. For thirty-four years, he stopped the invasions of the surrounding empires. We had peace and prosperity. God took his first two wives but he took a third, to show his people the importance of a strong marriage. His son, Leon, felt the same loyalty to the Empire but, poor man, he was ill from birth. He lacked the strength of body and of character to lead the country."

Abbess Pulkeria's face darkened. "Empress Irini brought icons back into holy worship. Because of her, icons are in every home and church. But her loyalty has never been to the Empire. Her loyalty has always been to herself alone. She used icons to make herself popular with the people and the monks. She thought would keep her in power. She was wrong from the start."

She fixed her eyes on us. "Abbess Thekla, Efrosini, I know that Irini plans to use this stolen jewellery and coin to fight her way back to the throne. I am complicit, but not for Irini. I hide this wealth for the sake of the Empire. One day, you, Efrosini, will sit on the throne. I feel this in my bones. You will need this wealth. I hope that you use it wisely. Do not waste it by giving it to Irini to start another civil war."

"Thank you, Abbess," I breathed.

She held up her hand. "Do not thank me. I am not doing this for you. Loyalty is a difficult path that has many crossroads. Make sure that you take the right turning."

We returned quickly to Irini's palace. As soon as we stepped inside, she handed me a packet wrapped in oilskin and a gold coin. "Take this to the Jews in the Copper Market. Pay them to deliver it."

Efrosini and I went some distance away before looking at the name on the packet. "Bardanes Tourkos," I read, disbelieving. I shook my head in wonder. "She really believes he will help her escape."

"Do you believe that he actually will put her on the throne?"

I threw up my hands. "Why would he? More likely, he will take her wealth and never come for her. He could even be a spy for Emperor Nikiforos."

"What shall we do with this letter?" she frowned.

"We will take it to the Jews. They have their ears to the ground. They can decide whether to deliver it or throw it on the fire."

The merchant recognized me and quickly let us in. He read the name on the packet and looked at us soberly. "Bardanes Tourkos has left Constantinople, we heard. We have not heard where he has gone. I cannot promise that we can find him."

"Do whatever you think is best," I said, and handed over a gold coin. He bit it gently to make sure it was gold and slipped the packet into his desk.

We went silently back to Irini's palace—and just in time. Emperor Nikiforos soon arrived. With him were the traitors who had vowed loyalty to Irini, then joined in her arrest. I recognised Irini's cousin, Leon, as well as Nikitas Triphillios and his brother. I knew the faces of the others from Irini's reception where I had been a shadow, unseen in my abbess garb, unheard in my silence.

Emperor Nikiforos bowed to Irini and spoke with respect. "Allow me to express my deep regret at the situation in which we find ourselves. I have only good will towards your person. This honour that has been bestowed upon me, I greatly regret. I had no desire to be named Emperor. How could my humble person follow your esteemed father-in-law, or your esteemed husband? How could I possibly take the throne that belonged to your son Constantine? My position is thrust upon me. Do you see these black shoes I wear? Had I aspired to the throne, they would be purple." He lifted his long tunica to show his simple black shoes.

"What do you want?" Irini asked calmly.

"That you acknowledge me as your sovereign. If you do, you will live out your life in comfort and dignity." He snapped his fingers and Nikitas Trifillios stepped forward with a parchment. "Please read this aloud and sign it."

Irini seated herself at the table. She arranged the papyrus and candle carefully before her and read aloud in a clear voice, sliding her slender fingers down the page. The topaz ring that I had returned to her gleamed in the candlelight. "'I acknowledge you, Emperor Nikiforos, as my sovereign and emperor. I make this vow as a symbol of the instability of human fortunes and the need of submission to the Divine Will.'"

She carefully dipped her quill into the ink, drew her name, blotted it, and placed her hands in her lap. Nikitas Trifillios picked it up and tucked it with a satisfied smile into his leather bag.

Emperor Nikiforos bowed slightly. "Now if you will reveal where you have hidden the gold and jewels and plate that you have been taking from the Palace these many years. It is the property of the Treasury."

Irini smiled. "The imperial jewellery is in Daphne Palace. Surely you have found it already. My personal jewellery is in my bedchamber upstairs."

Emperor Nikiforos moved his chin slightly and the men clattered up the steps. I could hear doors banging and furniture scraping on floors.

"Grant me one request," Irini said. "Allow me to live out my years in this palace. I built it as a refuge to rest and pray. It will be consolation for my incomparable misfortune."

Emperor Nikiforos barely smiled. "This palace was built with Treasury funds and it belongs to the Empire. You will retire to the convent on Prinkypos. It was built as a prison—well suited for your situation. You will share the exile of your two daughters-in-law and your grandchildren. I recommend that you spend your days reflecting on the instability of human fortunes and the need of submission to the Divine Will."

A slight smile of triumph twitched Irini's lips. Her ploy had succeeded. She had secured her escape to her island refuge. Now she would make me help her escape from the Empire. Nearly thirty years before, I had vowed to do whatever she commanded and to protect her with my life. Elias's voice came into my ears. "There are many kinds of loyalty. One is loyalty to yourself and what you think is right."

Chapter XIII

They came for her a week later, seven traitors who had sworn their loyalty to Irini of Athens and now stood with Emperor Nikiforos.

I was down at the quay buying fish for supper. High winds and rain mixed with snow had kept the fishermen idle for days and the sea was still dark and studded with whitecaps. The day's catch was meagre, just sardines that Aspasia could mash into a fish paste. At least we wouldn't be eating carrot and leek soup thickened with trahana. The fisherman was filling my basket when Elias's tiny boat blew into the harbour. He was soaked to the skin. I tried to walk away but he caught my arm.

"I have a letter for you," he said curtly and pointed at the priest's cottage. Once inside, he dug into his pouch and handed me a tiny leather purse. He dripped by the fire while he and Father Dimitrios watched me tip the contents into my palm. "Irini's topaz ring," I blurted, then

I found a bit of papyrus. This I read silently, with rising fear. "Old monastery. Before dawn."

"Where did you get this?" I heard the quaver in my voice.

"A stranger came into the postal waystation in Pendykion and gave me three silver milaresia to bring it out in this weather.'"

"Did you read it?"

"Of course."

His answer so frightened me that I bolted out of the cottage without a word and up the hill without feeling the rain pelting me. To my surprise, two novices were waiting at the convent gate. They pulled me to the outer corner of the wall and pointed at the sea below, thrashing white with rain. I gasped. An imperial warship was making the turn into the harbour.

"Are they coming to take Empress Irini away?" The novice's voice trembled from the cold rain and fear.

"If they can," I said grimly. "Lock the gate and bar it." I ran for the study.

Irini was sitting by the fire with Efrosini, holding a glass of elderberry wine. I dropped the tiny purse in her lap, then collapsed in a chair. She read the note and threw back her head. She drew a gasping breath. The relief in her face shook me.

"Bardanes Tourkos has come for me!"

"He's too late," I choked. "An imperial warship is dropping anchor outside the harbour even as we speak. Soon there will be soldiers at our gate."

Irini didn't move. Only her eyes flickered as she took that in and reviewed her options. I had seen her do this many times over the years. Her eyes rested on the fire. Under those flames lay the steps to the escape tunnel.

"Grandmama," Efrosini said. She was twelve, nearly marriageable age, a young woman who could read Irini's intentions and had the courage to speak her mind. "You cannot hide in the secret room. The soldiers will torture Auntie Thekla until she tells them where you are."

"Thekla will say I have left on a fishing boat."

"The villagers will say you are here. The soldiers will drive us into the sea to drown."

"Tell them that I left from the old monastery harbour. In this weather, the villagers couldn't possibly know." She knelt before the hearth and picked up the tin shovel that we used to remove ashes from the hearth. She scooped up some glowing coals and slid them into the tin box we kept for ashes. "Put the coals back after I am gone," she ordered over her shoulder.

I couldn't move, watching her hands.

"Grandmama, you can't escape," said Efrosini slowly.

"Nonsense, child. Take this shovel and clear out the hearth while I put on my coat and boots."

A sharp knock on the door brought me to my feet. I opened the door a crack. Sister Matrona was outside with the soaking wet novices who were biting their fingers in fear.

"Abbess Thekla, there are men outside the gate. They are shouting that we must open it or they will scale the wall."

"I am coming. Call everyone into the kitchen. Keep them there." I closed the door even as I saw Sister Matrona's eyes take in Irini moving coals from the hearth to the tin box.

I went to my desk and took Saint Thekla from the secret drawer. I tied her into the corner of my scarf. I had failed my vow to Irini before. I had not gone to prison with her. Now I could make up for my disloyalty. When the men took her away, Saint Thekla and I would go with her. Efrosini was pulling on her boots.

"I am coming with you," she said.

I took her hand as we crossed the pasture to the convent gate. "Irini will be opening the secret steps and escape through the tunnel even as I speak," I said. "This is what she planned when she was eighteen and ordered the stone mason to repair the escape tunnel. I will tell the men that she left a few days ago from the little harbour by the ruins of the old monastery. I will take the blame for her escape. I vowed to protect her with my life and that time has come."

"She won't leave through the escape tunnel," said Efrosini. "It's too late."

We reached the gate then and pulled it open together. My heart sank when I saw who was standing in the rain. Irini's cousin Leon was there with Sisinnios and his brother Nikitas Trifillios who had falsely accused Irini of giving the throne the brother of Aetios. Constantine's loyal friend Petros was there, and the other Leon who had come with Emperor Nikiforos to Irini's palace to search for her jewellery. Behind them stood Grigorios and Theoktistos who had searched with them. Emperor Nikiforos was letting these seven traitors prove their loyalty to him by taking Irini of Athens to her death.

Petros bowed politely to me. Even though he was siding with Nikiforos, I had a soft spot in my heart for him because he had helped Constantine arrest Stavrakios. They had failed and Irini had stripped Petros of his titles and exiled him. So many shifting loyalties, I thought.

Efrosini and I led them across the sodden pasture. I stopped in front of the basilica, stalling for time to let Irini get away. "Will you light candles for your souls?" I demanded in the stern tone of an abbess.

Shamed, they went inside. Their eyes widened seeing the wall icons and they whispered to each other. Back in the rain, we continued to the convent courtyard. I let them peer into the hospice and the weaving room, again stalling so Irini could get away. Maria flung open the door to the scriptorium and glared at them. They snickered at her layers of tunicas and her wild hair held back with thistles but they backed away when she cursed at them. She slammed the door.

At the door to my study, I took Efrosini's arm and drew a breath, preparing to lie to the men that Irini had left days before from the harbour by the ruins. But when I opened the door, I barely choked back a cry of surprise. Irini was sitting in her chair. A fire flickered in the hearth.

The seven men crowded in, shaking the rain off their cloaks. I watched them take in the tapestries and maps on the walls, the heavy wool curtains half-pulled over the tall glass windows, and the rugs that muffled the clatter of their boots. Irini smiled, the gracious sovereign.

"Cousin Leon! Former loyal friends! What brings you here?"

Leon bowed. "Cousin Irini, I must inform you that you are being transferred."

"To where?" She raised her eyebrows.

"The island of Lesbos."

"This very moment?" Her eyebrows arched higher.

"In the morning. Prepare your belongings. You will need that blanket." He gestured at the fur rug over her lap.

Nikitas cut in, always the greedy one. "Emperor Nikiforos wants the treasure you stole from the Palace. We know it's here. It belongs to the Empire."

"The Emperor has taken all my wealth."

"The Treasury inventory shows much is missing: gold and silver plate, bolts of silk, a fortune in jewellery and gold coins."

"Ask Evdokia," she smiled. "You remember your former Empress? She took a great deal with her when she left."

Petros spoke up. "Highness, forgive me, but long ago, my beloved Dino told me of a secret chamber under this room. He went down there as a child. He said that there is a trunk filled with treasure."

Nikitas interrupted. "Constantine described this room when he and Petros arrested that vermin Stavrakios. You recall that event, surely. Petros and Constantine tried to rid the Empire of that pig and you had them beaten and imprisoned."

"Search the convent since you think it is here." Irini waved her arm graciously.

"This room will suffice. Constantine said the entrance is from here."

Efrosini and I stood behind Irini and watched the seven men lift the maps and tapestries so they could tap the walls with the hilt of their knives, listening for a hollow sound indicating a space underneath. They rolled up the rugs and tapped the flagstones. They opened the trunk that held Irini's clothing and tossed the lovely garments on the floor.

Frustrated and angry, they stared at each other. Petros went to the fire and held out his hands to the warmth. He reached for the poker and poked up the flames. Then he gasped and began scraping aside the coals. "Now I remember! There is a trick with the poker, Dino said."

The others gathered around. They shovelled the coals into the tin box and tapped on the fireplace floor and walls. "Aha!" Petros shouted when he found the hole. He inserted the tip of the poker and pressed down.

Nothing moved. He jiggled the poker. Nothing. He flung it down and inserted his knife between the stones. No success. He glared at Irini.

"How does it open? Steps go down, I'm sure of it. Dino told me."

She smiled and lifted her palms. "It's just a hearth."

They all went at it with the poker and their knives but the stones didn't budge. Finally, Nikitas Trifillios stood up and brushed the soot off his hands.

"Get your keys, Abbess. You will open every door of this convent to every room until we find the treasure."

Petros stayed behind to keep an eye on Irini while Sister Matrona, Efrosini, and I led the others through the convent. In the supply room, they threw the nuns' seasonal clothing and school supplies on the floor. They upended the looms in the weaving room and tapped the flagstones with the hilts of their knives. They ventured into the scriptorium and cautiously tapped the walls and floor, nervous under Maria's mad stare. They clattered up the steps to the two imperial suites, bowed to Tula who was clutching her son, then dumped out her chest containing her meagre belongings and tapped her walls and floor with the hilt of their knives. They did the same in each dormitory room, upending the narrow beds to look under them.

The sky was darkening into dusk and Sister Efthia was leading the nuns in procession to the church in the courtyard for Esperinos prayers. The men pushed in front of them and banged on the church floor with the hilt of their knives. They searched the guards' rooms at the entrance into the convent enclave and went on to the basilica. Sister Matrona took a beeswax candle from the devotional candle box and lit it from the oil lamp hanging over the altar. I lit mine from hers, surprised at my steady hand.

"What's down there?" Leon pointed down the crypt steps.

"Ossuaries of the nuns who died here." I led him down the steps and unlocked the gate. He peered at the stack of wooden ossuaries and went up again.

It was fully dark and the rain was mixed with snow when we got back to the kitchen door. I was shaking with cold and nerves. Nikitas Trifillios pointed down the steps to the root cellar.

"What's in there?"

"Vegetables and preserved foods."

"Too dark. We'll search in the morning." He turned away.

The nuns and novices were having supper around the long kitchen table so I made the men wait outside in the wet until the nuns had cleaned their bowls and left. Then I opened the door. The six men sighed with relief at the warmth and the fragrance of soup bubbling in the pot hanging over the fire. Aspasia pointed at the table.

"Supper."

They eagerly filled the benches and reached for the mugs and jugs of our elderberry wine. It was full strength, potent stuff, and would hit them hard, as cold, wet, and hungry as they were. I sent Efrosini to get Petros.

"Stay with the Empress," I murmured. I didn't like the way the men were looking at her. They could very well decide to take her with Irini.

We fed them soup, fish paste, and warm flatbread. "You will sleep here tonight," I told them while they were stuffing their mouths. "We will bring mattresses and blankets. You cannot go anywhere else in the convent. You have already violated the law of religious seclusion. If you need to relieve yourself, go outside the kitchen door."

"I have to guard where she sleeps," Nikitas said sullenly.

"She sleeps in my study. We will put a mattress and blankets against the door for one man. But he cannot move except into the kitchen."

Sister Matrona, Aspasia, and I dragged wool mattresses and blankets from the storage room into the kitchen then we left the men for the night. We carried our own supper into my study: a pot of soup, hot flatbread, and fish paste, and all we ate together: Efrosini, Aspasia, Sister Matrona, Irini, and I. Then Aspasia and Sister Matrona went to their beds in the dormitory. I locked the door and made up Irini's bed on the couch, while Efrosini spread blankets over the two wool mattresses where she and I would sleep. It would be our last night together, the three of us, before the men took Irini and me away. Efrosini started to add a log to the fire but Irini stopped her. She spoke in a low, urgent tone.

"Put out the fire, child. It's time for me to go."

Efrosini and I stared at her in astonishment.

Irini grew impatient. "Didn't you hear me? Put out the fire. I have to leave now, or never. In the morning, those thugs will go down into the root cellar and find the door to the tunnel. I will never be able to escape. Bardanes's boat will come soon, if it isn't there already. I am going down there now." She pulled on her boots.

Efrosini and I looked at each other. "What will Auntie Thekla tell the men in the morning when they see you are gone?" Efrosini asked evenly.

"You will say that you don't know how I escaped. Tonight, you both will sleep in your own beds. The man outside the door will watch you leave this room and go up to bed. He will see me here by the fire. In the morning, when they find me gone, they will know that you had nothing to do with my escape. Move aside, Efrosini. I don't want Bardanes's ship to leave without me."

"Why didn't you escape out the tunnel before we came back?" I stammered.

"Because I couldn't open the hearth. I will open it now to make sure that I can, before you leave." She inserted the poker in the hole and pushed down. The floor didn't move. She frowned at me. Then came a smile of understanding.

"Thekla, you blocked the trapdoor from below, didn't you, when you went to get my purse of gold coins? That's why I couldn't open it—and neither could those brutes. I remember years ago when you showed me how to block it from below with bricks."

"I haven't blocked it," I frowned, puzzled.

Irini turned to Efrosini. "You did it, clever child! You will make a strong empress. Now go through the kitchen and through the root cellar and remove the bricks so I can go down these steps."

"She cannot. The men are in the kitchen," I said woodenly. My lips felt stiff.

"You go, then. Tell them you are bringing them more wine. Now go!"

"Grandmama, you are not opening this trapdoor," Efrosini said firmly.

Irini scowled at her. "Don't be afraid of those creatures. They came for me, not you. Now go release the trapdoor!"

Efrosini shook her head. "No, Grandmama. Auntie Thekla will be beaten and thrown in prison for letting you escape. I won't let that happen."

"How will I get out of here, child? Fly like a seagull? In the morning, those traitors will put me on their warship and take me to that convent on Lesbos. I will die there. Or they will save themselves the trip and throw me into the sea."

"Perhaps they will gouge out your eyes, like you gouged out Papa's eyes."

Irini took a deep breath. "No, dear heart. I ordered Doctor Moses to make a tiny cut in the corner of one eye. Aetios defied my order. Aetios killed Constantine."

"You sent Aetios to get there before Doctor Moses. You knew what Aetios would do."

Irini sat down and folded her hands. "Are you angry at me for your exile here, child? Your father exiled you, not me."

"Papa wanted to keep us at the Palace. You wouldn't let him."

"I brought you there many times. You sat beside me for the Easter ceremonies."

"Then you sent me back here."

Irini's voice grew strained. "We will rule together, dear child. But only if I leave on that ship. Thekla, go open the trapdoor."

"No, Grandmama. If you go with Bardanes, the deaths will start again."

"My child, you know nothing of how I survived all these years. From the moment I stepped off that warship when I was seventeen, everyone was against me. Only my cousin Theo stood by me and he was writing reports to my uncle. My husband Leon did everything he could to get rid of me. When Leon died, his advisors and military commanders subverted whatever I tried to accomplish. I managed to do much good despite them. Because of me, the Chalke icon is back over Chalke Gate. Icons are in churches and homes. The monasteries and convents are repaired and filled with monks and nuns. The orphanages and old people's homes have sufficient funds. I had mosaics installed in churches around the empire.

I built a basilica in Athens and made it the seat of the bishop. Because of me, Jews don't have to take oaths on the Christian Bible."

"You poisoned my great-grandfather Constantine with your poultice for his skin sores. You murdered my grandfather Leon with a poisoned crown. Many people say so."

"People lie. Don't believe everything you hear."

"I believe what I see. I saw my father's eyes after Aetios gouged them out. Now I see that you will send Auntie Thekla to prison and death so that you get back on the throne. I will not allow it, Grandmama."

Irini rose and faced me. "Thekla! Go release the trapdoor."

I had vowed in the name of God to protect her; I could not deny God. Or her. Slowly, I turned towards the door. Then before me, I saw my beloved Constantine. I saw him with my eyes, just as I saw the room around him. His face shone with compassion and sadness and love. "Dino," I breathed and I reached for him but he dissolved like salt in water. I turned to Irini.

"I will not open the trapdoor, Empress."

"Do not be a traitor, Thekla," she said harshly. "You vowed to do whatever I wanted, even if you had to die."

"I cannot be a traitor to Efrosini and the nuns of this convent. If those men find you gone, they will drive us into the sea."

"Soldiers die in battle for their emperor."

"People died because you wanted to be Empress in your own right," said Efrosini. "My father died and Alexios died. The people of Amorion and the villages around

Amorion died or became slaves because you told my father that Harun was retreating. You lied so you could throw Papa in prison and have the throne to yourself."

"Any Emperor would have done the same."

"No Isaurian emperor would abandon their people to the enemy."

Irini stared at Efrosini. She looked at me. Then she sat down and stared into the fire. Exhaustion overcame me. I stumbled to my mattress, pulled the quilt over my head, and fell into the dark tunnel of sleep.

In the morning, Nikitas Trifillios hammered on the door and barged in with the other six men. Efrosini and I were packing Irini's trunk. They stopped us and searched every pocket and seam. Then they made me and Sister Matrona take them around the convent again so they could search every room, even under the straw in the goat shed. When they went down into the root cellar, I waited outside with Sister Matrona in the cold December sunshine. I feared that my eyes might lead them to the latch that opened the tunnel.

"I am going with Irini to Lesbos," I said in a low voice.

Sister Matrona gaped at me. "Whatever are you thinking, my dear? You cannot leave your responsibility to your convent."

"You will make an excellent Abbess."

"Of course I would. That is not the point. You have always believed that your Saint Thekla brought you here to care for the women of this convent. How can that have changed?"

I looked at the faint tinge of snow on my boots. "I could have helped her escape last night. I refused. I failed my vow to protect her with my life. A vow I made before God."

"You have made equally powerful vows. You vowed to protect your nuns and Efrosini and Irinoula. These vows you made to your soul."

This confused me but I could not think about it then because the men came out, shouting with anger that they had not found the treasure. I followed Sister Matrona as she led them through the kitchen to my study.

We dressed Irini in layers of wool trousers and tunicas and a long sheepskin coat. We pulled on her fur-lined boots and fur coat and put on her mink hat that had been a gift from the Rus.

"These are too warm for Lesbos, even in the worst of winters," Irini protested.

"Use them as bribes," said Efrosini.

We all walked her down to the harbour—nuns and novices, Aspasia, Megalo, Maria, Tula, and their children. Nikitas Triphillios led us, and his men followed with Irini's trunk. I searched the faces of Maria and Tula for any gloat of victory. Irini had destroyed their lives and now they were watching her go to her death. But Tula's face showed only sorrow and I wasn't certain that Maria knew what was happening.

Half-way down, Nikitas Trifillios pointed through the bare branches. People filled the plateia where we had to pass. "Stones are coming, lads. Keep your heads down," he groaned. They drew their swords.

But when we got there, no one was holding stones. They were holding icons. They lifted them high and soft whispers floated through the cold December air.

"God be with you, Irini of Athens."

"Bless you for bringing back our icons."

Irini smiled to one side and the other. I felt bewildered. She didn't believe in icons. She had brought them back only because it would give her the throne. Her reason didn't matter, she had told me, because the people got what they wanted. I didn't know if she was right. I still didn't know.

Father Dimitrios made the sign of the cross over Irini. "The Almighty God who is all-knowing and all-seeing and ever-present sees into your soul and knows everything that you have done. He will judge you. But we will remember that you brought back our icons."

As we moved on, the women lifted their voices in that high-pitched quivering keening that rises from the soul and pierces the air in a long vibrating wail. Irini leaned towards me and gripped my hand. Her topaz ring dug into my flesh through her mittens. I thought she was going to say goodbye. As usual, I was wrong.

"Listen, Thekla," she whispered. "Bardanes's ship is out there somewhere, waiting. His men will come for my treasure. Give it to them. Bardanes will come to Lesbos and take me away. Soon I will be back on the throne."

A lump of sorrow at her illusion choked my throat. "Yes, Empress," I whispered.

She continued, her voice firm and steady. "If Bardanes fails to take the throne, Nikiforos will have me killed. He will send my body back here to be buried. He will need witnesses and evidence that I am dead. Promise me one thing."

"Yes, Empress." Another promise, another vow.

"Promise me that if you leave this place, you will take my bones with you. I cannot stay here without you."

"Yes, Empress," I choked. We had reached the quay. Irini tightened her grip.

"I have reached this place in my life because I lost the one person who could have shown me the right path."

My heart twisted. The grief in my throat would permit only a whisper. "You never lost me, Empress. I am going with you into exile. I will protect you and keep you safe."

But she wasn't listening. "My father-in-law, Emperor Constantine, could have taught me all I needed to know to stay on the throne. If only he had lived longer, what an empress I would have been!"

Fury filled me. Suddenly, I saw my life clearly, as if I was looking through clear water to the bottom of the sea. Abbess Pulkeria had said that Saint Thekla had brought us together so that I could guide Irini on the right path. I had believed her. I had spent my life trying to be Irini's conscience. But Irini had listened to none of it. All she wanted was a slave who would do whatever she wanted. I had been a fool from the start.

Irini moved her lips close to my ear. "Give Saint Thekla to me," she murmured. "She belongs to me more than to you. She made you push her into my hands when I found you in prison so she could protect me in the Palace. She brought me to Prinkypos so you could protect me. You took a vow before God to obey me and do whatever I want. Keep your vow. Give Saint Thekla to me so she can protect me in exile."

I was shocked nearly breathless. "No!" I gasped. "Saint Thekla has been near me ever since I was baptised. I would be lost without her." My fingers found the little icon tied into the end of my scarf and I gripped her tightly.

But the familiar form felt strange under my fingers. No warmth or comfort came into my heart as it had my entire life. I frowned, confused. Then the answer came. Saint Thekla wanted to go with Irini. After a lifetime of my protecting her, my saint was abandoning me.

My voice shook with anger. "You lied to me, both of you," I hissed. "You made me care for you and protect you so that you could be together. You used me."

I yanked off my scarf and flung it around Irini's neck. "Have each other," I choked. "I am through with both of you."

A dingy was coming from the ship, two sailors fighting the choppy waves. When they reached the quay, Nikitas Trifillios and Sisinnios climbed in and handed Irini down. I didn't move. I was not going with her into exile. For that, she had Saint Thekla. I watched the sailors row them out to the warship and help her climb the ladder. She disappeared into the cabin. The sailors rowed back for the other men and we watched them climb the ladder, too.

The sails went up and the warship disappeared into the dark December horizon. Aspasia took my arm, as she had done so often, and we climbed the hill. Behind us came everyone from the convent: Sister Efthia, Sister Evanthia, Sister Filothei, and Sister Matrona, nuns who had known me since I was a young abbess. We went into my study—all of us together—and built a great hot fire of olive and apple wood. Sister Matrona lit the candles and oil lamps. The novices brought mugs of hot mountain tea and sweet lemon preserves and we sat and ate while the pinecones snapped and flashed sparks just like the sunlight had flashed on Irini's rings when she stood on the warship over thirty years before and waved to the crowds calling her name.

I went to my desk and drew a sheet of papyrus from the drawer.

"I have known Empress Irini of Athens for thirty-two years," I said. "I have kept a record of her acts and my reflections on those acts. Today will be my final entry. When the truth gets tumbled over time, as it always does, my words will set the record straight."

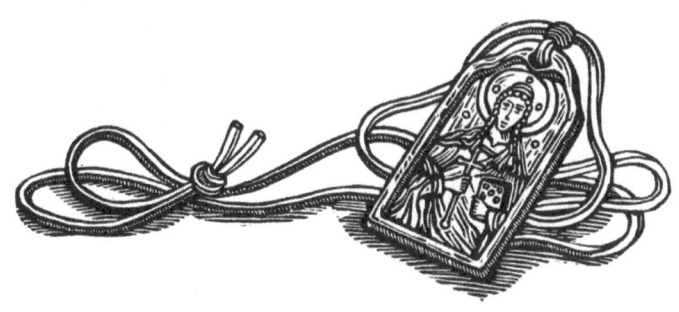

Chapter XIV

They came for her a week later, seven traitors who had sworn their loyalty to Irini of Athens and now stood with Emperor Nikiforos.

I was down at the quay buying fish for supper. High winds and rain mixed with snow had kept the fishermen idle for days and the sea was still dark and studded with whitecaps. The day's catch was meagre, just sardines that Aspasia could mash into a fish paste. At least we wouldn't be eating carrot and leek soup thickened with trahana. The fisherman was filling my basket when Elias's tiny boat blew into the harbour. He was soaked to the skin. I tried to walk away but he caught my arm.

"I have a letter for you," he said curtly and pointed at the priest's cottage. Once inside, he dug into his pouch and handed me a tiny leather purse. He dripped by the fire while he and Father Dimitrios watched me tip the contents into my palm. "Irini's topaz ring," I blurted, then I found a bit of papyrus. This I read silently, with rising fear. "Old monastery. Before dawn."

"Where did you get this?" I heard the quaver in my

voice.

"A stranger came into the postal waystation in Pendykion and gave me three silver milaresia to bring it out in this weather.'"

"Did you read it?"

"Of course."

His answer so frightened me that I bolted out of the cottage without a word and up the hill without feeling the rain pelting me. To my surprise, two novices were waiting at the convent gate. They pulled me to the outer corner of the wall and pointed at the sea below, thrashing white with rain. I gasped. An imperial warship was making the turn into the harbour.

"Are they coming to take Empress Irini away?" The novice's voice trembled from the cold rain and fear.

"If they can," I said grimly. "Lock the gate and bar it." I ran for the study.

Irini was sitting by the fire with Efrosini, holding a glass of elderberry wine. I dropped the tiny purse in her lap, then collapsed in a chair. She read the note and threw back her head. She drew a gasping breath. The relief in her face shook me.

"Bardanes Tourkos has come for me!"

"He's too late," I choked. "An imperial warship is dropping anchor outside the harbour even as we speak. Soon there will be soldiers at our gate."

Irini didn't move. Only her eyes flickered as she took that in and reviewed her options. I had seen her do this many times over the years. Her eyes rested on the fire. Under those flames lay the steps to the escape tunnel.

"Grandmama," Efrosini said. She was twelve, nearly

marriageable age, a young woman who could read Irini's intentions and had the courage to speak her mind. "You cannot hide in the secret room. The soldiers will torture Auntie Thekla until she tells them where you are."

"Thekla will say I have left on a fishing boat."

"The villagers will say you are here. The soldiers will drive us into the sea to drown."

"Tell them that I left from the old monastery harbour. In this weather, the villagers couldn't possibly know." She knelt before the hearth and picked up the tin shovel that we used to remove ashes from the hearth. She scooped up some glowing coals and slid them into the tin box we kept for ashes. "Put the coals back after I am gone," she ordered over her shoulder.

I couldn't move, watching her hands.

"Grandmama, you can't escape," said Efrosini slowly.

"Nonsense, child. Take this shovel and clear out the hearth while I put on my coat and boots."

A sharp knock on the door brought me to my feet. I opened the door a crack. Sister Matrona was outside with the soaking wet novices who were biting their fingers in fear.

"Abbess Thekla, there are men outside the gate. They are shouting that we must open it or they will scale the wall."

"I am coming. Call everyone into the kitchen. Keep them there." I closed the door even as I saw Sister Matrona's eyes take in Irini moving coals from the hearth to the tin box.

I went to my desk and took Saint Thekla from the secret drawer. I tied her into the corner of my scarf. I had failed my vow to Irini before. I had not gone to prison with her. Now I could make up for my disloyalty. When the men took her away, Saint Thekla and I would go with her. Efrosini was pulling on her boots.

"I am coming with you," she said.

I took her hand as we crossed the pasture to the convent gate. "Irini will be opening the secret steps and escape through the tunnel even as I speak," I said. "This is what she planned when she was eighteen and ordered the stone mason to repair the escape tunnel. I will tell the men that she left a few days ago from the little harbour by the ruins of the old monastery. I will take the blame for her escape. I vowed to protect her with my life and that time has come."

"She won't leave through the escape tunnel," said Efrosini. "It's too late."

We reached the gate then and pulled it open together. My heart sank when I saw who was standing in the rain. Irini's cousin Leon was there with Sisinnios and his brother Nikitas Trifillios who had falsely accused Irini of giving the throne the brother of Aetios. Constantine's loyal friend Petros was there, and the other Leon who had come with Emperor Nikiforos to Irini's palace to search for her jewellery. Behind them stood Grigorios and Theoktistos who had searched with them. Emperor Nikiforos was letting these seven traitors prove their loyalty to him by taking Irini of Athens to her death.

Petros bowed politely to me. Even though he was siding with Nikiforos, I had a soft spot in my heart for him because he had helped Constantine arrest Stavrakios. They had failed and Irini had stripped Petros of his titles and exiled him. So many shifting loyalties, I thought.

Efrosini and I led them across the sodden pasture. I stopped in front of the basilica, stalling for time to let Irini get away. "Will you light candles for your souls?" I demanded in the stern tone of an abbess.

Shamed, they went inside. Their eyes widened seeing the wall icons and they whispered to each other. Back in the rain, we continued to the convent courtyard. I let them peer into the hospice and the weaving room, again stalling so Irini could get away. Maria flung open the door to the scriptorium and glared at them. They snickered at her layers of tunicas and her wild hair held back with thistles but they backed away when she cursed at them. She slammed the door.

At the door to my study, I took Efrosini's arm and drew a breath, preparing to lie to the men that Irini had left days before from the harbour by the ruins. But when I opened the door, I barely choked back a cry of surprise. Irini was sitting in her chair. A fire flickered in the hearth.

The seven men crowded in, shaking the rain off their cloaks. I watched them take in the tapestries and maps on the walls, the heavy wool curtains half-pulled over the tall glass windows, and the rugs that muffled the clatter of their boots. Irini smiled, the gracious sovereign.

"Cousin Leon! Former loyal friends! What brings you here?"

Leon bowed. "Cousin Irini, I must inform you that you are being transferred."

"To where?" She raised her eyebrows.

"The island of Lesbos."

"This very moment?" Her eyebrows arched higher.

"In the morning. Prepare your belongings. You will need that blanket." He gestured at the fur rug over her lap.

Nikitas cut in, always the greedy one. "Emperor Nikiforos wants the treasure you stole from the Palace. We know it's here. It belongs to the Empire."

"The Emperor has taken all my wealth."

"The Treasury inventory shows much is missing: gold and silver plate, bolts of silk, a fortune in jewellery and gold coins."

"Ask Evdokia," she smiled. "You remember your former Empress? She took a great deal with her when she left."

Petros spoke up. "Highness, forgive me, but long ago, my beloved Dino told me of a secret chamber under this room. He went down there as a child. He said that there is a trunk filled with treasure."

Nikitas interrupted. "Constantine described this room when he and Petros arrested that vermin Stavrakios. You recall that event, surely. Petros and Constantine tried to rid the Empire of that pig and you had them beaten and imprisoned."

"Search the convent since you think it is here." Irini waved her arm graciously.

"This room will suffice. Constantine said the entrance is from here."

Efrosini and I stood behind Irini and watched the seven men lift the maps and tapestries so they could tap the walls with the hilt of their knives, listening for a hollow sound indicating a space underneath. They rolled up the rugs and tapped the flagstones. They opened the trunk that held Irini's clothing and tossed the lovely garments on the floor.

Frustrated and angry, they stared at each other. Petros went to the fire and held out his hands to the warmth. He reached for the poker and poked up the flames. Then he gasped and began scraping aside the coals. "Now I remember! There is a trick with the poker, Dino said."

The others gathered around. They shovelled the coals into the tin box and tapped on the fireplace floor and walls. "Aha!" Petros shouted when he found the hole. He inserted the tip of the poker and pressed down.

Nothing moved. He jiggled the poker. Nothing. He flung it down and inserted his knife between the stones. No success. He glared at Irini.

"How does it open? Steps go down, I'm sure of it. Dino told me."

She smiled and lifted her palms. "It's just a hearth."

They all went at it with the poker and their knives but the stones didn't budge. Finally, Nikitas Trifillios stood up and brushed the soot off his hands.

"Get your keys, Abbess. You will open every door of this convent to every room until we find the treasure."

Petros stayed behind to keep an eye on Irini while Sister Matrona, Efrosini, and I led the others through the convent. In the supply room, they threw the nuns' seasonal clothing and school supplies on the floor. They upended the looms in the weaving room and tapped the flagstones with the hilts of their knives. They ventured into the scriptorium and cautiously tapped the walls and floor, nervous under Maria's mad stare. They clattered up the steps to the two imperial suites, bowed to Tula who was clutching her son, then dumped out her chest containing her meagre belongings and tapped her walls and floor with the hilt of their knives. They did the same in each dormitory room, upending the narrow beds to look under them.

The sky was darkening into dusk and Sister Efthia was leading the nuns in procession to the church in the courtyard for Esperinos prayers. The men pushed in front of them and banged on the church floor with the hilt of their knives. They searched the guards' rooms at the entrance into the convent enclave and went on to the basilica. Sister Matrona took a beeswax candle from the devotional candle box and lit it from the oil lamp hanging over the altar. I lit mine from hers, surprised at my steady hand.

"What's down there?" Leon pointed down the crypt steps.

"Ossuaries of the nuns who died here." I led him down the steps and unlocked the gate. He peered at the stack of wooden ossuaries and went up again.

It was fully dark and the rain was mixed with snow when we got back to the kitchen door. I was shaking with cold and nerves. Nikitas Trifillios pointed down the steps to the root cellar.

"What's in there?"

"Vegetables and preserved foods."

"Too dark. We'll search in the morning." He turned away.

The nuns and novices were having supper around the long kitchen table so I made the men wait outside in the wet until the nuns had cleaned their bowls and left.

Then I opened the door. The six men sighed with relief at the warmth and the fragrance of soup bubbling in the pot hanging over the fire. Aspasia pointed at the table.

"Supper."

They eagerly filled the benches and reached for the mugs and jugs of our elderberry wine. It was full strength, potent stuff, and would hit them hard, as cold, wet, and hungry as they were. I sent Efrosini to get Petros.

"Stay with the Empress," I murmured. I didn't like the way the men were looking at her. They could very well decide to take her with Irini.

We fed them soup, fish paste, and warm flatbread. "You will sleep here tonight," I told them while they were stuffing their mouths. "We will bring mattresses and blankets. You cannot go anywhere else in the convent. You have already violated the law of religious seclusion. If you need to relieve yourself, go outside the kitchen door."

"I have to guard where she sleeps," Nikitas said sullenly.

"She sleeps in my study. We will put a mattress and blankets against the door for one man. But he cannot move except into the kitchen."

Sister Matrona, Aspasia, and I dragged wool mattresses and blankets from the storage room into the kitchen then we left the men for the night. We carried our own supper into my study: a pot of soup, hot flatbread, and fish paste, and all we ate together: Efrosini, Aspasia, Sister Matrona, Irini, and I. Then Aspasia and Sister Matrona went to their beds in the dormitory. I locked the door and made up Irini's bed on the couch, while

Efrosini spread blankets over the two wool mattresses where she and I would sleep. It would be our last night together, the three of us, before the men took Irini and me away. Efrosini started to add a log to the fire but Irini stopped her. She spoke in a low, urgent tone.

"Put out the fire, child. It's time for me to go."

Efrosini and I stared at her in astonishment.

Irini grew impatient. "Didn't you hear me? Put out the fire. I have to leave now, or never. In the morning, those thugs will go down into the root cellar and find the door to the tunnel. I will never be able to escape. Bardanes's boat will come soon, if it isn't there already. I am going down there now." She pulled on her boots.

Efrosini and I looked at each other. "What will Auntie Thekla tell the men in the morning when they see you are gone?" Efrosini asked evenly.

"You will say that you don't know how I escaped. Tonight, you both will sleep in your own beds. The man outside the door will watch you leave this room and go up to bed. He will see me here by the fire. In the morning, when they find me gone, they will know that you had nothing to do with my escape. Move aside, Efrosini. I don't want Bardanes's ship to leave without me."

"Why didn't you escape out the tunnel before we came back?" I stammered.

"Because I couldn't open the hearth. I will open it now to make sure that I can, before you leave." She inserted the poker in the hole and pushed down. The floor didn't move. She frowned at me. Then came a smile of understanding.

"Thekla, you blocked the trapdoor from below, didn't

you, when you went to get my purse of gold coins? That's why I couldn't open it—and neither could those brutes. I remember years ago when you showed me how to block it from below with bricks."

"I haven't blocked it," I frowned, puzzled.

Irini turned to Efrosini. "You did it, clever child! You will make a strong empress. Now go through the kitchen and through the root cellar and remove the bricks so I can go down these steps."

"She cannot. The men are in the kitchen," I said woodenly. My lips felt stiff.

"You go, then. Tell them you are bringing them more wine. Now go!"

"Grandmama, you are not opening this trapdoor," Efrosini said firmly.

Irini scowled at her. "Don't be afraid of those creatures. They came for me, not you. Now go release the trapdoor!"

Efrosini shook her head. "No, Grandmama. Auntie Thekla will be beaten and thrown in prison for letting you escape. I won't let that happen."

"How will I get out of here, child? Fly like a seagull? In the morning, those traitors will put me on their warship and take me to that convent on Lesbos. I will die there. Or they will save themselves the trip and throw me into the sea."

"Perhaps they will gouge out your eyes, like you gouged out Papa's eyes."

Irini took a deep breath. "No, dear heart. I ordered Doctor Moses to make a tiny cut in the corner of one eye. Aetios defied my order. Aetios killed Constantine."

"You sent Aetios to get there before Doctor Moses. You knew what Aetios would do."

Irini sat down and folded her hands. "Are you angry at me for your exile here, child? Your father exiled you, not me."

"Papa wanted to keep us at the Palace. You wouldn't let him."

"I brought you there many times. You sat beside me for the Easter ceremonies."

"Then you sent me back here."

Irini's voice grew strained. "We will rule together, dear child. But only if I leave on that ship. Thekla, go open the trapdoor."

"No, Grandmama. If you go with Bardanes, the deaths will start again."

"My child, you know nothing of how I survived all these years. From the moment I stepped off that warship when I was seventeen, everyone was against me. Only my cousin Theo stood by me and he was writing reports to my uncle. My husband Leon did everything he could to get rid of me. When Leon died, his advisors and military commanders subverted whatever I tried to accomplish. I managed to do much good despite them. Because of me, the Chalke icon is back over Chalke Gate. Icons are in churches and homes. The monasteries and convents are repaired and filled with monks and nuns. The orphanages and old people's homes have sufficient funds. I had mosaics installed in churches around the empire. I built a basilica in Athens and made it the seat of the bishop. Because of me, Jews don't have to take oaths on the Christian Bible."

"You poisoned my great-grandfather Constantine with your poultice for his skin sores. You murdered my grandfather Leon with a poisoned crown. Many people say so."

"People lie. Don't believe everything you hear."

"I believe what I see. I saw my father's eyes after Aetios gouged them out. Now I see that you will send Auntie Thekla to prison and death so that you get back on the throne. I will not allow it, Grandmama."

Irini rose and faced me. "Thekla! Go release the trapdoor."

I had vowed in the name of God to protect her; I could not deny God. Or her. Slowly, I turned towards the door. Then before me, I saw my beloved Constantine. I saw him with my eyes, just as I saw the room around him. His face shone with compassion and sadness and love. "Dino," I breathed and I reached for him but he dissolved like salt in water. I turned to Irini.

"I will not open the trapdoor, Empress."

"Do not be a traitor, Thekla," she said harshly. "You vowed to do whatever I wanted, even if you had to die."

"I cannot be a traitor to Efrosini and the nuns of this convent. If those men find you gone, they will drive us into the sea."

"Soldiers die in battle for their emperor."

"People died because you wanted to be Empress in your own right," said Efrosini. "My father died and Alexios died. The people of Amorion and the villages around Amorion died or became slaves because you told my father that Harun was retreating. You lied so you could throw Papa in prison and have the throne to yourself."

"Any Emperor would have done the same."

"No Isaurian emperor would abandon their people to the enemy."

Irini stared at Efrosini. She looked at me. Then she sat down and stared into the fire. Exhaustion overcame me. I stumbled to my mattress, pulled the quilt over my head, and fell into the dark tunnel of sleep.

In the morning, Nikitas Trifillios hammered on the door and barged in with the other six men. Efrosini and I were packing Irini's trunk. They stopped us and searched every pocket and seam. Then they made me and Sister Matrona take them around the convent again so they could search every room, even under the straw in the goat shed. When they went down into the root cellar, I waited outside with Sister Matrona in the cold December sunshine. I feared that my eyes might lead them to the latch that opened the tunnel.

"I am going with Irini to Lesbos," I said in a low voice.

Sister Matrona gaped at me. "Whatever are you thinking, my dear? You cannot leave your responsibility to your convent."

"You will make an excellent Abbess."

"Of course I would. That is not the point. You have always believed that your Saint Thekla brought you here to care for the women of this convent. How can that have changed?"

I looked at the faint tinge of snow on my boots. "I could have helped her escape last night. I refused. I failed my vow to protect her with my life. A vow I made before God."

"You have made equally powerful vows. You vowed to protect your nuns and Efrosini and Irinoula. These vows you made to your soul."

This confused me but I could not think about it then because the men came out, shouting with anger that they had not found the treasure. I followed Sister Matrona as she led them through the kitchen to my study.

We dressed Irini in layers of wool trousers and tunicas and a long sheepskin coat. We pulled on her fur-lined boots and fur coat and put on her mink hat that had been a gift from the Rus.

"These are too warm for Lesbos, even in the worst of winters," Irini protested.

"Use them as bribes," said Efrosini.

We all walked her down to the harbour—nuns and novices, Aspasia, Megalo, Maria, Tula, and their children. Nikitas Triphillios led us, and his men followed with Irini's trunk. I searched the faces of Maria and Tula for any gloat of victory. Irini had destroyed their lives and now they were watching her go to her death. But Tula's face showed only sorrow and I wasn't certain that Maria knew what was happening.

Half-way down, Nikitas Trifillios pointed through the bare branches. People filled the plateia where we had to pass. "Stones are coming, lads. Keep your heads down," he groaned. They drew their swords.

But when we got there, no one was holding stones. They were holding icons. They lifted them high and soft whispers floated through the cold December air.

"God be with you, Irini of Athens."

"Bless you for bringing back our icons."

Irini smiled to one side and the other. I felt bewildered. She didn't believe in icons. She had brought them back only because it would give her the throne. Her reason didn't matter, she had told me, because the people got what they wanted. I didn't know if she was right. I still didn't know.

Father Dimitrios made the sign of the cross over Irini. "The Almighty God who is all-knowing and all-seeing and ever-present sees into your soul and knows everything that you have done. He will judge you. But we will remember that you brought back our icons."

As we moved on, the women lifted their voices in that high-pitched quivering keening that rises from the soul and pierces the air in a long vibrating wail. Irini leaned towards me and gripped my hand. Her topaz ring dug into my flesh through her mittens. I thought she was going to say goodbye. As usual, I was wrong.

"Listen, Thekla," she whispered. "Bardanes's ship is out there somewhere, waiting. His men will come for my treasure. Give it to them. Bardanes will come to Lesbos and take me away. Soon I will be back on the throne."

A lump of sorrow at her illusion choked my throat. "Yes, Empress," I whispered.

She continued, her voice firm and steady. "If Bardanes fails to take the throne, Nikiforos will have me killed. He will send my body back here to be buried. He will need witnesses and evidence that I am dead. Promise me one thing."

"Yes, Empress." Another promise, another vow.

"Promise me that if you leave this place, you will take

my bones with you. I cannot stay here without you."

"Yes, Empress," I choked. We had reached the quay. Irini tightened her grip.

"I have reached this place in my life because I lost the one person who could have shown me the right path."

My heart twisted. The grief in my throat would permit only a whisper. "You never lost me, Empress. I am going with you into exile. I will protect you and keep you safe."

But she wasn't listening. "My father-in-law, Emperor Constantine, could have taught me all I needed to know to stay on the throne. If only he had lived longer, what an empress I would have been!"

Fury filled me. Suddenly, I saw my life clearly, as if I was looking through clear water to the bottom of the sea. Abbess Pulkeria had said that Saint Thekla had brought us together so that I could guide Irini on the right path. I had believed her. I had spent my life trying to be Irini's conscience. But Irini had listened to none of it. All she wanted was a slave who would do whatever she wanted. I had been a fool from the start.

Irini moved her lips close to my ear. "Give Saint Thekla to me," she murmured. "She belongs to me more than to you. She made you push her into my hands when I found you in prison so she could protect me in the Palace. She brought me to Prinkypos so you could protect me. You took a vow before God to obey me and do whatever I want. Keep your vow. Give Saint Thekla to me so she can protect me in exile."

I was shocked nearly breathless. "No!" I gasped. "Saint Thekla has been near me ever since I was baptised. I would be lost without her." My fingers found the little icon tied into the end of my scarf and I gripped her tightly.

But the familiar form felt strange under my fingers. No warmth or comfort came into my heart as it had my entire life. I frowned, confused. Then the answer came. Saint Thekla wanted to go with Irini. After a lifetime of my protecting her, my saint was abandoning me.

My voice shook with anger. "You lied to me, both of you," I hissed. "You made me care for you and protect you so that you could be together. You used me."

I yanked off my scarf and flung it around Irini's neck. "Have each other," I choked. "I am through with both of you."

A dingy was coming from the ship, two sailors fighting the choppy waves. When they reached the quay, Nikitas Trifillios and Sisinnios climbed in and handed Irini down. I didn't move. I was not going with her into exile. For that, she had Saint Thekla. I watched the sailors row them out to the warship and help her climb the ladder. She disappeared into the cabin. The sailors rowed back for the other men and we watched them climb the ladder, too.

The sails went up and the warship disappeared into the dark December horizon. Aspasia took my arm, as she had done so often, and we climbed the hill. Behind us came everyone from the convent: Sister Efthia, Sister Evanthia, Sister Filothei, and Sister Matrona, nuns who had known me since I was a young abbess. We went into my study—all of us together—and built a great hot fire of olive and apple wood. Sister Matrona lit the candles and oil lamps. The novices brought mugs of hot mountain tea and sweet lemon preserves and we sat and ate while the pinecones snapped and flashed sparks just like the sunlight had flashed on Irini's rings when she stood on the warship over thirty years before and waved to the crowds calling her name.

I went to my desk and drew a sheet of papyrus from the drawer.

"I have known Empress Irini of Athens for thirty-two years," I said. "I have kept a record of her acts and my reflections on those acts. Today will be my final entry. When the truth gets tumbled over time, as it always does, my words will set the record straight."

Chapter XV

The full moon shone on the snow on the convent roofs and my breath was as white as the snow under our boots. Sister Matrona and I stood arm-in-arm looking over the low part of the wall as we had done every night since Irini left. My eyes searched the silver sea for the shadow of a foreign ship or the flash of a candle signal.

"Irini believes that Bardanes Tourkos will come to Lesbos and rescue her," I said.

"She was deluded about a lot of things, not the least of which was her belief that the Empire could be ruled by a woman," noted Sister Matrona.

"Do you think Bardanes will come here for her treasure?"

"It is more likely than rescuing her from Lesbos. But do not indulge in speculation or hope, Thekla. Both are illusions. Either his ship will come or it won't."

My teeth began chattering with cold and nerves. I had hardly slept since Irini left. I kept awakening with a start, twisted with guilt that my anger had caused me to send Irini into exile alone.

Sister Matrona guided me to my study. She and Sister Evanthia wrapped me in quilts on the couch where Irini had slept. Efrosini built up the fire and Aspasia put hot bricks at my feet and along my back. Even then I shook with cold. The warmth had left my heart.

"Enough of this foolish watching for phantom ships," said Sister Efthia sternly, holding an herbal concoction to my lips. "Sister Matrona, you should know better than to encourage these illusions."

"Perhaps it isn't an illusion," said Efrosini, gazing into the flickering fire. "Perhaps Bardanes Tourkos is chasing the warship. He may think that those men found the treasure. He will rescue Grandmama and take her with him into battle."

"Bardanes doesn't want Irini," snorted Aspasia. "She would give him nothing but trouble. He wants her treasure. One day, his men will bang on our gate and make us hand it over."

"Don't give it to them, Auntie Thekla," Efrosini advised. "You will need every coin to keep this convent going. Emperor Nikiforos will cut off our funding."

Aspasia poked up the fire. "Give Bardanes's men only the coins, Thekla. Sell the jewels and the silver and gold plate to the Jews in Constantinople."

"I told Irini I would give it all to Bardanes," I muttered.

"She will never know," said Sister Matrona. "No one returns from that prison convent on Lesbos."

"She will die because of me," I said in a low voice. "I didn't help her escape. I didn't go with her. I broke my vow to protect her with my life."

"No, Auntie Thekla." Efrosini's voice was calm and

assured. "The reason she didn't escape was me, not you. I am heir to the throne. The decision was mine."

The nuns left then and Efrosini curled up on her mattress by the fire. She had slept by me in my study since Irini left. I kept waking in panic at the slightest sound and she calmed me until I slept again. Every morning, we waded through the snow down to the village but no one had seen a foreign ship. All we heard were rumours gathered by the fishermen when they sold their catch in the villages along the mainland: Irini had exchanged clothing with a prostitute on the ship and had escaped in a foreign port. Pirates had boarded the vessel and Irini was a pirate queen. Elpidios had rescued her and she was living with him in North Africa. Each rumour was more absurd than the last.

Elias disappeared and Lent came before we saw him again. Maria spotted the little boat from her window and I went down with her, Efrosini, and Irinoula. I longed to feel his arms around me but I was an abbess and all I could do was smile at him and feel his hand brush mine as he handed me the mail. It was a letter bearing the seal of Emperor Nikiforos.

"Is Irini dead? Is this how we will learn of her passing?" I whispered, staring at it.

"Do not let your imagination run away with you." Elias broke the seal and read aloud. "Emperor Nikiforos grants Tula's petition to return to her parents with her seven-year-old son."

Relief made me dizzy and Efrosini steadied me. "The Senate had already declared the boy illegitimate. He is no threat to Emperor Nikiforos. Still, I hope Tula's family takes her and her son far from Constantinople."

Elias had more news. "Nikitas Trifillios has died horribly of poisoning."

"Emperor Nikiforos had him poisoned," Efrosini declared. "No one trusts a traitor. The others who had sworn loyalty to Irini and betrayed her should get food tasters and leave Constantinople."

She went off to talk to her friends and Elias and I walked along the sea path away from the village. We sat on a driftwood log facing the waves. Elias took my hand.

"Do not blame yourself for Irini's arrest. Your infinite capacity for loyalty to her makes you believe that you should have helped her escape through that secret tunnel." He smiled at my exclamation of surprise. "Oh, I know all about that tunnel. I found it when my grandfather was exiled here by Constantine's grandfather. The tunnel was only partially blocked then. My uncle could have crawled through. I had arranged for a boat to take him from the little harbour and bribed the monks to look the other way. But he refused to escape. He said a patriarch should not run from death."

"I had vowed to die for her and I handed her over to them," I whispered, and then I wept, tears that had been blocked inside me and now came pouring out in sobs. He put his arms around me and rocked me as my words poured out. "I broke the vow that I made in the name of God. That means I have denied that God exists."

Elias shook me gently. "You did not deny God. You finally accepted that your loyalty to your conscience was greater than your loyalty to her."

Tula's parents came by yacht to collect her and their

grandson. They had never visited and her mother gasped when she saw her daughter's hands hardened by work. She went pale when she saw the plain room and two narrow beds where Tula and her son had slept for his seven years. She stood mutely by the grave of Constantine while Tula placed her final flowers on his ossuary. After five years, the village bone-scraper had dug up the bones, scraped them, and now they lay in a stone ossuary at the head of the empty shaft. The villagers continued to bring flowers.

We all carried Tula's belongings down to the harbour to say goodbye. The clothing her parents had sent was still new; Tula had preferred a nun's tunica. Her son wept when he said goodbye to his friends. We all wept. Tula had become one of us. Her gentle voice and sweet nature had eased our days. Now she was a lovely and mature woman ready for a new life.

"You will find a good husband," I told her. "I know you suffered during your exile here. Now we will suffer because you are gone."

Elias sailed in on the mail boat as Tula's yacht was leaving the harbour. We sat on the bench by the church with Father Dimitrios and watched Maria chase a butterfly down the sea path.

"Perhaps Maria will return to sanity, now that both her rivals are gone," Elias commented.

Father Dimitrios shook his head. "The poor woman feels safer when she is mad."

I gave a letter to Elias to deliver to Emperor Nikiforos. "It is a petition to release Maria and Efrosini to her parents in Paphlagonia. Maria wrote it with her own hand. Her script has improved. When she copies a scroll, she uses the miniscule script that Abbott Theodore invented."

Elias shook his head. "Emperor Nikiforos will never let Maria or her daughters leave here. They are the last of the Isaurian dynasty and he needs to keep an eye on their activities."

"Do you continue to worry about Irini?" Father Dimitrios asked, glancing at me.

My eyes strayed to the horizon where she had gone. "I keep wondering how she is faring, what she is plotting. Every day I expect a letter saying that she has escaped and wants me to come to some hiding place."

Elias laughed but Father Dimitrios frowned. "Control your imagination. Those thoughts cannot help her and they will harm you in the same way that Maria's thoughts harm her."

"Have you asked Saint Thekla how Irini is faring?" smiled Elias. "Or does Irini change her plans so often that even a saint cannot follow?"

I thought about my icon of Saint Thekla with Irini somewhere beyond the horizon. I had told no-one that I had given her away. "Only once has Saint Thekla told me about Irini and that was when Irini was desperate to know if her unborn child was alive and male. But I don't know if Saint Thekla gave me the answer or if I imagined it."

"Stop thinking about Irini," chided Father Dimitrios. "Do not exhaust your spirit with your thoughts."

"What disturbs me is that she may be treated cruelly."

"She will be treated no more cruelly than she has treated others," snapped Elias. "Yes, you are alive because Irini freed you from prison when you were both young. But she did it because it pleased her to violate rules. She knew the Emperor would not punish her. He had other plans for her."

"So you knew what happened to her on the ship and at the Palace," I whispered.

"Everyone knew. That doesn't excuse what she did to Leon," he said grimly.

Father Dimitrios went off to visit a sick child and Elias and I walked along the sea.

"Come with me into the hills of Bithynia," he smiled. "We will sleep in the starry meadows and the stars will tell us our futures through our dreams."

I smiled. "I can tell you our futures, Elias. You will be postmaster in Pendykion until some young man takes your post. Then you will move to a cottage here and become a fisherman. I will be the Abbess here until a younger woman takes my place."

"Then you will come and live with me in my cottage by the sea, each of us loving the other as we have done all our lives."

In July, on the feast of the Holy Great Martyr Marina, six months after they took Irini away, Aspasia returned from the quay panting under the weight of a basket of fish and extraordinary news.

"Bardanes Tourkos has declared war on Emperor Nikiforos! He is gathering an army at Nikomidia."

"Bardanes will become Emperor! He will bring Grandmama back from Lesbos!" Efrosini cried.

But July became August and we heard nothing more. The tension strained our nerves. Elias knew nothing and the fishermen heard no rumours. In late August, I spotted the mail boat coming and I called all the nuns and novices to come down to the village. We needed a break from the strain of waiting. Elias was in the plateia.

"Bardanes Tourkos has joined forces with Thomas the Slav, along with Mihalis the Stammerer and Leon of the Armenian theme. Their combined forces have nearly reached Pendykion. They will camp there tonight and tomorrow they will march to Chrysopolis across the narrowest part of the Propontis Sea from Constantinople. Bardanes has sent a message to the Chrysopolis city fathers to open the gates and acknowledge him as Emperor. When they do, Bardanes will send a message to Emperor Nikiforos to step down. He and his armies will cross by barge to Constantinople and enter through open gates."

My heart went cold. I remembered the prophesy of the monk in Filomelion. Bardanes would never become Emperor, Mihalis the Stammerer and Leon of the Armenian Theme would both become Emperors, and Thomas the Slav would become Emperor but never sit on the throne.

"Is there any hope they will succeed?" Father Dimitrios asked.

Elias grimaced. "Hope is all they have. The mail couriers coming from Nikomidia report that Bardanes has gathered an army but is not as large as expected."

"Irini said that Bardanes had the backing of the armies of the five themes," I faltered.

"The rest are probably waiting to learn if the Chrysopolis city fathers acknowledge Bardanes as Emperor.

If they refuse to open the gates, Emperor Nikiforos will send the imperial army after Bardanes. He will have to retreat."

The next day, we all stood at the top of the lane and watched the flutter of military banners along the road passing through Pendykion and marching towards Chrysopolis. Only two days later, Elias brought the result—and it was fact, not rumour. Bardanes Tourkos had failed.

"Chrysopolis did not open its gates," he reported. "The city fathers refused to acknowledge Bardanes as Emperor. Bardanes is retreating to Nikomidia where he has supporters. Emperor Nikiforos will blockade the city and starve Bardanes out."

The next day, we watched the scattered bunches of soldiers moving along the white line of sea road, this time with no valiant banners. A day later, we watched warhorses of the Palace regiment riding swiftly towards Nikomidia. "There was never any hope," said Sister Evanthia.

Some weeks later, Elias confirmed her words. "Bardanes has retreated to Malagina. He has surrendered and asked Emperor Nikiforos for a pardon. He begs to be allowed to retire to his monastery on Proti."

It wasn't long after that when Maria shouted that an imperial warship was dropping anchor off Proti. Father Dimitrios and his sons rowed over to get the news.

"Bardanes is on Proti," he reported later. "He has cut his hair like a monk and taken the name of Sabas. Emperor Nikiforos has ordered him to be imprisoned in his monastery."

I swayed, as if some invisible walls that had protected us had collapsed. "Bardanes Tourkos was all Irini had who could save her."

"No-one could have saved her," said Aspasia. "Not you, and certainly not Bardanes Tourkos."

"She will come back," I said. "She will find a way."

"Emperor Nikiforos has guaranteed Bardanes's safety," Father Dimitrios went on. "Patriarch Tarasios has signed his name to the guarantee. So have all the senators."

Maria laughed her mad-woman's laugh. "Their guarantees are written on the sea."

The mad can see more clearly than we. This we learned in September when Patriarch Tarasios came to our gate and asked that we let him in.

Chapter XVI

It was late September when I heard the clang of the bell on the convent gate. I was in my study with Sister Evanthia, Sister Filothei, and Sister Matrona, discussing their proposal to bring an expert weaver to the island to teach the nuns and school girls more intricate weaving. Our rugs were selling well in Constantinople. Now that Emperor Nikiforos had cut off our stipends, we had to produce more and better rugs.

I sent a novice with the key to find out who was ringing the bell. Sister Efthia had a wide reputation for healing and people came from far away. A fisherman had told me there was plague in Proussa and I didn't want that disease getting inside the convent. We would treat patients outside the walls, somehow. More likely, the visitor was a villager or someone from another island with an injury or illness. But the novice was quickly back, panting in haste.

"Three men from the Palace are here. One says he is

Patriarch Tarasios. I didn't believe him so I told them to wait outside."

I laughed. How would she know Patriarch Tarasios? The three patriarchs in my lifetime had rarely left Constantinople. Patriarch Tarasios certainly wouldn't visit a small island convent. Sister Efthia and I took our time but when I opened the gate, I saw that the novice was right. Patriarch Tarasios was indeed outside. He was kneeling beside Constantine's ossuary, bowing his grey head. The fine silk of his green tunica shone in the sun.

The two men standing behind him looked hot and thirsty in their fancy brocade tunicas and red leggings. With a flash of hatred, I recognized the traitors, Leon and Sisinnios, who had taken Irini away to Lesbos.

Patriarch Tarasios ceremoniously rose from his knees and brushed the dust off his knees. He moved his right hand slightly forward. Sister Efthia went over, knelt, and kissed it. I remained blocking the gate.

"Good you have come, Patriarch Tarasios." I gave a standard greeting.

"Good to find you here, Abbess Thekla," he replied with his usual lack of expression. His long beard had gone grizzled but his body was as thin as ever. My mind slid back to the last time I had seen him. It was in the Purple Chamber and Constantine's blood had been draining his life out through his eyes. Patriarch Tarasios had not moved to help Doctor Moses staunch the blood.

"What do you want?" I demanded, not politely. Sister Efthia shot me a reproving glance.

"To talk about Irini of Athens. May we enter?"

We walked through the pasture and I paused at the

door to the basilica. "Built by Empress Irini," I said.

The Patriarch nodded slightly but made no move to enter. We continued through the courtyard. He glanced through the open doors of the scriptorium and weaving rooms but gave barely a glance at our little church. Patriarch Tarasios had never come to the convent that I could remember. Obviously, he didn't want a tour today. I opened the door to my study. Sister Evanthia and Sister Filothei were still inside with Sister Matrona.

"Patriarch Tarasios," I murmured. They rose swiftly, knelt, and kissed his hand.

"Please have Aspasia prepare refreshments for our guests," I said as they left.

Leon and Sisinnios went over to the fireplace and began examining the scrubbed hearth. Patriarch Tarasios was running his eyes around the room, taking in the thick coloured rugs, the gleaming chairs and tables, and the polished silver and brass plate.

"You still have Empress Irini's maps," he noted.

"We use them to teach the village girls about the Empire." That wasn't strictly true. Efrosini wanted them to stay on the wall. She still believed what Irini had told her—that she would be Empress. What we are told as children lingers in us.

Tarasios lifted an icon on a side table and peered at the elaborate script around the saint's halo. "Saint Efthia."

"I bought it in Nicaea during the Evangelical Council that Empress Irini organized. Perhaps you bought some icons at the time?"

He didn't answer. He was fingering a tapestry, covetously, I thought.

"Our nuns wove that," I noted. "The wool is from our sheep. It belongs to the convent, as does everything in this room."

The Patriarch's response was curt. Gone were the soft speeches that had soothed the bishops' tempers at the Council at Nicaea and led them to bring back icons. "This is an imperial convent, Abbess Thekla. All moveable property belongs to the crown. That includes spinning wheels, looms, and sheep."

I smiled. "I suggest you read our typikon, esteemed Patriarch Tarasios. It was signed by Emperor Constantine and registered by the Eparch of the Monasteries. It states that both immovable and moveable objects are the property of the convent. That includes furnishings and equipment. And sheep."

"Emperor Constantine has been dead for decades. Emperor Nikiforos signs typikons."

"Emperor Nikiforos has read our typikon and has no difficulty with the contents."

Suddenly I understood why Emperor Nikiforos had made that surprise visit. He was considering sending Irini into exile here. He wanted to see for himself if she could be securely imprisoned on this rock.

Patriarch Tarasios seated himself where Irini used to sit, in the chair by the hearth. Efrosini brought in a silver bowl of grapes and a silver pitcher of water with lemon slices. She set them on a side table next to the brass tray holding six green glass goblets. She came to stand by me.

"Efrosini," I introduced her. "The younger daughter

of Emperor Constantine and Empress Maria. Their other daughter will join our convent. Maria also lives here."

Patriarch Tarasios knew this perfectly well but he hadn't seen Efrosini since the day her father was blinded in the Purple Chamber. She was fourteen now and taller than me. She had her grandmother's thick chestnut hair and dark intense eyes. And Irini's frightening resolve.

Efrosini knelt and kissed his hand. Then she returned to stand by me. We watched Sisinnios pace the room, counting his steps. He went outside and his thick figure crossed the windows. He returned wearing a smug smile.

"The outside wall is longer than the inside. There is a passage within the walls."

"The walls are two building blocks thick, which accounts for the difference," I corrected.

Patriarch Tarasios turned his gaze on me. I could feel him debating the value of throwing an elderly abbess in prison in hopes that she would reveal the site of treasure that might not exist. His calculating eyes shifted to Efrosini. She was filling the glasses with water and carrying the tray around. Sisinnios and Leon each took a glass but didn't drink, suspicious of poison. I took a glass and drank all the water. Patriarch Tarasios drank. Then Leon and Sisinnios finished theirs with thirsty slurps. Efrosini refilled them. She placed the bowl of grapes on the small table at the Patriarch's elbow, then poured our elderberry wine into four tiny glasses. She took these around on a tray. Patriarch Tarasios took an experimental sip, nodded in satisfaction, and placed it on the small table beside the grapes. He selected a grape and ate it.

"Lovely study, Abbess Thekla. As comfortable as my own."

"One of Empress Irini's many achievements."

"You place excessive value on the achievements of our former Empress."

"She brought back our icons."

"A temporary accomplishment. She thought it would keep her on the throne. She failed to understand that only the army decides who stays on the throne, and the army didn't want Irini. No woman can lead an army. Women cannot rise through the ranks and gain a soldier's trust. Her disastrous military decisions drove two excellent commanders to defect to the Caliph. Then she tried to force the theme armies to vow loyalty to her and only her. The morale among the troops fell so low that we were losing battles for no reason. She distrusted men so much that she believed the lies of unscrupulous eunuchs like Stavrakios and Aetios. The size of the ransom she paid to free Stavrakios, plus the tributes she was paying Harun al-Rashid and the Bulgars to keep the peace nearly broke the Treasury. Her treachery to her son to gain the throne allowed Harun to devastate Amorion. As for her skill as an administrator, she had none. Her decisions to reduce taxes robbed the Treasury of funds needed for salaries and military supplies. The money she spent on jewellery and clothing for herself could finance years of military campaigns. For the sake of the Empire, she had to be replaced."

"She raised you to Patriarch. She gave you the highest power in the church."

"She wanted the Council at Nicaea to bring back

icons and she knew I could do that."

He sipped his elderberry wine and turned to Efrosini. He spoke gently, as if she were still a little girl. He miscalculated. She was an adult of marriageable age and well versed in Palace wiles.

"Efrosini, dear, I saw you the day you were born. I knew your father and your grandfather and your great-grandfather, God rest their souls." He crossed himself, as did we all. "Now I am searching for your grandmother's possessions. Do you know where they are?"

Efrosini gestured at the trunk in front of the couch. "In there, Patriarch Tarasios."

"We searched that trunk over and over," Leon interrupted.

"I am referring to her jewellery and gold." Patriarch Tarasios didn't take his eyes off Efrosini.

"She never wore jewellery on Prinkypos, Patriarch Tarasios. There is no one here to impress but goats."

He shot her a sharp look but her expression remained bland. He forced the corners of his thin mouth to lift. "Where are the bolts of silk she removed from the Palace? Silver bowls. Gold chalices. Purses of coins."

"You might ask the ghost of Patriarch Constantine. He is said to wander through these rooms. He may speak to a fellow patriarch." I hid my smile. Now she really was being impertinent.

He adopted a stern tone. "Whenever your grandmother came here from Constantinople, she brought valuables that belong to the Treasury. Tell me where they are."

"Will you release me and my mother from this exile?

Will you allow us to go to our family in Paphlagonia?"

He sneaked a look at me but I hid my thoughts under the half smile that nuns wear in a closed community where there is no privacy. He began again, but it was too late. Maria stood in the doorway. Her wild hair was pinned back with thistles, her filthy nun's tunica was askew, and her dirty feet were bare. However, I saw no crazed look in her eyes. I wondered if this might be a day of sanity.

Patriarch Tarasios rose and bowed slightly. "Empress Maria. Good to see you looking so well."

"Let me and my daughter go home, Patriarch Tarasios," Maria said in a firm but polite tone. "My husband is dead. The Isaurian line is finished. How could a woman and her daughter possibly harm Emperor Nikiforos?"

Patriarch Tarasios lifted his hands. "I will discuss the issue with the Emperor. This is his decision, not mine. He may be in favour, under certain conditions."

"Such as?"

"You tell me where to find the treasure that Irini systematically stole from the Great Palace and hid in this convent."

Maria gave up her brief moment of good manners. She lifted the pitcher and splashed water into my glass, then drank it down thirstily. She smacked it on the tray and threw herself onto the couch, flinging her dirty bare feet onto the trunk. "If I tell you, will take Efrosini and me today to Constantinople? Will you arrange our journey to my parents in Paphlagonia? Promise me that and I will show you where the treasure is. Then I will instruct my servants to pack my belongings, such as they are after eight years in exile."

The Patriarch glanced at me. I could feel him calculating the depths of her madness. He bowed slightly. "Tell me where it is and you will return to Paphlagonia this very day. The imperial yacht sits in the harbour. You can be on it, you and Efrosini."

She smiled and drummed her heels on the trunk. "The treasure is here."

His eyes flicked to the chest. The ivory insets gleamed in the dark mahogany. "Leon, search the trunk."

"We searched it before, Patriarch," protested Sisinnios.

"Search it again."

Maria swung her feet off the trunk and sat cross-legged on the couch with a sly smile. "Search it again, Leon," she taunted.

Leon and Sisinnios threw open the lid and began flinging out Irini's clothes—the shimmering green tunica embroidered with silver thread, the red velvet cloak, her summer linen shoes. Every article brought a memory. My head fairly swam with them.

Maria picked the green tunica off the floor and held it up to her. I remembered the first time Irini had worn it. It was for her audience with Empress Evdokia after the birth of Constantine. The Empress's reception hall had been filled with silk-clad attendants whispering and giggling behind their fingers. Irini had marched straight through them, head high, with us behind her—the nurses carrying baby Constantine in his basket, three attendants, and me. One attendant had been Megalo. Empress Maria had not yet been born. I felt dazed at the passage of time.

Leon had reached the bottom of the trunk. He ran his hands over the wood, searching for a false panel. Patriarch Tarasios spoke in an even, quiet voice.

"Where are the jewels, Empress Maria?"

Maria slid her dirty fingers over her smile. "There's a secret tunnel."

The room went so silent that I could hear the scrape of a crow's feet walking across the courtyard. My face tingled. I forced myself not to look at Efrosini. Had Maria seen Irini or me open the hearth and go down the steps? For eight years, Maria had roamed the convent, soundless on bare feet in summer. I had been careful but the mad are cunning.

"A tunnel? In this room?" Patriarch Tarasios addressed her gently, carefully.

Her smile became as hard as her voice. "Guess, Patriarch. You signed my divorce decree. You cut off my hair. You made me a nun against my will. Guess." She could do that, switch from madness to sanity in a breath. Her swift change made him cautious.

He rose. Keeping his eyes on her, he moved towards the window and touched the wall by it. "Am I getting warm?" he smiled, playing the child's game.

She giggled. He lifted the tapestry and looked at her. She shook her head. He moved toward the fireplace. "Warmer?"

Maria laughed in glee and clasped her hands.

The Patriarch picked up the poker. He pointed at the hearth. "Is the tunnel under there, Empress? Your husband once told his friends about secret steps under this hearth."

My beloved Constantine dying in the Purple Chamber rose before my eyes. I saw the blood running from his eyes. I saw Aetios standing over him and Patriarch Tarasios standing in the doorway doing nothing. I stopped the game.

"Constantine told you all he knew," I said harshly. "You were there when Aetios blinded him. You heard Aetios refuse to allow Doctor Moses to give him opium unless he told you where the treasure was. He didn't know."

Patriarch Tarasios ignored me. He kept his eyes on Maria. He tapped the poker on the hearth. "Am I hot, Maria?"

Maria dropped her smile. She spoke with calm logic. "Perhaps my deceased husband was referring to one of the many hearths at the Great Palace. There are hundreds of them."

Her return to sanity shook him. He gazed at her warily, not sure whether to believe the sane woman or the mad one. He shifted the poker between his long fingers and tried again to reach her with words. That was his skill, words.

"Irini's servants showed us where she had hidden jewellery and gold coins in the Great Palace and in her private Palace. We found them behind sliding panels and in hollow statues and holes in the stone walls. But the Treasury has kept records of Empress Irini's gifts and purchases and a great deal is missing. Did you see her hiding anything in this room, Empress Maria? Was it under this hearth?"

Leon took the poker from him and found the hole he had found before. He pried and pushed until the edges of the stones crumbled and the poker clattered from his hands. "I will have this fireplace taken apart!" he shouted.

Maria burst into wild laughter. I clasped my hands to hide their shaking.

"Take the entire convent apart, Patriarch Tarasios," I said, keeping my voice low to hide my hatred of the highest cleric in the church, the Patriarch appointed by Irini when she was the Hand of God herself. "Empress Irini spent a fortune to furnish this convent. She gave gifts. She wrote letters and paid fishermen to deliver them. If she brought any treasure here, that is where it has gone."

Patriarch Tarasios sat down. He picked up his elderberry wine and took a sip. He set it down. He selected a grape and ate it, his eyes on me. Juice trickled onto his green silk tunica. He dabbed at it with an embroidered handkerchief. "Emperor Nikiforos has decided to bring Irini back to Prinkypos. She will arrive in a month or so."

For a moment, I couldn't breathe. "Then she can tell you herself if there is any treasure to be found," I managed.

He smiled.

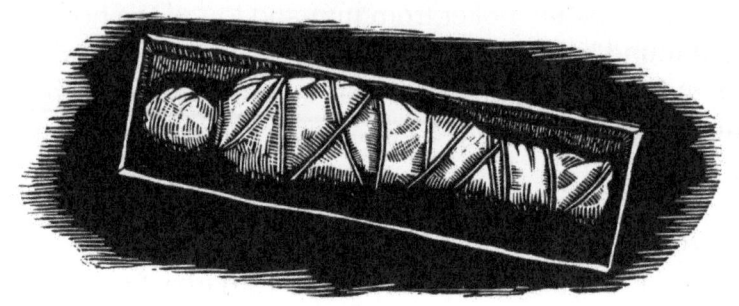

Chapter XVII

All of October, November, and well into December, we watched the sea. Everyone on the island watched. From dawn until dusk, eyes searched for the ship bringing Irini home. Wild speculating came from all sides: "She is coming by warship, she is coming overland through Nicaea, she has been pardoned, Emperor Nikiforos is making her his co-empress, she has been forcibly tonsured as a nun."

I swung from hope to despair. I wanted her alive yet I wanted her dead and her deception gone forever. The nuns and novices, however, were desperate for her return to the throne. Emperor Nikiforos had cut off our funds and the nuns feared that he would shutter the convent. They would have to find new homes. Sister Matrona tried to reassure them that many convents in Bithynia would welcome them, that she herself had found a convent there after Commander Mihalis the Dragon had burnt down her convent. But the nuns' fears would not be calmed.

So I avoided them. I waited until the last minute to come to prayer services and I left before the last echo of the final chant had faded. At meals, I did not speak. Sister Matrona said archly that she wasn't aware that the convent enforced silence at meals. Aspasia finally told me that I was giving everyone indigestion and she would bring my meals to my study.

Nights were the worst. Worried thoughts swarmed like bees through my head. In December, we moved into the kitchen, fleeing the freezing dormitory. I lay awake listening for the splash of an anchor. I was up at dawn lifting the blankets off the windows and scanning the sea for an unfamiliar vessel.

I was at my desk when the ship came. I was calculating our expenses and deciding how much gold to take from Irini's hoard to pay the nuns' stipends and our other expenses. I didn't spend much. We ate from our garden and orchard. Our sheep and goats gave us milk which we also made into cheese. Our chickens provided eggs and a meat meal when they were too old to lay eggs. We gathered mussels and other sea creatures and cut wild greens from the hillsides. We made our wine and cheese. Some of our olives we stored in vats and the rest we pressed into oil on the village olive press. We wove our tunicas and blankets and knotted our rugs. But flour and fish were our staples and flour came from Pendykion and fish was bought from the local fishermen. Linen thread for summer tunicas came from shops in Pendykion. The cobbler from Pendykion came out to fit us for boots and sandals. I had to pay the stonemason and carpenter for repairs to the buildings and pay Father

Dimitrios for his monthly service in the basilica and to hear our confessions. Finally, there were the yearly stipends for the nuns which they sent home to their families. I was totalling this up when Aspasia threw open my door.

"A merchant ship is dropping anchor. If she's on it, she's not coming with an army."

Sister Matrona was right behind her, pulling on her cloak. "Of course she's not bringing an army," she snapped irritably. "Patriarch Tarasios said Emperor Nikiforos was having her brought home."

My heart leapt. Until that moment, I had not realized how strong was my certainty that Irini was alive, that she would walk off a ship into our arms, that we would climb the hill together and sit by the convent cemetery and look out over the chain of islands to the mountains of Bithynia. I opened the secret drawer in my desk to get my icon of Saint Thekla, then remembered, with a wrench of my heart, that I had sent her away with Irini. I missed her terribly. I felt like part of my body was gone. I pulled on my shawl and cloak. But my legs wouldn't take the first step. Aspasia gripped my arm.

"Let's go see if Irini is really on that ship," she said in a matter-of-fact voice.

Sister Matrona took my other arm and we followed the nuns hurrying across the pasture. At the top of the lane, we stopped to look down at the merchant ship anchored outside the harbour. The quay was solid with people. Father Dimitrios was standing by his sons. Nuns were already crossing the plateia. By the time the three of us got to the quay, we had to fight our way to the front.

Everyone was strangely quiet. We watched sailors splash a dinghy into the water and unroll a rope ladder into it. The captain and an officer came out of the cabin, settling their hats and fastening their coats. They climbed down the ladder and waited in the dinghy, bobbing in the sea. Whispers swarmed around me.

"Look, a door is opening. She's coming out." The universe stood still. The sea stopped moving. The seagulls stopped swooping.

A sailor backed out of the cabin door. He was holding something. The sailor kept backing.

There is no mistaking the shape of a coffin.

A cry rose from my heart. My knees gave out and I sank to the quay, my arms over my head. Someone was wailing; it was me. Aspasia yanked my arm. Her insistent voice hurt my ears.

"Maybe it's not her! Make the captain get that lid off! Somebody else could be in that box."

Sister Matrona was pulling my other arm and hissing in my ear. "Tarasios is a born liar. Who knows whose corpse is inside that coffin? Irini could be alive! Make the captain open the coffin so we can see!"

Understanding pierced my grief and I got to my feet. The sailors had lowered the coffin into the dinghy and they were trying to balance it, a struggle with an unwieldy box on a restless December sea. Fishermen rowed out in rowboats and steadied the coffin. Then everyone rowed with all their worth into the calmer harbour. The fishermen hoisted the coffin onto the quay at my feet and handed up the captain and his officer.

I stared at the plain wooden box, numb, unable to

think or feel. Aspasia shook my arm.

"The captain is speaking to you! Tell him to open the coffin!"

I forced my eyes to the captain's bearded face. He was saying something.

"You are Abbess Thekla of the Convent of the Theotokos on Prinkypos?"

"Yes. She is Abbess Thekla." Sister Matrona shook my arm.

He saluted me briskly, then opened his logbook. "I am delivering into your authority the body of Irini of Athens. Date of death, ninth of August, eleventh indiction, year of Our Lord six thousand two hundred and ninety-five. Place of receipt: Convent on the island of Lesbos. Place of delivery: Prinkypos Island. Date of delivery, tenth December, twelfth indiction, year of Our Lord six thousand two hundred and ninety-five. Kindly sign here to acknowledge receipt."

A sailor bent over and the captain placed the logbook on his back. The officer dipped a quill into an ink bottle and held out the quill to me.

"What took you so long?" Aspasia interrupted. "Five months to come from Lesbos?"

I found my tongue. "Yes," I fumbled. "Why so long?"

The captain lifted his hands. "We are a merchant vessel, Abbess. We pick up goods from one port and deliver them to another, then pick up goods from there destined for another port. We don't sail a direct route. Now if you will kindly sign to acknowledge receipt."

The officer dipped his quill again and held it out. Around me lay silence and watching eyes. Sister Matrona was whispering in my ear.

"Tell them to open the coffin! Tell them!"

I pulled myself together. "I must ask you to open the coffin, Captain. I have to be certain that the physical remains are those of Irini of Athens."

The captain frowned. "Abbess Thekla, please God, the body has been in there for five months. Rot has surely sent in. Also, the priest did not state the cause of death. Could have been pox. Or plague."

Gasps came from around me and movements backwards. Father Dimitrios stepped forward.

"We will take the coffin into the church and open it there. Saint Nikolaos will protect us." He ignored the protest of his son, the young priest.

Fishermen pulled oars from their boats and slid them cross-wise under the coffin. They lifted it onto their shoulders and carried it down the quay and into the church. Father Dimitrios followed—along with me, Efrosini, Irinoula, Maria, Aspasia, Sister Matrona, and Sister Efthia. Father Dimitrios and his son placed two chairs the right distance apart and the fishermen placed the coffin on them. They crossed themselves and hurried out.

Father Dimitrios took a handful of candles from the prayer box. He lit his from the oil lamp hanging over the altar and handed the other candles around. We carefully lit ours from his candle. The dark church softened into shadows. My nerves steadied.

The carpenter and his sons returned carrying crowbars. Under the wavery candlelight, they jammed the tips under the lid. The stiff wood groaned and screeched.

The wax that had sealed it peeled away and suddenly the coffin lid clattered onto the stones. With an oath, the two men stepped backwards and flung their bent arms over their mouth and nose. The odour of putrefaction struck me like a blow, but it wasn't as bad as a rotting sheep. I covered my mouth and nose with my shawl and moved closer.

The physical remains of Irini of Athens had been sewn into a linen shroud and spread with a heavy layer of sage and rosemary. Their scent blended with the fragrance of thyme incense and scented oil. Some priest had administered last rites and some abbess had prepared the body for burial. The stitches closing the shroud over the face were loose and wide, as if someone knew we would open them. Father Dimitrios took his knife and slit them. He folded back the linen, then retreated and covered his mouth and nose with his sleeve. I lifted my candle higher.

A black shawl wrapped the head and throat and tied up the jaw. The eyes were sunken, the cheekbones stuck out like knives, and the skin stretched across them was paper thin. But there was no mistaking that face. "It's her," I breathed. "Irini of Athens." I crossed myself.

Sister Matrona lifted her candle higher and Sister Efthia peered over the face. She spoke with strong assurance. "No purple blotches, no oozing sores. Not plague or pox, thank the Lord."

The young priest hurried to the door and whispered through the crack. I could hear a murmur from outside before he shut the door again. With trembling fingers, I folded the shroud back further. Irini was wearing her black tunica with the purple ribbon stitched around the collar. Her hands were folded over her heart. Her fingers were bare. The topaz ring and the gold band had paid for food or a bit of fresh air. Or for the coffin.

Father Dimitrios's deep voice broke into my thoughts. "Abbess Thekla, we must bury her immediately. Put the lid back on. Rot has set in."

"Wait!" Sister Matrona's sharp voice echoed through the church. "Lift her hand, Thekla!" She placed her hand over mine and forced it onto the hands folded over the heart.

I recoiled but Sister Matrona tightened her grip and pushed my hand onto those cold bones.

My flesh crawled. But as I felt those cold bones under my fingers, I saw that something lay under them. With trembling fingers, I slid it out. There in my hand lay Saint Thekla. She looked up at me with her quiet smile. I lifted her to my lips and kissed her.

"You came home," I whispered. "You went with Irini so you could bring her home."

Back outside the church and gulping fresh air, I signed the ship captain's logbook with a firm hand. The captain and his officers saluted me and climbed into the dingy. Father Dimitrios gripped my arm.

"The burial must be today. The whole coffin has to go in the ground. The physical remains will fall to pieces if we lift the shroud." He turned to the stonemason. "Can you get the lid off the empty shaft?"

Ritual says that the deceased must lie for a day in the church so all can pay last respects. But the state of decomposition had made that impossible. So the carpenter hammered down the coffin lid and we left Irini alone in the church where she used to thank Saint Nikolaos for her safe arrival. Efrosini and Irini and I went to Father Dimitrios's cottage to get warm, the others from the convent went to various cottages, and the men climbed the hill to the convent cemetery to open the shaft.

The merchant vessel had been spotted by people on the other islands and boats started coming. Elias arrived and found me shivering by the fire. He put his arms around me. I closed my eyes and leaned against him.

"She's truly gone," I whispered. "I can rest."

It was dusk when the men came to report that the grave shaft was open. They loaded the coffin onto the donkey cart and heaved it up the frozen lane. Father Dimitrios and his son walked in front. His son carried the tall, gold cross.

For the last time, I climbed the hill with Irini of Athens and stopped at the cemetery. I thought of all the times we had sat on the bench and leaned our tired backs against the convent wall to catch our breath and rest our eyes on the islands spilling out at our feet like a handful of green figs.

The shaft where Constantine had lain was empty now; his bones lay in the stone ossuary at the head of the shaft. The slab of stone over the shaft had been tipped to the side and beside it lay a mound of earth. The men wrapped ropes around the coffin and lowered it into the shaft while Father Dimitrios chanted Irini to her eternal rest. I dropped in the first handful of earth to send her on her journey to the Underworld. Everyone, even the children, dropped their handfuls of earth, as we had done when we had buried her son, my beloved Constantine.

Our own hand writes our fate. We die as we have lived, some in peace and some in struggle. As I stood there, I wondered how Irini had died. I don't mean, was she poisoned or did her heart just stop beating? Had she died in peace? That's what I wanted to know. Or was her spirit out there somewhere, still struggling?

After that, I grew absent-minded and forgetful. At meals, I stared at my bowl, forgetting to lift my spoon. I held the chicken feed in my hand and forgot to toss it to the fowls. I remained standing in the church after prayers until Sister Efthia led me out. A strange pressure closed my ears and my breath became short at the slightest exertion. My throat swelled and I could swallow only broth. I fell asleep at the refectory table, at my desk, stirring the broth.

One morning at Orthros prayers, my eyes closed and I could not open them. Aspasia and Efrosini led me to bed. I heard Sister Matrona praying beside me. I slept and woke but my eyes would not open, even when Efrosini and Sister Efthia led me to the latrine and washed my hands and face. So they sat me on my bed and fed me broth and tucked me under the blankets.

Day became night and day and night again. I dreamed that I saw Irini of Athens falling into the dark well of time, growing smaller and smaller. Others fell into the well after her: Emperor Constantine who had brought Irini from Athens, Leon her husband, Constantine her son. I saw all the people in my life passing before me in a long stream. I saw my parents and my brothers walking with the nuns in the convent. I saw the six Palace eunuchs who had been locked in the stocks walking with Father Dimitrios. I saw Andreas and Doctor Moses walking next to Emperor Leon who was holding little Constantine by the hand. I saw the three dead Patriarchs walking arm in arm. My beloved Constantine passed me as an adult, his face sad and blood-streaked, holding in his arms his dead son. Behind him walked his two wives, arm and arm.

I saw myself as a child pass in that column of people, and then I saw myself again as a young woman with my betrothed, holding him in my arms in the sweet grass and my heart overflowed with warmth and happiness. I saw my parents and the places I would never again see and sorrow flooded my arms and legs and the bones of my back and my fingers and my heart. Then a strange tingling passed through my body from heart to toe as if I were being rolled in sand-charged waves. Two more strong tinglings passed through me and then my body jerked and I awoke.

I lay unable to move—indeed, not wanting to move for fear of disturbing the peace that filled my body. I saw the ceiling beams as if I had never before seen them, rough wooden poles with slender sticks between. I saw the plaster walls that the builders had coloured pink by stirring red clay into the plaster. I sat up feeling clear-headed, slightly dizzy, but calm. Efrosini was sleeping in the second bed. I pushed open the shutters and watched the red sun rise from the winter-blue sea. I smelled the cold sea air and heard the gulls' cries.

"I didn't understand the meaning of loyalty," I said

to Efrosini who had awakened and was wrapping me in my quilt. "That's why I became ill. She was a tyrant over my heart. She made me her accomplice and she called it loyalty. She made me spy for her and lie for her. In return, she made me the abbess of a convent where she could escape. Now she is dead. It is over."

A great relief came over me to say this and at the same time a great sorrow. A sense of grief hung about my heart through breakfast and into the afternoon, but when I went to watch the sun set into the sea, it had gone.

Chapter XVIII

One wet day the following autumn, Maria, ever vigilant at her window, shouted that two monks were rowing a small boat over from Proti Island. Sister Efthia, Efrosini, and I went down to find out if someone in the monastery was ill. We found the monks in Father Dimitrios's cottage, drying themselves at his fire.

"Emperor Nikiforos sent out his thugs," they told us, lips tight with anger. "They dragged Brother Bardanes from his cell and blinded him. We could not stop the bastards."

"But I thought that the Emperor and the senators had guaranteed his safety!" I exclaimed in horror. "Patriarch Tarasios signed his name to the guarantee!"

One monk burst out, "Patriarch Tarasios is not a man of God. He is a politician who changes his course with the wind. He is no better than the lying senators."

Shaken that the Emperor's butchers had come so near to us, Efrosini and I locked ourselves in my study that evening and unblocked the steps to the secret room. We brought up the leather and silk pouches and spilled out their shining contents over my desk.

"The gold coins we can value, but the jewels are a mystery," I said helplessly.

Efrosini draped a string of pearls and sapphires around her lovely young neck and gazed at her reflection in a polished silver hand mirror she had found in the chest. She lacked the sculptured beauty of her grandmother; she had inherited her mother's round features. But she had her father's gentle expression which is where her beauty lay.

"Take the precious stones to Constantinople and ask the Jews," she suggested.

"Why not?" I said impulsively. "I want to see Constantinople again. My life with Irini began there. This will close the door on it."

So, shortly after that on a warm autumn day, when we saw the little mail boat sailing into our harbour, Efrosini and I went down to the quay with a small pouch of jewels tied in my scarf. "We're going to Constantinople," I told Elias with a smile. "Can you put us on a coach?"

"I'll take you there myself and bring you straight back. Emperor Nikiforos shouldn't know of your presence." He handed the mail to Father Dimitrios and turned the little boat to catch the wind towards the golden haze of Constantinople.

The wind was strong and we reached Rymin harbour by mid-afternoon. When we climbed out, Elias said, "Don't stay in the city tonight. I'll be here waiting."

We left him tying up his boat but I knew he would be

right behind us; he always was. Efrosini and I pulled our scarves over our faces and hurried through the Golden Gate. Memories struck me like blows. There was the lane to the prison where I had nearly died and where I had put my icon into Irini's hand thinking she was Saint Thekla coming to take me to Heaven. There was Studios Monastery where Abbott Theodore was spying on his monks. Farther up Mesi Street were the steps down to Ta Gastria convent where I had lived and worked.

My feet took us straight to the shop in the Jewish quarter where I had taken Irini's letters for the Jews to deliver to Charles of the Franks and others. The merchant quickly beckoned us inside and bolted the door. His dark, cautious eyes moved from me to Efrosini. I held out the little pouch of jewels.

"Please tell me the worth of these and if you will buy them. I needn't tell you from whence they came."

He lit a candle and waved us to stools before his desk. Then he lit another candle and seated himself. He laid out a strip of dark silk and carefully tipped out the stones. With small tweezers he lifted each to the candle-light, turning the stones to peer into their depths. Their brilliant colours flashed on the walls, just as the jewels on Irini's fingers had flashed on the white silk sails of the warship taking her to wed Co-emperor Leon.

The merchant took out an abacus and tapped on it. Then he sat back and gave us a sum. "I won't make any profit. These are known stones so I must take them out of the Empire to sell them. I do this only because she was good to us. Jews need not make any more vows on the Christian Bible."

I accepted his offer, having no idea of the worth of the stones. He deftly slid them into a small, silk pouch. Then he removed a leather purse from a drawer and counted out the thin gold coins aloud onto the black silk, glancing up at me to make sure that I was paying attention. He slid the coins into my little pouch and pushed it back to me. My hand was shaking as I fastened it onto the leather strap around my neck that held my wooden cross.

"I will take you out through the back," he said gently. "I never saw you."

"Nor we you," smiled Efrosini.

He smiled then and I saw that he was much younger than I had thought. It was hard to tell through the dark beard and his sombre expression. "I am sorry for what happened to her," he said. "She deserved better. She had a difficult life in Constantinople and she survived longer than we expected. Her husband and her son made far worse mistakes than she did when they sat on the throne."

I started to rise, but Efrosini put a hand on my arm and addressed the merchant. "How much is passage on a ship to the island of Lesbos?" she inquired.

He raised his eyebrows in surprise and caution. "Are you certain you wish to go there? The voyage is long and you will find the destination painful."

"Passage for two women," said Efrosini firmly. "To Lesbos and on to Athens."

He gave us a sum and I reached for my pouch but he shook his head. "We have no ships leaving for those ports until spring. I will send you a message."

He let us out onto an alley so narrow that my shoulders touched both sides. We pulled our scarves over our faces and found our way to Mesi Street and out the Golden Gate. I took Efrosini's arm as we crossed the broad square under the shadow of the golden angels looking down upon us from the towers.

"One day, Efrosini," I declared, "You and I will sail to the island of Lesbos. We will find the convent where Irini was imprisoned and meet the abbess who spread rosemary and sage over her shroud. We will ask how Irini lived and how she died."

"Then we will sail south to Athens." Efrosini picked up our story. "We will dock at Piraeus where she climbed aboard Emperor Constantine's warship filled with dreams of Constantinople. Uncle Theo will meet us and we will walk up the slope to Athens between the walls that Themistocles built."

I nodded. "Theo will show us where Irini grew up and where she gazed over the ancient walls to the hills carpeted with olive trees. We will look into the glittering onyx eyes of the painted statues of goddesses and philosophers and we will stand in the Temple of Athena at night and hear the whispers of the ancients."

"Yes," continued Efrosini. "We will climb the hill she called the Sanctuary of the Wolves and hear their silent howls. We will swim in the bay of Salamis where the Athenians sank the Persian fleet. We will walk down the Sacred Way to Elefsia where our ancestors stepped through the veil into eternity. And we will lay flowers inside the cave where the god of the Underworld dragged Persephone down into his darkness, causing her mother to turn summer into winter with her tears."

***

We covered our faces until Elias had got our sailboat well away from Constantinople. "Emperor Nikiforos is purging the official records of anything about Irini," he said. "We must rely on Yiorgos the Synkellos to write about her in his history of the world."

"Will Emperor Nikiforos again ban icons?" wondered Efrosini.

Elias shrugged. "He is too busy fighting the Bulgars to worry about icons. But keep a cistern dry in case you need to hide your wood icons. And keep plenty of whitewash to paint over the icons that Brother Grigorios has brought to life on your church walls."

Efrosini sighed. "I feel like everything I have loved has been taken away—my father, my mother's wits, my life in the Palace, my grandmother—and possibly icons."

"The people will remain in your memory," I said. "As for the icons on our church walls, we may have to hide them again under whitewash. We will not see them but we will know they are there."

The End

The Empress Irini Series

Book 4:
The Price of Eyes

Fictional characters are in *italics*.

Aetios – based on Aetios, eunuch appointed by Empress Irini to command the Palace Guard
Alexios – based on Alexios Mousoule, Palace Guard commander under Constantine VI
Anthusa – based on Princess Anthusa, only daughter of Emperor Constantine V and Empress Evdokia, became a nun in a convent in Constantinople
Aspasia – cook at the Convent of the Theotokos on Prinkypos Island
Bardanes Tourkos – based on the esteemed military commander by that name who served under Emperors Constantine V, Leon IV, Constantine VI, and Empress Irini
Brother Yiorgios – based on George Synkellos, monk who began writing *A History of the World* which was completed by Theophanes the Confessor
Brother Grigorios – monk who paints icon frescos on the walls, pillars, and ceilings of the churches on Prinkypos Island in the story
Charles of the Franks – also called Charlemagne, King of the Franks during the reigns of Emperor Leon IV, Emperor Constantine VI, and Empress Irini, crowned by

Pope Leo as "Emperor of the Holy Roman Empire" in 800 A.D., briefly engaged to Empress Irini

Constantine V – based on the second emperor of the Isaurian Dynasty of the Roman Empire of the East, powerful military commander and skilled administrator, had one son from his first wife who died, a second wife who died, and five sons and a daughter from his third wife, brought Irini of Athens from Athens to Constantinople to marry his son Leon

Constantine VI – based on the fourth Emperor of the Isaurian Dynasty of the Roman Empire of the East, only child of Emperor Leon IV and Empress Irini, died aged 26

Doctor Moses – based on a physician by that name who was also a deacon of the Antioch church under the caliphate of al-Mansour during the time of Irini of Athens

Efrosini – based on the second daughter of Emperor Constantine VI and Empress Maria of Amnia, exiled to Prinkypos Island as a child

Elias – from a wealthy Constantinople family, postmaster in the seaside fortress of Pendykion, confidant and lover of Thekla

Elpidios – based on Elpidios, Consul of Sicily, who was accused of having illicit relations with Empress Irini, defected to the Caliphate

Evdokia – also Eudokia, based on the third wife of Emperor Constantine V and mother of his five sons and one daughter

Fanis – based on Theophanes the Confessor, married to Megalo, became a monk and established his own monastery

Father Dimitrios – village priest on Prinkypos island, friend and confidant of Abbess Thekla

Harun al-Rashid – Leader of the Caliphate during the reigns of Empress Irini and Emperor Constantine VI

Irini of Athens – also Irene or Eirene, based on the Byzantine Empress who was born in Athens, orphaned, raised in the house of her uncle, taken by Emperor Constantine V to Constantinople to marry his son, Leon, became Empress Regent for her only son after the deaths of her father-in-law and her husband, became Empress in her own right

Irinoula – Based on Irini, the elder daughter of Emperor Constantine VI and Empress Maria of Amnia, called Irinoula in the book to distinguish her from her grandmother Irini, exiled to Prinkypos Island as a child

Leon IV – also called Leo, heir to the throne, based on the son of Emperor Constantine V and his first wife who died, husband of Irini of Athens, father of Emperor Constantine VI, reigned for five years after the death of his father, died suddenly at age 30

Infant Leon – also called Leo, based on the first son of Emperor Constantine VI and his second wife Empress Theodote, died as a young child

Maria – Based on Maria of Amnia, first wife of Constantine VI and mother of his two daughters, exiled to Prinkypos Island with her young daughters

Megalo – based on Megalo who married Theophanes the Confessor and was sent by him to live in the Convent of the Theotokos on Prinkypos Island

Medea – ancient Greek play by Euripides

Mihalis the Dragon – based on Michael Lachanodrakon, distinguished military commander under Emperors Constantine V, Leon IV, Constantine VI, and Empress Irini

Nikiforos – Based on the Minister of Finance appointed by Empress Irini, became Emperor Nikiforos I

Nikiforos and Christoforos – based on the two eldest uncles of Emperor Constantine VI who never stopped trying to become emperor

Nikitas Triphillios – based on the officer in the Palace guards appointed by Empress Irini

Platon – based on Abbott Platon, uncle of Abbott Theodore the Studite

Pope Leo – Bishop of Rome (Pope) during part of the reign of Empress Irini

Pulkeria – Abbess of the Ta Gastria Convent in Constantinople, friend and advisor to Thekla

Romans of the East – people later labelled "Byzantines" by a scholar, lived in the eastern part of the Roman Empire which Constantine the Great broke away from the Roman Empire in 330, declared himself Emperor, and built his capitol, Constantinople

Sister Matrona – nun, Ekonomis, second in command, at the Convent of the Theotokos

Sister Efthia - nun at the Convent of the Theotokos who directs the hospice

Sister Evanthia – nun at the Convent of the Theotokos who supervises the weaving

Sister Filothei – nun at the Convent of the Theotokos who teaches the village girls

Stavrakios – also Staurakios, based on the eunuch

appointed by Empress Irini as Minister of the Imperial Post and Foreign Affairs, patrikios, and holder of a seat in the Senate

Tarasios – based on Patriarch Tarasios who was appointed by Empress Irini as Patriarch of Constantinople

Thekla of Ikonion – fictional Abbess of the Convent of the Theotokos, based on an actual nun named Thekla who lived in a convent near Constantinople and wrote hymns during the reign of Irini of Athens

Theo – based on Theophylaktos, cousin of Irini of Athens who accompanied her from Athens to Constantinople

Theodore – based on Theodore the Studite, Abbott of the Monastery of Studios in Constantinople

Tula – based on Empress Theodote, second wife of Emperor Constantine VI and mother of their two sons

Note: The IRINI OF ATHENS series covers the years 752 AD – 803 AD. During this time these people called themselves Romans of the East. We now call them Byzantines.

Biographical data is available at "Prosopography of the Byzantine Empire", www.pbe.kcl.ac.uk, URL.

Glossary

Aegean Sea – body of water between mainland Greece and Turkey

Amorion – wealthy walled city and military base in the Anatolikon theme, now Hisarköy, Turkey

Anatolikon theme – also Anatolia, province of the Roman Empire of the East bordering the Caliphate to the east and the Roman Sea (Mediterranean) to the south

Armeniakon theme – also Armenia, province of the Roman Empire of the East bordering the Black Sea to the north and the Caliphate to the east

anagrapheus – tax official

anassa – term of respect for an abbess

Antioch – wealthy city in the Caliphate near the Roman Sea, now Antakya, Turkey

artopios – bread vendor

Akimeti monks – monks who never sleep so they can continually pray

Augustaion – large walled area between the Church of Holy Wisdom and the Great Palace, now part of the Topkapi Palace Museum

biblioamphiastis – bookbinder

Bithynia – farming region across the Propontis Sea from Constantinople, part of the Opsikon Theme by Mount Olympus (Turkish: Uludag)

Blachernae Gate – most northern land gate into Constantinople, by Blachernae Palace

Blachernae Palace – imperial palace in Constantinople on the Golden Horn

Bosporus Strait – also Bosphorus, narrow waterway connecting the Propontis Sea and the Pontus Sea (Sea of Marmara and Black Sea)
Bulgars – people who lived in the Bulgar Khanate, now called Bulgaria
Byzantine Empire – name invented by a German historian in 1557 for the Roman Empire of the East
Caliphate – empire located east of the Roman Empire of the East
Chalke Gate – entrance to the Great Palace opposite the Church of Holy Wisdom
Chalkidon – also spelled Chalcedon, city on the Bosporus Strait across from Constantinople, now Kadikoy, part of Istanbul, Turkey
Chrysopolis – walled city on the Bosporus Strait opposite Constantinople, now Uskudar, Turkey
clamys – triangular cloak worn over one shoulder and fastened with a broach
Church of the Virgin of the Copper Market – church in Constantinople said to have the belt of the Virgin Mary
Church of Holy Apostles – church with many domes on Fourth Hill in Constantinople, contained the tombs of the emperors, built in 330 A.D. demolished in 1461
Church of Holy Wisdom – church built in 537 A.D. dedicated to the Wisdom of God, now a mosque officially called the Hagia Sofia Grand Mosque
Church of Saint Irini – also called Hagia Irine, Eastern Orthodox church now located in Topkapi Palace in Istanbul, popular tourist site

Consistory – group of advisors to the emperor
Constantinople – "City of Constantine" founded by Constantine the Great in 330 A.D. as the capitol of his empire, conquered in 1453 by the Ottoman Empire, now Istanbul, Turkey
Convent of the Theotokos (Convent of the Mother of God) – convent on Prinkypos Island near Constantinople which Empress Irini of Athens converted from a monastery and used as her religious retreat and refuge
codex – book that came after scrolls (pl. codices)
Dalmatiou Prison – prison in Constantinople
Daphne Palace – residence palace of the imperial family inside the Great Palace, now lies under the Sultan Ahmed Mosque in Istanbul
despina – title of respect for women
diapompefsi – public humiliation consisting of putting the victim naked backwards on a donkey and driving it through the streets
Dorylaion – walled city on Thekla's route to Constantinople
Ekloga – book of laws of the Roman Empire of the East issued by Emperor Leon the Isaurian in 726 A.D in his name and that of his son Constantine, replaced the 6th-century Code of Justinian
ekonomis – nun second in authority in a convent after the abbess
Saint Emmelia convent – invented convent in the hills of Bithynia
evkrata – drink made from early sour apples
Evdomon – military base seven miles outside Constan-

tinople, also called Hebdomon
folles – copper coin
forum – large square or oval space in a Roman city with statues, fountains, or important buildings (pl. fora)
Galatas – residential area on the steep hill on the opposite side of the Golden Horn from Constantinople, location of the summer Palace of Saint Mamas, now a popular residential and tourist area
garum – fish sauce
gerokomion – old people's home
Golden Gate – largest and most southern gate in the land walls of Constantinople
Golden Horn – narrow waterway inlet off the Bosporus Straits which formed the NE side of Byzantine Constantinople
Great Palace – built by Constantine I and expanded by other emperors, walled enclosure containing palaces, administrative buildings, and workshops producing silks, weapons, clothing, now part of Topkapi Palace Museum, popular tourist destination
Hall of Nineteen Couches – vast reception hall inside the Great Palace
haristikaris – manager of a convent
heteria – prostitutes
Hippodrome – arena in Constantinople for chariot racing
hiremporia – pork vendor
Holy Week – in Eastern Orthodoxy, the week before Easter Sunday
hypourgia – nurses

Ikonion – walled town in the centre of the Empire of the Romans of the East, now Konya, Turkey, known for rug-making and Whirling Dervishes, popular tourist destination
ikthyopratia – fish store
inopios – wine vendor
Kallipolis – "beautiful city" in Greek, town at the eastern end of the Dardanelles strait between the Aegean Sea and the Sea of Marmara, Gallipoli (Italian), now Gelipolu, Turkey
kandilli – candelabra
kapelarion – family restaurant (pl. kapelaria)
kapelarios – owner or waiter in a kapelarion
Kappadokia – region in Anatolia known for its caves where people live, also called Cappadocia, now Kapadokya, Turkey, popular tourist destination
kathisma – covered stand in the Hippodrome for the emperor and his family
Kherson – also called Cherson, part of the Empire of the Romans of the East in the Crimea, now Kherson, Ukraine
kinammomo – cinnamon
kitron – similar to a lemon
koukla – little doll, term of affection
kouritzaki – my little girl, term of affection
krasopatera – "wino monk", a curse
kithara – stringed instrument like a guitar
Lesbos Island – Aegean Sea island known during Byzantine times for its prison convent
Lycus River – river that flowed through Constantinople and provided a water source

lyre – hand-held harp
maforion – head scarf of a nun (pl. maforia)
magerissa – nun in a convent who manages the kitchen and shops for provisions
magirio – bread bakery
makelarion – lamb and mutton vendor
Malagina – imperial army horse breeding farm
malakismeni – a foul curse, wanker
Magnavra Palace – also Magnaura, large hall in Constantinople where emperors were crowned and received visitors, near Chalke Gate
Markellon – site of two battles between the Bulgars and the Romans of the East, the first in 756 headed by Emperor Constantine V who won, and the second in 794 headed by his grandson Constantine VI who lost, site now near the town of Karnobot, Bulgaria
Master Builder – professional builder and architect at the top of his field
milaresion – silver coin (pl. milaresia)
mizoteris – paid housekeeper
Nakoleia – walled market town on Thekla's route to Constantinople, now Seyitgazi, Turkey
Nicaea – walled city in Bithynia where the First Council of Bishops formulated the Nicene Creed in 325 A.D. and where the Seventh Council of Bishops convened by Empress Irini in 787 A.D. restored the use of icons, now Iznik, Turkey
Nikomidia – busy market city in Bithynia on Thekla's route to Constantinople, now Izmit, Turkey
omorfia mou – my pretty girl
Opsikon theme – province in the Empire of the

Romans of the East near Constantinople, their soldiers were first to arrive in defence of the city
oxygala – sour milk cheese like yogurt
Palace of Saint Mamas – summer palace across the Golden Horn from Constantinople in an area called Galata, now a neighbourhood and popular tourist area called Karakoy.
pandoheus – innkeeper
pandohion – inn
pandokissa – innkeeper's wife
Paphlagonia – region of the Empire of the Romans of the East south of the Pontus (Black) Sea, now Paphlygonya, Turkey
patrikios – position of honour granted by the emperor, (female, patrikia)
paximadia – dried bread rusks softened with liquid, popular modern Greek food
Pelagios Cemetery – cemetery outside the walls of Constantinople where the bodies of executed criminals were thrown into an open pit
Pelekitis – monastery in Bithynia near Constantinople
Pendykion – walled town on the Propontis (now Marmara) Sea, now Pendyk, Turkey
Phiale prison – prison inside the walls of the Great Palace
Piraeas – port city for Athens
plateia – open area in a village where people gather
polykandillon – flat hanging chandelier with glass holders for lamp oil
Pontus Sea – now Black Sea

Pornovoskos – "girl-shepherd", man who buys girls from their fathers for prostitution
protarch – physician chief of staff of a hospital
proyevma – breakfast
Propontis Sea – now the Sea of Marmara
Proussa – town in Bithynia in the foothills of Mount Olympus (Turkish: Mount Uludag) known for its hot springs, now Brusa, Turkey
Prinkypos Island – large island in a chain in the Propontis (Marmara) Sea near Constantinople, now Buyukada, popular tourist day trip
raptaina – seamstress
Roman Empire of the East – called the "Byzantine Empire" by a German historian in 1557, founded by Constantine the Great in 330 A.D. and continued under the same administrative system for 1,123 years until it was conquered by the Ottomans
Saint's Eortologion – yearly calendar listing the saints' days
Sampson Hospital – large public hospital behind the Church of Holy Wisdom
Selefkia – also spelled Seleucia, port for Antioch on the Roman (Mediterranean) Sea
skaramangion – long, sleeveless garment worn over a tunica
skatopsychi – crude curse
stratiotis – wife of a soldier
Studios Monastery – Monastery of Saint John the Forerunner at Studios, founded in 462, the largest and one of the oldest monasteries in Constantinople, located near the sea in the Istanbul district called **Psamathia,**

ruins now under restoration
Syke – port on the Roman (Mediterranean) Sea near the Caliphate border
szingi – fritters
Ta Gastria – or Gastria, large convent in Constantinople in the district of Psamathia, became Sancaktar Hayrettin Mosque in the 15th century, damaged by earthquake, restored in 1973
Tagmata – Emperor Constantine's personal guard
theme – province of the Empire of the Romans of the East
Thessaloniki – also Salonika, second largest city in the Empire of the Romans of the East, located on the Aegean Sea, now Thessaloniki, Greece.
thymelikia – dancers
tonsure – shaved area on the head of a monk or nun
trahana – mixture of a grain and dried milk used to thicken soup and stew
tunica – article of clothing cut in one piece including sleeves, worn by men and women short or long, embroidered or plain depending on wearer's wealth
typikon – founding documents of an Eastern Orthodox convent or monastery which states the rules of living and duties of the residents
valanissa – attendant in a public bathhouse
Veil of the Virgin – scarf kept at Blachernae Palace said to belong to the Virgin Mary
verjuice – drink made from unripe grapes
xenodohos – admitting clerk in a hospital
zamnykistria – player of an ancient stringed instrument called the sambuca

Explore the Empress Irini Series

Book 1
Betrothal & Betrayal
Seventeen-year-old Thekla needs her quick wits and knife to track down her betrothed, a soldier who has left her at the altar for the third time. Elias the monk travels with her to Constantinople where she meets Irini of Athens, an extraordinarily beautiful orphan her same age who has been brought by powerful Emperor Constantine to marry his son, Co-emperor Leon. The two women join forces to survive this vigorous capital of the Roman Empire of the East which is rocked by religious and political strife. But will Thekla help the ambitious and ruthless Irini of Athens find the power that she craves?

Book 2
Poison is a Woman's Weapon
Irini's conniving mother-in-law, her five jealous step-brothers, and her own husband threaten Irini's safety in Constantinople. She summons Abbess Thekla, her knife-wielding friend, to bring her sharp wits and courage to get Irini safely through childbirth in the Great Palace. Thekla owes Irini her life and thus her loyalty but she is staggered by Irini's powerful ambitions which far exceed being docile wife and mother. Can Thekla survive Irini's vengeful nature and the bloody aftermath of Irini's ruthless ambition?

Book 3
Seizing Power
Constantine's father, Co-emperor Leon, dies unexpectedly, making Constantine emperor at age nine with Irini as Empress Regent. Abbess Thekla's loyalty to Irini shifts to Constantine as she watches Irini block his authority and keep the power herself. Irini makes Constantine wed the disliked Maria, prevents the Senate from naming him Emperor in his own right at age 18, and imprisons him when he tries to stop her henchmen from amassing wealth and power. Constantine's army friends free him, arrest her, and raise him to the throne. Resourceful as ever, Irini will not be thwarted. Can Thekla prevent them from murdering each other?

Book 4
The Price of Eyes
In the final book, Irini returns to the throne. She tricks Constantine into divorcing Maria and exiles her and Constantine's two daughters to Abbess Thekla's island convent where Maria goes mad. Irini misleads Constantine into taking revenge on the soldiers who arrested her and the empire erupts into civil war, army against army, Irini against Constantine. Fearing for her life, Irini traps Constantine, wounding his eyes, but Thekla rescues him. Irini is finally empress in her own right. But will Thekla help her hold the throne?

Janet McGiffin lives in Manhattan and Washington State. She can be reached through her website at https://janmcgiffin.com/, https://janetmcgiffin.com/, or janmcgiffin.com